# Indio

# Indio

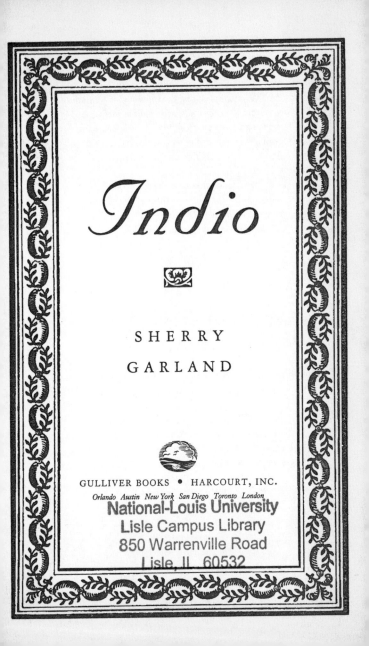

SHERRY

GARLAND

GULLIVER BOOKS • HARCOURT, INC.

Orlando  Austin  New York  San Diego  Toronto  London

Copyright © 1995 by Sherry Garland

www.HarcourtBooks.com

*Gulliver Books* is a registered trademark of Harcourt, Inc..

Library of Congress Cataloging-in-Publication Data
Garland, Sherry.
Indio/by Sherry Garland.—1st ed.
p.   cm.
Summary: Teenage Ipa struggles to survive a brutal time of change
as the Spanish begin the conquest of the native people
along the Texas border.
ISBN 0-15-238631-9   ISBN 0-15-200021-6 (pb)
1. Pueblo Indians—Juvenile fiction.  [1. Pueblo Indians—
Fiction.   2. Indians of North America—Texas—Fiction.
3. America—Discovery and exploration—Spanish—Fiction.]
I. Title.
PZ7.G18415In  1995
[Fic]—dc20     94-38429

Text set in Granjon
Designed by Lisa Peters
Printed in the United States of America
D F H J L M K I G E

*For Marj Gurasich,*

who has been lured into history's tangled web

many times

# *Author's Note*

*A*LONG THE banks of the Rio Grande, in the mountainous desert country of far west Texas, dwelled a peaceful farming people. They lived in square, flat-topped adobe houses and eked out a living by growing maize, beans, and squash in limited areas near the river. They supplemented their diet with desert plants such as yucca, agave, sotol, cactus pears, mesquite beans, berries, nuts, and various wildlife such as rabbit, deer, antelope, fish, and buffalo. Archeologists believe they were related to some of the larger, more complex Pueblo societies of New Mexico located on the Upper Rio Grande.

The largest concentration of the Texas *pueblos*

(the Spanish word for villages) occurred in a valley at the junction of the Rio Grande and the Rio Conchos. Called *La Junta* (the junction) by the Spanish, the area was estimated by one explorer to have a population of ten thousand residents. Smaller pueblos spread up the rugged Rio Grande to El Paso, other pueblos spread along the Rio Conchos southward into Mexico for many miles.

The first Spaniard to meet these Texas pueblo builders was Alvar Núñez Cabeza de Vaca in 1535. In the late 1500s, several Spanish *entradas* (expeditions) passed through *La Junta* on their way north. Spanish chroniclers remarked that the men were handsome and the women beautiful, that they were merry and friendly, singing as they walked and generously giving presents to visitors. Unfortunately, illegal expeditions by slave hunters also entered the region, searching for laborers for the newly discovered silver mines of Northern Mexico.

Very little is known about the culture or language of these peaceful river farmers. The Spanish called all the Texas pueblo dwellers by the general name Jumanos. But the Spaniards also called several nomadic, buffalo-hunting peoples by the same name. All these groups painted or tattooed themselves in a similar way and spoke a similar language. This discrepancy has caused historians much difficulty in sorting out the lifestyle of the Jumanos. Some historians believe that *La Junta* residents formed buffalo-hunting parties that traveled north from spring to fall and returned to their villages during the winter. Other historians believe that the nomadic hunters were a completely separate and culturally distinct group of people who simply wintered at *La Junta*.

In either case, historians agree that the nomadic Jumanos were renowned traders, traveling hundreds of miles over well-established trade routes. They were able to communicate with most of the other indigenous peoples of Texas and even held large trade fairs. The Spanish explorers relied heavily on the Jumanos as guides and interpreters. Today most historians refer to the nomadic hunter-traders by the name Jumanos, and call the pueblo dwellers by specific names—Patarabueye, Abriache, Caguates, Otomoacos, Julimes, Mansos—depending on which part of the river was their home.

Although some events depicted in this novel are based on recorded facts, *Indio* is first and foremost a work of fiction. I have taken the liberty of condensing history into a very short time span. In truth, it took over a hundred years for the culture of the Jumanos to vanish as they changed from *indios* to *mejicanos* or joined their old enemy, the Apaches.

Also, to give the novel a sense of time and place, I have used words from other indigenous New World peoples. For example, the words *cacique* and *yucca* originated in the Caribbean. The word *Apache* is a Puebloan word meaning enemy. *Ocotillo* comes from the Aztec word *ocotl. Adobe* is an Arabic word, brought to Spain by the Moors. And, of course, many Spanish words are dispersed throughout the text— *arroyo, caballo, mano, pinyon, playa, sierras,* to name but a few.

And lastly, since very little is known about the religion, ceremonies, or legends of the river farmers, I have borrowed liberally from the ancient cultures of the Upper Rio Grande Pueblos of eastern New Mexico to fill in the gaps. The rest comes from my own imagination, stirred within my heart while standing on the canyon rim overlooking the Rio Grande.

Today, at first glance, it looks as if the culture of the Texas river farmers is gone forever. All that remains physically are the ruins of a few adobe pit houses. But look closer and you will find women on both sides of the Rio Grande grinding corn on stone *metates* as their ancestors did; you will find them gathering agave bulbs and ripe red cactus pears, and using yucca roots for soap. You will see them weaving baskets from reeds and wearing yucca-fiber sandals. And you will see modern-day healers, *curanderos,* using the same medicine plants that Ipatah-chi used four hundred years ago.

# Chapter One

PALE BEAMS of dying moonlight fell upon the canyon path. Ipa-tah-chi knew the trail so well that her yucca-fiber sandals found the hidden notches and unseen rocks without the help of her eyes. But Ipa's younger brother, Kadoh, was only five summers old and had not climbed the path in darkness before. He stumbled, making pebbles rain to the canyon below, where flat-roofed adobe houses squatted beside the Great River.

"Come, Little Brother. The top of the canyon is near," Ipa whispered as she helped her brother up and brushed a layer of red sand from his bare legs.

The boy's breath came in little gasps until he

reached the flat ground at the canyon rim. Ipa's own breathing was calm as she drew in the deliciously cool predawn air heavy with the fragrance of tangy creosote bushes and sweet purple sage and dusty cactus.

"We are here!" Kadoh cried out. His sharp echo ricocheted off the rocky walls beneath their feet.

*"Shh!"* Ipa put her hand over his broad, grinning mouth. "You will scare away the panther."

"Is this where the panther comes to drink?"

"No, Brother Panther drinks from the river below. We are going to a secret place to watch him."

"Why don't we hide in the canes beside the river?"

"Brother Panther is far too smart for us. The wind would carry our scent to his nose and he would run away. Give me your hand. We still have many paces to walk."

Ipa took the boy's small, sweaty hand into her own and walked along the rim of the canyon. To her left, beyond the space of nothingness, the far canyon wall seemed to move in the opposite direction. Ipa felt the rush of giddiness that always came when she looked over the edge. She turned her face away and continued walking until they came to broken boulders tumbled on top of one another. Kadoh broke away and ran toward the formation.

*"Ay!"* Ipa called out after him. "Watch out for snakes and yucca spears."

As Kadoh ignored her advice and scrambled up one of the boulders, Ipa sighed heavily. She had not wanted to bring Kadoh with her, but he had heard her sneaking up the notched tree ladder that led from their beds to the flat roof of their grandmother's house. His prying questions and excitement would have jeopardized waking the old woman if Ipa did not bring him along. Even threatening him with stories of a bogeyman who snatched away disobedient children in a shoulder basket would not make the curious little boy change his stubborn mind.

As Kadoh leaped down, he cried out softly.

"*Ay!* It is a yucca spear," he said in disbelief, and rubbed his kneecap. "How did you see it, Sister? Do you have the eyes of an owl that can see at night?"

Ipa chuckled. "Perhaps I do. Or perhaps I have been up and down this trail more years than you have been alive, Little Beetle." Ipa called her brother by a special name that only she used. Rarely did anyone call him by his Sun-Name, Kadoh, which had been bestowed on him at his naming ceremony. Ipa remembered that dawn their grandmother had presented the naked baby to the Great Spirit for blessing. Even back then, Ipa thought the precious little bundle looked like a beetle as he squirmed and kicked in his cradleboard, his large black eyes twinkling over the top of the soft rabbit-fur lining.

"I am not a beetle," Kadoh insisted, jutting his chin out.

"Oh, yes you are—always crawling into places where you do not belong. I saw you creeping down the corn rows yesterday when you were supposed to be scaring away the crows."

"I was stalking a rabbit. I almost caught him with my bare hands."

"Your bare hands?" Ipa laughed lightly. "It is a good thing you did not succeed, Little Beetle. Someday you will learn that Brother Rabbit's hind legs are a better weapon than your bare hands. But we must not talk. The animals have ears even bigger than our uncle's."

Kadoh started to laugh but quickly put his own hand over his mouth to stifle the sound.

Soon they reached a jagged crevice in the canyon wall, wider than ten men stretched on end, where a great hunk of earth had caved in and fallen below. No one knew when it had happened. The gap had been there as long as anyone in the village could remember. The Old One—a woman with only one good tooth and white hair—said that Panther Spirit had stepped there one day while chasing a buffalo over the canyon's edge, and the earth had given way beneath his great paws. But some elders said the old woman was not right in the head. Everyone knew that buffalo did not come to the canyon. Every year the hunters of the village traveled to the northern plains to seek the endless buffalo herds whose hooves shook the earth like thunder. For many suns the hunters dragged the buffalo hides and dried meat on travois before reaching their village. And even though her own father was the hunting captain, only once in all of Ipa's ten summers had she tasted fresh bison meat.

And yet there was some truth in the Old One's words, for one day Ipa and her older cousin, Xucate, had discovered buffalo bones at the bottom of the canyon—many bones, so old they had turned to stone, half buried under layers of dirt. Perhaps the legend was true. Perhaps Panther Spirit still roamed this part of the canyon. This thought was what made Ipa risk walking the canyon rim at night. If only she could find the panther and beg his mighty spirit to call down the rain, then her village's corn would be spared from the drought that ravaged the land.

At last Ipa reached the secret place where she often came during the day. She had cleared away sharp stones and cactus pads and smoothed the earth so she could sit quietly and look out over the canyon.

"Here is the place," she whispered to Kadoh. "We will stay here until Grandfather Sun wakes up and walks over the mountains."

"Will the panther come this morning?"

"I do not know. I saw a footprint down by the river yesterday on my way to fill my water gourd. I know the mark was not there the night before. Once I saw a shadow and heard a growl in the canes along the river. It must have been the panther."

"But have you seen the panther's face?"

Ipa sighed. "No, but I know he is out there. We must be patient."

"I do not like the dark, Sister. Is it true that evil spirits come out at night and steal children away? Do they carry children down into deep holes in Earth-mother's back, where it is dark and there is no air? I could not bear to be in such a place."

"*Shh,* do not be afraid, Little Beetle. I am here. I will always protect you from evil spirits. But now we must be quiet and watch for the panther."

Ipa pulled Kadoh in front of her and rested her chin on top of his thick, black hair still worn in the way of small boys. It smelled of *ocotillo* and *agarita* plants. Her grandmother had ground their roots and mixed them with cactus pulp and smeared them on a cut on Kadoh's head. Yesterday morning, in his hasty climb up the ladder that led to the roof hatch of their adobe house, he had scraped his head against the underside of the ceiling. The medicine had worked its magic, and the cut was healing quickly.

Ipa smiled to herself as she imagined her small, sturdy grandmother crawling along the canyon walls or sifting through the riverbed or stooped over some tangy-smelling plant in the desert, mumbling to her-self as she searched for secret medicines. The old woman had more knowledge of magic plants than anyone else in the village. Ipa never felt happier than when she walked beside her grandmother, learning which berries were used for healing and which ones were poisonous.

Every season, Ipa learned more of her grandmother's secrets. Although she had lived only ten summers, already Ipa knew how to pound the roots into powder and how to boil leaves into medicinal teas for fever or for chasing away bad dreams. And most wonderful of all, Ipa accompanied her grandmother when she traveled to other villages up and down the river to heal the sick. The old woman's reputation was renowned among the people who spoke her language. But there were still many seasons of learning to come before Ipa dared try to heal the sick alone.

As Ipa's eyes adjusted to the darkness and the eastern sky turned gray, the outline of the canyon became clearer. Below, square adobe houses with flat roofs clustered around a central plaza. A narrow strip of corn grew along the riverbank and up the dry branch of another, smaller canyon. The stalks covered every patch of good earth available, dispersed between stretches of rocky, arid ground. Between the cornstalks grew squash and bean vines. One patch of corn grew on a tiny island in the middle of the river. This would be the sweetest corn of all and would be saved for sacred ceremonies. The corn nearest the river grew tall and green, rustling happily. It had shallow roots and the easy life of river corn. But the stalks were few and their precious seeds would be gone before the first frost of winter.

The other corn grew in the fields out in the desert or in dry arroyos at the bottom of hills, where sometimes the stalks were lucky enough to catch runoff from summer rains. That corn was withering from thirst. In late spring the shaman had jabbed his prayer stick covered with songbird feathers into the soil, then scratched lines that radiated out in the six sacred directions. The men had plunged their digging sticks deep into the soil so that tender new roots would find moisture. They dropped many seeds into each hole, keeping the corn colors separate. The shaman sang his secret song to the seeds to make them grow. He prayed to Mother Corn and to the Great Spirit, then spread sacred juniper twigs in the fields to instruct the corn how to stay green.

At last the plants had come up—ugly, squatty bushes of tough, dark green leaves with deep roots. But when the thirsty corn had sucked up all the moisture from below, there was nothing left. The Rain Spirit turned his dark, brooding back on the shaman's prayers. He rolled up his great gray turkey-feather cloak and walked away, leaving behind Brother Wind. Brother Wind puffed up his cheeks and tore away the outer leaves of the corn, exposing tiny budding ears that would never mature unless the Rain Spirit returned very soon.

Ipa looked up at the heavens filled with fading stars. As usual, the sky was clear above, with no sign of rain clouds except over the distant purple mountains. She remembered the last rain as clearly as if it were yesterday. The men had pounded their hands against their thighs and had worn bonnets made of goose feathers. They had captured songbirds and released them to carry prayers to the Rain Spirit. For days they had chanted, and when at last they had sung down the rain, they danced until their feet were covered with mud. Everyone laughed and stayed out in the rain like dumbfounded turkeys that day. Even the Old One turned around a few times with the help of her gnarly juniper cane and smiled her toothless grin. Later, the Great River swelled with water and spoke in angry, rushing voices. It burst over its banks and flooded the canyon and gushed into their pit houses. But still the people rejoiced and thanked the Rain Spirit for his gift. That had been last summer.

A little scraping noise startled Ipa out of her daydream. She felt Kadoh's body go tense.

"Was that the panther?" he asked.

"*Shh!*"

The noise came again, louder. This time Ipa was sure it was not from the river below. It was behind them. She rose to her feet and spun around. A shadow leaped at them and said, *"Ay!"*

"Ximi!" Kadoh chirped as he leaped to his feet. He ran to the shadowy boy and wrapped his arms around the slender waist.

"What are you doing here, Older Brother?" Ipa asked the boy, trying to calm her voice. "Are you not on watch at the end of the canyon?"

"I am watching. Why do you think I am here now? Your walking and your talking carries across the canyon walls. Your great noise could awaken a deaf coyote."

"Ha! And you could not sneak up on a deaf coyote, Brother." Ipa tossed her long hair over one shoulder, for she had not yet taken time to bind it back. "We heard you coming for a long way."

"No, we did not hear you, Brother," Kadoh interrupted. "Sister is teasing. You sneaked up on us with the feet of a mouse."

Ximi laughed and lifted his small brother into the air and slung him around. Ximi was tall like their father. Everyone knew that someday he would be the village leader, the *cacique*. Their uncle was the *cacique* now, but he had no sons and loved Ximi like his own.

*"Shh!"* Ipa protested when Kadoh let loose a yelp of joy. "Now you have surely frightened off the panther."

"Panther?" Ximi lowered Kadoh to the ground.

His arms rippled with small, hard muscles. His body was bare except for a deerskin breechcloth that almost touched the tops of his knees. Around his neck hung his medicine pouch, filled with secret things to give him power. A long, curved bow and a quiver of arrows hung over one shoulder. He leaned gracefully on a curved club made of *tornillo* wood, waiting for an explanation.

"We are watching for Panther Spirit," Kadoh boasted before Ipa could reply. Ximi raised one eyebrow and crossed his arms. A tattoo rose on his left cheek. It had been etched there during his twelfth summer, signifying his initiation into manhood after he had slain his first deer.

"I thought if we saw the panther getting a drink of water . . . " Ipa paused. Her idea, so clear and brilliant in the night, now seemed foolish in the gray dawn. She stared at the rocky ground, grateful that the dimness would not allow her to see Ximi's dark eyes and scolding expression. He waited, saying nothing. Ipa drew in a long breath and continued.

"I thought if we saw the panther, we could pray to its spirit for rain."

"Pray for rain?" Ximi laughed. "You, a little girl of how many summers? Seven? Eight?"

Ipa swallowed hard and felt her cheeks grow hot. She was indeed small for her age, but her own brother should remember how old she was. It seemed to Ipa that everyone in the village remembered her birth in great detail, for she had been one half of a set of twins—the first twins born to the village in the memory of the Old One. To be a twin was considered the luckiest thing that could happen, and a twin child was destined for great things. It was a time for much rejoicing, and she had been named Ipa-tah-chi, which meant Moonlight-on-River-Water, and her twin had been named Ona-tah-chi, which meant Starlight-on-River-Water. But the joy soon turned to sorrow when Ipa-tah-chi's twin sister died. Even now, Ipa was called She-Who-Lived by the older villagers. Ipa remained smaller than the other girls her age. Sometimes she felt that half of her strength had been buried with her twin sister.

Ipa drew in a deep breath before answering Ximi's question.

"I have ten summers," she replied softly, still staring at the ground.

"Ten summers. And a boy of only five summers. Ha! You would pray to the Panther Spirit and bring rain when our pueblo elders have been singing and dancing for more days than hairs on Little Brother's head? Ha!"

Ipa lifted her face.

"I thought Panther Spirit would feel pity for hungry children."

Ipa saw a flash of white spread across Ximi's

shadowy face and knew that he was smiling, as he often did when teasing the children of her village.

"You will need strong medicine to help you when our grandmother finds that you have brought Little Brother to the canyon rim in the darkness. It is far too dangerous."

Ipa knew in her heart that Ximi was right. Since the death of their mother when Kadoh was still in his cradleboard, their grandmother had raised them with a stern, loving hand while their father was away on long hunting and trading journeys.

Ipa sighed. "You are right, Older Brother. I should not have brought him. He is afraid of the dark."

"I am not afraid," Kadoh protested in a loud voice.

"You should be," Ximi said, turning to his brother. He showed his teeth and growled. "Animals may eat you alive up here. Or Apache raiders from the North Mountains may shoot you through the belly with arrows." He drilled a lean, brown finger into Kadoh's pudgy stomach. Kadoh twisted, then tugged at Ximi's bow.

"Let me shoot your bow. I am big enough. Let me shoot a rabbit for Grandmother."

"No, Little Brother, we use sticks for killing rabbits. We must save our precious arrows for big game like deer and buffalo."

Kadoh's lips drooped and his eyes clouded. Ximi sighed in resignation, then lifted the bow from his shoulder.

"Go, Sister-Who-Lived; sit on the rock and watch for Panther Spirit. Sing all day for rain. I am going to teach this young hunter how to bring home a deer." He placed the bow in Kadoh's hands. "On a real hunting trip we would bathe in the river first to wash away our scent and to cleanse our hearts. Then we would dance the hunter's dance and promise the deer that we would be kind to them and respect them, so they would return another day."

Kadoh's small fingers could not pull the bowstring, or lift the bow off the ground. Ximi turned it sideways, fixed the arrow notch into the sinew string, and helped Kadoh draw it back. When released, the arrow flew only a short distance before plummeting into the dry, yellow grass.

"I think Brother Deer has nothing to fear this morning," Ximi said, and gave Kadoh another arrow.

Ipa turned away from her brothers and returned to her special observation place. She sat down and rested her chin on her hands and stared across the desert. On the other side of the Great River lay Sacred Panther Mountain, the place where the ancient ones had drawn pictures of the panther on cavern walls and held secret council to worship his spirit. Below her, the canyon walls still lay in deep shadows, though the sky was turning gray in the east. The panther could be at the river this very moment, lapping up cool water.

Ipa strained her eyes, wishing she could see in the darkness as well as Kadoh believed she could. Beside the river, a stand of cane and the leaves of a cottonwood tree rustled and clacked. The wind moved down the canyon in swishing sounds, sometimes light, sometimes strong and fierce enough to bend the willow trees. Farther up, in the dry branch of the canyon and behind her on the flat plain, the voices of the thirsty corn called to her, pleading for rain. The river water rippling over stones and around boulders sang a joyful song, but the dry cornstalks sang sad songs like the eerie whispers of the dead.

Ipa moved closer to the edge of the wall. Removing a handful of finely ground cornmeal from a pouch made of two cactus pads sewn together, she sprinkled it in the six sacred directions—north, south, east, west, northwest to signify above, and southeast to signify below. She closed her eyes, spread her hands toward the sky, and began chanting a rain prayer.

Ipa repeated the sacred words again and again, until the scream of an eagle pierced the air and she heard the soft flap of its wings. The soft cooing of doves and the call of the quail rose from the canyon. Ipa opened her eyes. The east was soft pink and gray.

Soon Grandfather Sun would rise from his bed, trailing blankets of orange and red and pink across the mountaintops, and the sounds of morning would fill the air. Old men would climb out onto rooftops to greet the sun with morning prayers. Boys Ipa's own age would run in the sacred directions to sprinkle cornmeal and pollen, then splash into the river for a morning swim. Women and girls would rise and roll up their beds and hang them on the hanging pole in the house. They would rinse their faces and bodies in cool water from jars and start the endless tasks of grinding corn and fetching firewood. Little children would laugh and chase one another through the plaza, or play with corncob dolls, or kick sticks or stones. The village would come alive with the sounds of life.

But for the moment all was quiet. Even the wind was gentler now, as if it had gone to bed for the day. Ipa looked down. The pale gray light was spreading, caressing the tops of the tall cottonwood trees under which the village women often sat and talked while pounding their deerskin clothes on the rocks. The dawn swathed one canyon wall in a blanket of gray, leaving the other wall and most of the river still in deep shadows.

Suddenly Ipa caught her breath. She leaned forward and squinted. She wished her brothers would stop their noise behind her, so she could hear the sounds below, where a shadow was moving through the canes. She knew the shadow was alive, for even when the wind stopped and the corn did not rustle, the canes bent. She had not imagined that the panther would come through the canes. Maybe that was why she had never seen him before.

Ipa leaned as far as possible over the canyon rim. She watched the moving pattern in the cane come closer to the river. Then she saw something dark in the water itself. But the form did not stop to drink. It moved down the river, safely hidden in the shade of the canyon wall. Then Ipa saw another dark figure rustling the canes. Quickly Ipa rose. Two panthers! It was surely a sign of great things to come, of rain for days and crops of abundance. Her grandmother and her uncle would be very pleased.

As Ipa smiled and started to turn to call her brothers, the shadowy form stepped into the light. Her heart jumped to her throat, then pounded like war drums in her ears.

"Apaches! Apaches!" she screamed with all her might.

Ipa spun around, only to crash into Ximi. His black eyes pierced the scene below. More figures were coming down the canyon at the far end. Ximi's face was as gray as ashes when he turned to his sister.

"Take Little Brother to our uncle's house," he said as he grabbed his bow and arrow from Kadoh's hands and began to run.

With the speed and grace of a stag in flight, Ximi

raced along the rim of the canyon toward the main trail. He paused once, cupping his hands over his mouth, and screamed out a warning cry that was half human, half eagle. The warble echoed off the walls. Suddenly the tiny figures below, dressed in moccasins and deerskin clothing, broke into a run toward the granaries. They all wore their hair long, tied back with headbands, and some of them looked like women. *Only Apache women would be so arrogant and haughty,* Ipa thought. Among other peoples, women were peaceful and neutral. Even in times of war they did not take up weapons and kill.

As Ipa grabbed Kadoh's hand and ran, he stumbled and fell. Tears filled his eyes, but he said nothing. Ipa scooped him into her arms and darted toward the main trail that led down the side of the canyon to the village. Below, women and children and men scrambled onto the flat roofs of their adobe houses to see what was causing the noise.

As panic swept through the village, the women frantically began gathering the drying corn and beans and other valuables from the rooftops. Men carrying clubs and spears charged toward the Apaches who by now had broken into the granaries. The remaining men pulled ladders up onto the rooftops, where they knelt and shot arrows at the enemy. Soon the chilly cries of the raiders mingled with the angry cries of the villagers.

Blood surged through Ipa's temples and her

knees trembled as she heard the bloody battle cry of the warriors. Suddenly, visions of last year's Apache raid flashed through her mind, leaving a sickening feeling in her stomach. She squeezed Kadoh closer and ran faster toward the canyon trail, until her breath was gone.

"It is too late to go to our uncle's house," she said between gasps. "Our aunt has already drawn the ladder up. It will be safer up here behind this boulder. The Apaches will not come this way." Ipa put Kadoh on the ground. Though only five summers old, he was heavy for her slender arms.

"No! I want to go with Brother." Kadoh jerked his hand free from hers and scampered down the canyon trail like a frightened rabbit.

"Little Beetle! Come back!" Ipa shouted, but Kadoh ignored her cries.

Kadoh darted down the trail, stumbling and sliding in his eagerness to reach the pueblo.

As Ipa raced after her brother, her eyes swept over the houses below, but she did not see the familiar small figure of her grandmother, nor did she hear the familiar high-pitched voice. Grandmother must have heard the battle cries by now. She was old, but she still had the ears of a fox. Since Ipa's father was away on a hunting trip and there was no man to stand on her roof, surely the old woman had sought refuge in the *cacique*'s house. After all, she had lived through many Apache raids and knew what to do.

Suddenly Ipa wished her grandmother were by her side telling her what to do about Kadoh, who had ignored all her commands and had already reached the bottom of the trail.

At last Ipa saw her grandmother climb through the opening in the roof of her adobe house. For a moment the old woman stood on the roof shouting, "Grandchildren! Where are you!"

A wave of guilt swept through Ipa's heart. She cried out and waved her arms, but she was too far away to be heard. She saw the old woman hurrying toward the *cacique*'s house, her arms loaded down with baskets of medicine plants. Of course, that was why she was so late seeking refuge. She would never leave her precious medicines behind. The old woman valued them more than anything.

Before Ipa had reached the bottom of the trail, she saw an Apache woman running toward her grandmother, warbling a high-pitched cry. The enemy's tall deerskin moccasins came to her knees, meeting the fringes of her deerskin skirt.

"Run, Grandmother!" Ipa screamed with all her strength. But the old woman did not hear. Ipa threw caution to the wind and ran faster. Bumping against boulders and darting close to patches of cactus and yucca plants, shouting and crying, Ipa flew toward her grandmother. Her feet stung with the sharp needles, and she felt blood trickling down her exposed arms and legs. Ipa cursed her legs when she stumbled and fell to the ground at the foot of the trail. She helplessly watched the Apache reach the old woman and grab her baskets. But Ipa's grandmother would not give up her medicine plants. She screeched and flailed her arms against the tall enemy.

"No!" Ipa's voice came out no more than an airless squeak from her burning, aching lungs.

With an angry shout, the Apache brought her stone tomahawk down against the older woman's head. Ipa's grandmother fell to the ground and lay still. The Apache shouted her cry of victory and grabbed the baskets.

Ipa wanted to vomit. Her heart pounded so fiercely against her ribs that she was sure it would burst. Tears sprang into her eyes and a lump as sharp as a boulder cut her throat. For a moment Ipa sobbed into the dirt, her fingers digging into the dry earth. She could not bear to look up, to see the blood of her grandmother flowing onto the ground. She wanted to vanish, to fly into the sky and go with her grandmother's soul on the journey of afterlife. Ipa pressed her hands over her ears to drown out the screams of panic and agony as the men of her village fought the Apaches.

"Grandmother! Wake up!" a small, panic-filled voice cried out.

Ipa lifted her face and looked across the plaza. She saw Kadoh kneeling over the old woman's still body, his small face clouded with grief as he watched the pool of blood grow larger. The Apache woman saw Kadoh, too. She stopped her pillage on a nearby granary and strode back toward the boy in large, confident steps. To capture a fine boy like Kadoh would be a great feat for this enemy woman.

"Little Brother! Watch out!" Ipa screamed as she climbed to her feet. She pointed to the Apache woman. "Run, Little Brother!"

The boy stood up and turned around, but he did not run. He faced the Apache, his small legs braced. The enemy woman laughed in glee and charged at him, waving her tomahawk and screaming.

Ipa summoned all the courage her heart possessed and forced her legs to run again. Her lungs wheezed for air and her side throbbed with pain, but she dared not stop. She ran with all her strength, knowing she could not reach her brother before the swift Apache. Then Ipa heard the sound of sandals striking the sandy ground and the swish of a deerskin dress somewhere behind her. Out of the corner of her eye, Ipa saw her cousin Xucate running beside her.

"Cousin! Save my brother!" Ipa cried out to her taller cousin, who was one year older than she.

Xucate ran past Ipa, swifter than a fleeing deer. Ipa watched in amazement as the girl shoved the Apache woman from behind and knocked her sprawling to the ground. With a scream of rage Xucate wrenched the tomahawk from the enemy's hand

and struck her head again and again. Never had Ipa seen her cousin so full of fury and hatred, and for a moment Xucate's face became that of a demon child.

Xucate then scooped Kadoh into her arms and ran toward Ipa. Her long, strong legs devoured the ground in great gulps and soon she pushed Kadoh into Ipa's arms.

"He owes his life to me," she said between gasps for air, then ran back to her father's lodge.

Ipa fought back tears of joy as she wrapped her arms around her brother's trembling body and pressed her cheek to Kadoh's head. He pushed her away and struggled to get free, but Ipa held on to his arm with all her strength.

"I want to fight! I want to kill an Apache!" His voice screeched like an angry badger's. Ipa squeezed his arm hard. She knew she was hurting him, but he did not cry out.

"I want to help Ximi!" Kadoh screamed, and twisted like a speared fish as Ipa led him to the same house where Xucate waited on the roof, holding the ladder steady.

"No!" Ipa's voice trembled. "It is too dangerous."

"But the Apaches killed Grandmother!" Kadoh squealed indignantly. "How can you let them get away with killing Grandmother! You are a cowardly female!"

Even as her brother spoke, Ipa looked over his head and saw dust settling over her grandmother's body. She thought of her grandmother's special laugh, the twinkling black eyes always shining with wisdom and love. Tears filled Ipa's eyes, blurring her little brother's angry face.

There was no other woman in Ipa's house now—her mother, her grandmother were dead. Ipa was the only woman left. She must protect Kadoh. She must strengthen her heart and never let Kadoh know she was afraid. Ipa wiped her nose on her poncho and fought back the tears.

"Remember what Ximi told us before he left," Ipa said as she firmly held Kadoh's shoulders. "He said to go to uncle's house. Ximi wants you to grow into a man. He knows that a boy can do little damage, but as a man, you can be a great warrior and avenge Grandmother's death many times. Do you want me to disobey Ximi's commands?"

Kadoh stopped struggling and sighed. Ipa took his moment of indecision to scoop him up into her arms.

Ipa climbed up the ladder as fast as her aching legs would carry her. Kadoh looked over Ipa's shoulder, his eyes fixed on the plaza. His body trembled, but he said nothing.

When they had reached the rooftop, Ipa released Kadoh and helped Xucate pull the knotched tree ladder back up. Her uncle had already left the house to join the rest of the men chasing the retreating enemy.

As Ipa followed Xucate down a second ladder that led inside the house, she heard Kadoh whimpering behind her.

"What is it?" she asked, and paused.

"Ximi is gone," he said softly. His eyes stared blankly across the plaza.

Ipa did not want to look, for the thought of seeing her older brother dead, too, troubled her heart, but she forced herself to return to the roof. Smoke rose from the granaries, and bodies lay on the ground—her grandmother, two village warriors, and the dead Apache woman. The rest of the enemy were running back up the river from where they had come, loaded with baskets of maize and beans and arms full of tanned deer hides.

"I do not see Ximi," Ipa finally said in relief. "He must have survived."

"He is there," Kadoh said, pointing a pudgy finger to the far end of the canyon where the Apaches were running.

Ipa squinted. At first she only saw the running enemy, then she noticed that two of the runners did not have the long, loose hair of the Apaches. Their hair was cropped short and their hands were tied behind them. One of them was Ximi. The men of her village were following behind, shouting and shooting arrows that fell short of their marks.

Ipa felt a great sickness in her heart. To die in battle was honorable and desirable, but to be taken slave of an enemy was worse than death. Ximi, the pride of her family, the one who would someday be *cacique,* was now reduced to being lower than a woman in the eyes of the enemy.

Ipa fought a wave of sadness and guilt. If only she had not distracted Ximi from his watch, the village would have been warned in time. Her grandmother would still be alive, and Ximi would not be an Apache slave.

Ipa's heart felt so empty she wanted to sit down and weep; she wanted to pull her hair and cover her face in ashes and throw dust into the air and wail, but her hands lowered the ladder and her feet climbed down without her command. She silently picked up the basket of medicine plants that the Apache woman had dropped. In a daze, Ipa walked across the plaza to Old Uncle, who lay on his side, an arrow in his thigh.

She removed the arrow, then placed the powder of pounded roots on it. She gave him some leaves of the fever bush to chew, then walked on to the next man. One by one, Ipa treated the wounded men as best as she could, trying to remember which berries or leaves or roots her grandmother would have used.

By the time Ipa had seen to all the casualties, the air had turned cooler and dark clouds were gathering over the mesas. Ipa heard a rumble, then saw a flash of lightning in the distance.

While the women had carried the dead away and cleansed their bodies and dressed them in their best clothes, the sky was turning black. The shaman shook his dried gourd rattle as he chanted the death song over them. In his song, he gave directions to the departed spirits, so they would know how to reach the other world. He told them which direction to go, which trail to take, and which door to step through. For if they chose the wrong door, they would go down into a dark prison under the earth. If they stepped through the correct door, they would find a rope leading to the sky, which they must climb. And at the end of the rope were beautiful, peaceful fields, with sweet running streams and rustling green corn. There they would make their camps, and their campfires would glitter in the sky as stars.

Ipa worked swiftly, for if she tarried near the body too long, her grandmother's parting spirit might decide to force Ipa to go with her on the four-day journey to the Land of the Dead. During those four days, Ipa's family would bring food and water to the grave so her grandmother could make the journey comfortably. And on the fourth day, they would remove all things that had belonged to the old woman, they would burn *tobago* so its smoke would purify her house, and they would bathe in the river.

Her name would be spoken no more, and they would think of her no more.

Ipa's aunt painted and powdered the old woman's wrinkled face and brushed her long gray hair. In the desert, the villagers gently sat the dead in new graves with valuable possessions at their feet—bows and arrows for the two warriors, a new basket and drinking gourd for her grandmother. The village shaman placed a spirit stick in the hands of the dead and chanted again. Tears streaked Ipa's face as she stepped on the new basket to kill it so that no one would steal it, then gently placed it beside the old woman's sitting body. She added a bundle of her favorite medicine plants.

"May your cornfields be tall and green, and the river water sweet. I will carry on your work. Every time my hands tend a wounded warrior or heal a sick child, it will be your hands that guide me," Ipa whispered in a trembling voice, then stood aside and watched the men pile sand over the old woman's body.

"Grandmother wanted to die in her sleep," Kadoh said in a tiny voice.

Ipa took his hand and squeezed it. "That is every old one's dream; to die in their sleep when very old, with many children and grandchildren. But don't worry, in four days she will be as happy as ever."

Ipa peered into her brother's dark eyes, so full of questions. There were no old ones in their house now. No one to tell him stories of their ancestors, of sneaky coyotes and wise eagles. She would have to find someone suitable to teach Kadoh. But she did not have time to think about that now. The wailing of women filled the sky as the two warriors were buried. But, while the shaman sprinkled sacred pollen, Ipa thought of her captured brother. There would be no grave for Ximi, but surely he would be just as dead as the warriors very soon. Ipa knew Ximi would try to escape. He would refuse to obey his Apache masters and be starved or beaten to death— so many horrible things could happen to him. How much better if he had died on the battlefield like the warriors in the graves at her feet. And all because of her foolish desire to see the Panther Spirit and bring rain. How insignificant the thought of rain and dying cornfields seemed to her now.

But by midafternoon, as the villagers returned to their adobe houses from the burial field, fat drops of cool rain splattered against Ipa's face and blended with her salty tears. Ipa and Kadoh climbed up the notched tree limb that led to the flat roof of their uncle's lodge. They climbed down another ladder into the dark, one-room pit house that sank halfway under the earth. Ipa's aunt pulled a large, flat sandstone over most of the hatchway to keep out the fast, angry rain, then spun her fire stick over dry grass and started a small fire—for suddenly the air felt very cold. Smoke drifted upward toward the slight opening and the smell of it joined the sweet fragrance of wet earth as water trickled down the adobe walls and puddled on the dirt floor.

"Your prayer song has been answered, Sister," Kadoh said softly into the silence. "The Panther Spirit heard you after all."

"Yes, you did well, She-Who-Lived," Ipa's uncle said quietly. "The corn is saved."

Ipa looked at the faces around her, streaked with dancing firelight, but she said nothing.

*Chapter Two*

THREE SUMMERS passed. Three summers of watching creamy yucca flowers turn into sweet fruit to be peeled and pounded into blocks of sweetener for their food. Three summers of gathering juicy, red, prickly pear tunas, of eating until their stomachs ached with fullness. Three summers of rabbit hunts, where girls dressed their best, and chased and teased young men, and scrutinized them with eyes that searched for future husbands. Three summers of planting parties and hoeing parties, of harvesting parties, and husking parties. Three summers of separating the corn by color, of saving back the best corn for next year's seeds, and braiding the husks and hanging them from the ceilings. Three summers of drying the corn on rooftops, and storing it in granaries, and feasting on fresh ears of corn roasted in their husks.

And for Ipa-tah-chi, three summers of waiting for Kadoh and the other villagers to discover her secret, to realize the awful truth about the day of the Apache raid.

In her heart, Ipa carried the full blame for the raid and the deaths, for she had distracted Ximi from his watch. But instead of accusing Ipa and chastising her, the *cacique* had bestowed her with honors for saving his life and helping the wounded men. She received a small tattoo on her arm, signifying that she had done a great deed—the youngest female in the memory of the Old One to have won such a mark. Many said she was blessed because she was a surviving twin, that she had been chosen for greatness by the Great Spirit.

Ipa glanced down at her slender arms and legs protruding from the soft deerskin poncho and skirt. For a girl of thirteen summers, she was not much to look at. No matter how much she ate, she never grew plump, and she remained constantly hungry. Her aunt said it was because she climbed the canyon walls too often and walked in the desert or beside the river, searching for special medicine plants. But these were the things Ipa-tah-chi loved the most and could not live without. For each time she found a special plant, she felt as if her grandmother were smiling over her shoulder.

Even though the autumn air was pleasantly cool, the sun beat on Ipa's back and beads of sweat rolled down her temples and between her small, firm breasts. She had been laboring since early morning, yet her burden-basket was only half filled with yucca roots. Ipa's arms ached with fatigue, even though the roots she dug up were not as large or heavy as the agave bulbs the others struggled with. With pieces of flint rock and pointed deer antler and bones, the women jabbed and sawed at the fleshy bulbs, prying them from the rocky soil.

As Ipa watched her cousin, Xucate, tackle a stubborn bulb with vigor, a thorn of jealousy pricked her heart. Xucate dug faster than any other girl and was always the first to fill her basket to the brim. She could dig the troublesome agave bulbs without help from anyone. Every autumn, during the time of games and celebrations, there was not a girl in all the village who could defeat Xucate in a footrace or feats of endurance.

As if hearing her thoughts, one of the girls giggled and whispered, "Ipa-tah-chi's arms are as skinny as butterfly legs."

"Her basket is never as full as ours," another girl replied.

*"Shh!"* Xucate straightened to her full height and glared at her friends. "Ipa-tah-chi is small, but

she is special. She saved my father's life three summers ago when the Apaches attacked. And she
healed many men's wounds." Xucate jabbed a deer
antler in the air as she spoke.

Ipa bit her lip to keep from smiling. Her cousin's
tongue knew no boundaries when she was angry.
Like all the girls in the village, Xucate had been
taught to be silent and patient when the men spoke,
but among women her tongue could be as venomous
as the fangs of a rattlesnake.

"We are sorry, Xucate," one of the girls said. "We
did not mean to criticize."

But Xucate rudely ignored her apology. "And
didn't my cousin bring rain when our corn was dying from drought? I tell you, she is blessed by the
Panther Spirit." Xucate's perfect teeth flashed white
and strong against her smooth brown skin as she
smiled at Ipa.

Ipa did not want her cousin to defend her. It
only made her feel more like a child than ever. Xucate was only one summer older, yet she was the one
who always gave commands. Sometimes Ipa wanted
to protest, but then she would remember that, after
all, Xucate had saved Kadoh from the Apache
woman. And, besides that, it was far better to have
Xucate as a friend than an enemy.

"Thank you, Cousin," Ipa said. "But truly, I did
not bring the rain."

"I swear," Xucate said as she stood over Ipa,

"your modesty is too heavy a burden, Little Cousin. You must learn to take pride in what you have accomplished. Now, I say you brought the rain and that is that." She turned and pounced on the agave with all her vigor.

Ipa felt her face turn hot. She could not bear when people spoke of the rain that saved the corn crop three summers ago. It had been Kadoh who told everyone that Ipa had prayed to the Panther Spirit for rain. His heart had been too young and innocent to understand that her foolishness had also brought the death of their grandmother and the abduction of their brother, Ximi.

With renewed energy, Ipa jabbed the stubborn yucca root, but soon her arms ached again and she silently cursed their weakness. When Grandfather Sun was straight overhead and seemed to stop in his tracks, the girls and women moved to the shade of boulders to rest, for it was bad luck to be in the noonday sun. In the village, Ipa saw the old men standing on the roofs, praying to the sun, asking him to continue his journey across the sky.

Around midafternoon, the women straightened, rubbing their backs and stretching. Some of the girls adjusted the cradleboards of their babies on their backs to make room for yucca-fiber nets slung around their shoulders. Other women strapped their filled burden-baskets to their foreheads with strips of buffalo hide, but Ipa continued to struggle with her task. She did not stop even when she saw the sandaled feet of her cousin in front of her.

"Cousin," Xucate said. "We are returning to the pueblo now."

Ipa looked up into her cousin's face. Xucate was the perfect vision of what a girl should be—tall, strong, healthy, and beautiful. Her long hair, twisted back away from her face, shone in the sunlight like a raven's wing, for she washed it in the river often, using suds from the yucca roots. Many young men of the villages along the river knew of her beauty. Xucate had performed the becoming-a-woman ceremony the previous summer, and three young men had already proposed marriage to her. But Xucate was stubborn and was saving herself for the perfect husband. She had her heart set on a young man named Coyomo, the Brave One, who was famous in all the villages at the junction of the rivers. Coyomo was the son of the *cacique* in the second largest village. Ipa had visited the village with her grandmother once and remembered how the adobe houses sat high on a ridge overlooking flat fields of tall, green corn.

Ipa-tah-chi had performed the becoming-a-woman ceremony just four moons ago and was available for marriage, too. But by comparison to her cousin, Ipa felt unworthy of any young man.

"My basket is not full yet," Ipa said to Xucate as

she continued cutting the roots. "I will work until my chore is done."

"You do not have to fill your basket, Cousin. We know that you have worked as hard as you can. If you do not come along, my mother and father will worry about you. After all, you are their special one."

Ipa swallowed hard. "I am not special," she protested. "You are the daughter of the *cacique,* not I. Someday you will marry the son of a *cacique.* I will probably never find a husband at all."

"You underestimate your worth, Cousin," Xucate said as she shifted the heavy basket off her back and dropped it to the ground. "After the harvest games, I wager that you will receive so many proposals you will not be able to count them all." Xucate smiled her charming, confident smile.

"Ha! I will be fortunate to get one proposal from some old widower with many ugly, disobedient children."

Xucate tossed her head back and laughed hard like a man. Then she leaped to her feet and grabbed a piece of dead wood from the ground.

"Just tell me which young man you want. I will chase him and knock him down with my rabbit stick if he does not choose you. I will sit on his chest until he gives in." She swung the stick at an imaginary man, then dropped to her knees beside Ipa. Laughter spilled from Ipa's mouth until she thought she would not be able to stop.

Ipa wrapped her arms around Xucate and hugged with all her might. "Thank you, Cousin, for making me laugh. You are better than ever a sister could be."

Xucate's face turned pink and she shrugged off the hug. "Here, let me help you fill your basket or else you will still be here when Brother Coyote sings to the moon."

Xucate began ripping up the yucca root that Ipa had not been able to move. Ipa joined her cousin and stabbed the earth, using a long stick to pry the stubborn roots loose.

But after a short while, Ipa sat back on her heels, holding the sharp flint stone in one hand and a yucca root in the other. She stared dreamily toward the southeast, where the Great River merged with the Lesser River.

"Oh, I cannot concentrate on yucca roots today," Ipa said with a sigh. "Ever since the messenger arrived early this morning, announcing that the hunting party is almost here, I can think of nothing but my father's return."

Xucate smiled. "You miss your father very much, don't you?"

Ipa nodded and swallowed hard. "Before my mother died, he took us with him one time. I was very young, but I remember crossing over the mountains and the endless herds of buffalo. I remember sleeping inside buffalo-skin houses, and the taste of fresh buffalo meat. But most of all, I remember the strange people that we met and traded with along the way. Everyone respected my father."

"The old ones say he is the best hunting *cacique* the village has ever had. He negotiates shrewdly and trades the buffalo hides and our corn very well."

Ipa sighed. "But I only see him during the short winter season. As soon as the leaves start sprouting from tree branches, he is gone again. And he doesn't return until the leaves are falling."

"Well, I for one am glad that you and Kadoh came to live in my father's lodge. I enjoy having a little brother. And a little sister." She prodded Ipa's skinny arm, then leaned on her digging stick. "Oh, how I hope your father traded well. I cannot wait to see what he brings this time."

"And I hope the hunters fared well. The supply of dried buffalo meat is almost gone."

Talking about her father made Ipa's heart grow more eager. He had formed a party in the early spring to journey to the northeastern plains, where the buffalo lived. For days the men had sung and danced and held mock hunts. Some men dressed like buffalo and women pretended to lead them into the village. Kadoh still had some baby fat on him then. Now he was almost as tall as Ipa and had small, hard muscles. Their father would be surprised to see how much his younger son had grown since spring.

Ipa returned to her task of digging roots and thought about her father. He was the tallest man in their pueblo and had tattoos of honor etched across his arms, chest, and cheeks. Like other hunters of the village, he painted stripes across his cheeks. Even though he was known for his wisdom as a hunter, Ipa was sure her father enjoyed the trading and visits to the villages of strangers more than the buffalo hunt.

Ipa closed her eyes a moment and tried to imagine the places her father had told her about. From the direction of the rising sun, he told her, there were people who lived near a great water so immense that no man could see across it. He told her about people who lived where pine trees grew straight and tall instead of small and twisted as they did in the mountains near her home. Pines so thick you could not see the sun at day nor the moon at night. A place where people built their homes out of sticks and straw and made the roofs round instead of flat like those of their own adobe houses.

From the northwest, the land of the Corn People, Ipa's father often brought beautifully marked clay pots and little pouches of pigment used to make paint for their bodies. The people there lived in cities of white houses stacked on top of one another.

To the northeast was the land of the Buffalo

People, flat plains covered with grass and rivers. There, many other peoples traveled about, following the great herds, living in skin houses.

To the south, far beyond the Lesser River, was the greatest land of them all. The trees and flowers grew thick, for it rained every day. Colorful birds flew in the sky. Often her father brought red, blue, or green macaw feathers for the *cacique*'s sacred cane, and once he gave Ipa two golden parrot feathers, which she was saving for her wedding trousseau.

Ipa's father spoke many of the strange words of other peoples and knew how to communicate by sign language. He knew the trails that led out of the desert and over the mountains. Everyone in the village loved him, Ipa knew, even more than her uncle, who was older and very wise.

Ipa and Xucate worked until the sun sat on top of the distant purple-gray mountains. When they stood, Ipa's basket was full. As the girls returned to the trail that led down to the pueblo, Ipa paused to look a final time in the direction of the river junction. She saw a line of men walking across the desert, following the path of the river.

"The hunters are home!" she shouted, and pointed to the line.

Xucate cupped her hand over her mouth and sent out a high-pitched warble that carried to the pueblo below. The village crier climbed out on his roof and shouted the news in every direction.

Soon the entire village had crawled out onto the flat roofs.

With a pounding heart, Ipa unfastened her basket and dropped it to the ground, then raced as fast as her legs would carry her toward the small band of weary-looking men. Everyone climbed up the trail, laughing and talking. The men made music with their mouths and warbled like flutes in their traditional greeting.

Ipa saw the long poles of the travois laden with hides and other wonderful goods. A tall man led the band.

"Father!" Ipa shouted, guiding her legs skillfully around clumps of cactus and creosote bushes. A familiar laugh rocked the air, and the tall man quickened his step.

"My daughter!" he said, and hugged her. "You are more lovely than an antelope running across the desert." Large, straight teeth, separated by a tiny gap between the front two, filled his smile. Like all the men of the village, he wore his hair cropped short all around, with one long swath at the crown, into which brown turkey and white goose feathers were woven. A layer of red ochre mud had been smeared over the short hair, making it look like a snug skullcap. His broad, bare shoulders, marked with tattoos and painted stripes, glistened with sweat. Around his neck hung a string of tiny copper bells and pink and white bits of coral.

"Father!" Ipa heard her brother call out as he dashed across the desert. Even though he was only eight summers old, Kadoh was already as strong as Ipa and ran swiftly.

"My son!" Ipa's father hugged Kadoh with a fierceness that he had not shown her. His dark eyes glimmered with pride.

Ipa knew what her father must be thinking as he looked into Kadoh's eyes. He was thinking of Ximi and of how much Kadoh was beginning to look like his older brother. Ipa had to look away. She knew what question would come next, as it always did.

"Has there been any word of Ximi? Has he returned yet?"

Kadoh shook his head. "No, Father."

"Any more Apache raids since I last left?"

"No, Father." Kadoh glanced at Ipa and her heart jumped. Had he finally come to his senses and realized that she was responsible for the tragedy of the raid that day? That she was the one who had distracted Ximi from his watch that morning and allowed the enemy to go undetected until it was too late? Surely Kadoh was going to tell their father the truth and he would despise her.

"Daughter. Why so sad?" her father's voice cut into her thoughts. "I have brought you something from a special place. Do you not want to see it? Are you not pleased to see your father?"

Ipa peered into her father's kind face and felt ashamed for thinking he could ever hate her. She nodded and watched the tall man reach into the medicine pouch dangling around his neck. He held something concealed in his tattoo-notched hand. Cautiously Ipa held out her palm and felt something cool and hard drop into it.

"Ahh . . . a little turtle!" she whispered. The carving shimmered like the moon's face on water and changed colors as the light hit it.

"It comes from the people who live by the big water."

"What kind of stone is this?"

"It is not a stone. It is the shell of a clam that lives in the water. The people eat the meat and carve its shell into shapes of animals and wear them around their necks. I remember that you love to catch turtles in the river and that your favorite story is the tale of Turtle-Girl."

Ipa smiled and took her father's hand and gently breathed on it, a sign of her love and respect.

He lowered his voice so that only Ipa could hear.

"My daughter, I also have some news for you. I met a young man at the Otomoacas villages at the junction of the rivers. He would make a perfect husband for you."

Ipa felt heat rush to her face. Her father often teased her about young warriors and about getting a husband. As she searched his twinkling eyes she thought it was another jest.

"And who would want a skinny girl like me, Father?"

"A girl who knows the secrets of medicine plants and who brought the rain would make a good wife to any man. Perhaps even the son of a *cacique*." He touched her nose lightly with his fingertip. Red spots covered her cheeks and she could not speak.

"Do you not want to know his name? Are you too busy making rain to desire a husband?" he said in a teasing voice.

Ipa shook her head. "What is his name, Father?"

"Coyomo, the Brave One."

Ipa felt her heart stop, then start again, faster. Coyomo, the Brave One, was the prize that Xucate had her heart set on winning. He was the son of a *cacique* and his village was wealthy. Any girl would be pleased to have him as a husband, but what would Xucate say? Her tongue would burn hotter than the flames of a fire if she found out.

"We will speak of it more later," her father said, then turned to Kadoh, raising his voice.

"And for my son, something special." He walked to the travois and lifted up a new buffalo hide of curly brown hair. Beneath it lay bundles of long, straight tree branches, their bark already peeled off.

"We will choose the finest, strongest wood and make you a bow, my son. It is time you had one to be proud of, not that old one you have been carrying for years."

Kadoh's eyes reflected his joy as his fingers touched the slick, white wood.

Other villagers greeted the men and chattered merrily over the goods on the travois—wood and buffalo horns for the bows, colored feathers, clay pots, precious blue stones, buffalo hides and hooves, strips of dried buffalo meat, obsidian and flint, ochre, and a bag of salt. The children laughed as they hopped on top of the three travois, and the women lifted the long poles and dragged them toward the village. Ipa picked up her basket of yucca roots at the top of the trail and followed them down. At the open plaza in the middle of the village, everyone stopped. The women brought food and drink to the weary hunters, who sat on the ground around a fire prepared by the women. The orange flames lit the darkening sky.

The *cacique* greeted his younger brother warmly and told him the status of the corn. As always, the summer had been long and dry, with little rain. The corn had been harvested and husked, and now lay drying on rooftops before being stored in the granaries for the winter. The husks of the seed corn had been braided and now hung in the houses. They had seen far better harvests in the past, but it was not as bad as the drought that had afflicted the village the summer Kadoh was born.

46

"And now, Brother, tell us about your journey. Tell us of the strange people you met and the places you saw," the *cacique* said.

Ipa's father took a long draw from a gourd filled with sotol and finished his flat bread made from ground maize. He ran his arm across his mouth, then leaned forward. His eyes glimmered from the firelight dancing off his dark irises.

"I have news of a strange kind of man. They speak a tongue like no other. Their skin is as white as the belly of a fish. Their hair grows under their noses and over their chins. They wear hard shells around their trunks like turtles."

A murmur rippled through the crowd gathered around the fire.

"But strangest of all, they do not walk afoot like other men. They ride on the backs of strange animals that have four legs like dogs but hooves like buffalo. Animals bigger than deer and swifter. The turtle-shell men command the animals, telling them when to turn and when to run. Their speed is frightening and their tails fly in the wind like the hair of an Apache warrior."

The *cacique* stared at his brother's face.

"Have you drunk too much *mescal* wine, my brother? Have you been chewing on peyote buttons? Can this be true?"

"Yes, yes, it is true," the Old One said in her cracked voice as she nudged her way closer to Ipa's father. Her lips smacked over her toothless gums and her wrinkled chin trembled as she spoke. "When I was a young woman, such men came to my village at the junction of the rivers."

Another man stood and pointed to the south. "Once while we were hunting, we met a man from the village of the Cabri, on the Lesser River. He told me of such men, but I thought he had sun sickness. He told me their clubs were straight and shot arrows of fire and thunder. He said they rode upon sacred deer and captured his people as slaves many summers ago. Two of his own brothers were taken and he never saw them again."

Ipa swallowed. The smallest children scooted closer to their mothers and whimpered.

"They must be gods," the *cacique* said softly. "What do they want of us?"

Ipa's father shook his head, then took another drink of sotol.

"The word is out that these strangers are already at the village of the Shell People on the Lesser River. They are traveling in our direction, stopping at all the pueblos along the way."

"Perhaps they will not come here," one of the elders suggested. "They may turn southeast when they arrive at the Great River and get lost in Bear Mountains."

"Perhaps the Otomoacas villages will fight them and kill them before they reach us," another man suggested hopefully. The people nodded and spoke at once.

"And if they be gods?" The voice of Ipa's father cut through the noise and everyone turned silent.

The *cacique* told the women and children to return to their houses and the men assembled in the *kiva* to hold council and smoke a pipe.

Ipa reluctantly crawled through the hatch in the flat roof of her aunt's house and stepped down the ladder that led to the dark room below the earth. The fire was out and the light from the stars did not reveal the red-and-black stripes painted across the walls for decoration, but Ipa could smell the ochre. She smelled the dried corn and the earth and medicine plants hanging to dry. It reminded Ipa of her grandmother. Her aunt and uncle had been kind to take Ipa and Kadoh into their house, but still Ipa remembered happier days.

She crawled on her knees to her sleeping mat woven from reeds. Soon her aunt and cousin and Kadoh began to breathe the slow, deep breath of sleep, but Ipa still lay on her back, looking at the brilliant stars through the opening in the roof. How could anyone sleep while the men's voices rose to shouts then fell to silence in the council lodge? Far out on the desert, a coyote yelped and his notes echoed off the canyon walls, sending a chill through Ipa's body.

Ipa pulled her knees closer to her chin and closed

her eyes, but still she could not sleep. Her mind whirred with thoughts of white-faced men with turtle-shells, riding giant dogs. Why had they come to the river villages, and what would they do? Maybe they were gods. Perhaps they would bring rain with them and make the crops abundant. Perhaps they would bring death. Ipa trembled all through the night, but just before dawn, her weary mind turned to thoughts of being the wife of Coyomo, the Brave One. Suddenly a wave of comfort passed over her and she fell into a deep sleep.

## Chapter Three

ANOISE PULLED Ipa from her dream, a dream of giant turtle-men who devoured the people of her village as they waded up the river.

"Niece, wake up! Quickly!"

Ipa opened her eyes and saw the face of her aunt outlined against the opening in the roof.

"What is wrong?" Ipa asked as she rubbed her eyes.

"The council has made the decision. The women and children will go to the mountains to hide from the strangers."

Ipa sat up and watched her aunt flutter about

the room gathering her best pots and deerskins. She placed them in the middle of the floor.

"Auntie, what are you doing?" Ipa asked as an uneasy feeling crept over her.

"The council decided that we must offer gifts to the strangers so they will leave us in peace. A messenger from the lower village arrived last night. He told us that the strangers will take what they want anyway, so it is better to appease them early. Fetch those fancy baskets that I have been saving for your wedding day and put them in this pile."

Ipa crossed the room, her eyes finally adjusted to the dimness. She slipped two baskets from the wall, the ones made from the reeds along the river, the ones her aunt had worked on so diligently. Ipa traced her fingers over the beautiful pattern. Her aunt was the most talented weaver in the village. She could pull a weave so tight that no water could get through and her baskets always traded well with other villages.

Ipa gently laid the baskets on the pile. A stab of remorse filled her heart at the thought of the turtlemen having the baskets, but coveting possessions was not the custom among her people. Giving away a gift was more honorable and praiseworthy than receiving one.

The ladder rattled and shook as Xucate climbed down, carrying a basket of dried beans and a bag of *pinole,* finely ground corn.

"Where do you want this, Mother?" she asked.

"We will take it with us to the mountains. Niece, go fetch water from the river. There is no time to go to the spring."

Ipa picked up two long, sunbaked gourds with their tops cut off and insides removed. She climbed up the ladder onto the rooftop. Villagers hustled about like shadow spirits, whispering anxiously, piling their possessions into the plaza. Never had she seen their faces look so drawn and pale, not even when the crops failed and the people starved.

With a surge of urgency, Ipa darted to the river and filled the gourds with water. She had hardly had time to return to her aunt's house, when the women and children began the trek up the canyon trail. They would cross the yucca flats spotted with rocks and boulders, and then climb the nearest mountain.

Ipa had made the trip many times. Every autumn when the *pinyon* nuts ripened, the women journeyed to the cool mountains to gather them. It was a time of laughter; a time to make jokes about husbands and sons and brothers; a time to praise the worth of women; a time to prick your fingers on pinecones bursting with delicious seeds. It had been her grandmother's favorite time of the year, for certain medicine plants like juniper berries only grew in the mountains.

But this trip would be filled with anxiety. Perhaps some of the women would become widows while they waited. Ipa's stomach twisted into a tight knot as she thought about the village men, especially her father, facing the strangers. She loved and respected her father more than any man and could not bear the thought of never seeing his kind face again. Her heart told her to turn around and run back down the trail to beg her father to come with her. But she knew he would never do such a thing. Even Kadoh put up a struggle, for though he had only eight summers, he wanted to stay behind with the men. It was Xucate who had finally convinced him to come. Since she had saved his life, they had become very close.

Ahead on the flat plain, yucca plants stood against the reddening sky like stiff guards clutching their spears. In the village below, the men danced around the pile of possessions in the middle of the plaza, praying for protection from the strangers. The Old One had started a fire and was shuffling around it solemnly, beseeching guidance from the Great Spirit. Ipa felt sorry for the old people of the village who were too feeble to make the trek to the mountains. They were too old to fight and would be at the mercy of the turtle-men.

A little boy started to cry, but his mother hushed him.

"*Shh,* we must not shed tears," she said. "If you think bad thoughts, the god of ill fortune will hear you and make all your bad thoughts come true. We must think only good thoughts—thoughts of victory and reunion."

Ipa tried to follow the woman's advice, but at every little scrape or sound, Ipa jumped. She constantly glanced over her shoulder, expecting to see angry turtle-men on giant sacred dogs with teeth like those of a wolf coming after them.

But thoughts of fear did not seem to enter Xucate's mind. Carrying a twisted walking cane, she led the way with long, powerful strides, unconcerned that the other women and children could not keep up her strenuous pace. Only Kadoh trotted beside her, his hunting knife clacking against his narrow hips. *How much alike they are,* Ipa thought, *both stubborn and unwilling to bend.* Since the day that Xucate had rescued Kadoh from the Apaches, he followed her like a baby quail trailing its mother.

By the time they reached the mountains, the sun beat down on their heads. Ipa's deerskin cape kept the sun from burning her shoulders, but the back of her neck prickled with sweat, and the carrying strap of her burden-basket pressed into her forehead uncomfortably. Her long hair fell about her face and stuck to her damp cheeks. In the confusion, she had not had time to twist and coil it.

Near the foot of the mountains, the terrain grew rough with broken boulders as large as houses, and the climb grew steeper. The air grew cooler as they passed between fragrant junipers, pines, and shrubs.

A speckled snake-eater bird darted across their path, its long legs running smoothly and a partially devoured lizard hanging from its beak. Ipa heard the grunts of peccaries in the bushes as they ate succulent red cactus pears. If she were a man, she would have brought her bow and arrows and club and they would have fresh meat that night.

Soon the women reached the place where they gathered *pinyons,* but the cones were empty for they had already gathered them not long ago. The fresh smell of juniper tingled Ipa's nostrils as they stopped at a resting place. The women removed their burden-baskets and began preparing food for the children by mixing *pinole* with water to form a mushy paste.

Kadoh and Xucate sat under a twisted juniper tree and shared their food. Ipa sat on a gray rock in the shade of a small pine tree. She removed a strip of dried buffalo meat and chewed it slowly, savoring the juices. She could not see her village hidden beneath the canyon rim, but she could see the bend in the river. Beyond the bend, the Great River and the Lesser River joined. Many Otomoacas villages huddled along the low, fertile banks of the Great River at that place. The peoples of all the villages along the river spoke the same language, but Ipa's village was small by comparison and located farther up the river, where the canyon walls were steeper. Her little village was not as wealthy as those at the junction. Sometimes people from her village grew tired of the failing crops and moved to the junction, but Ipa did not want to live anyplace else. Of course, if she married Coyomo, the Brave One, she would have to go live with him in his village.

Ipa imagined Coyomo's tall, straight physique, his bright, fierce eyes, and his handsome face. She had seen him many times—once when she was only a child accompanying her grandmother to the junction villages. Coyomo's own father, *cacique* of the second village, had been stricken with a raging fever. Coyomo had stood beside his father's bed, his young face clouded with worry, his dark eyes full of fear. But Ipa's grandmother had worked a miracle that day and brought the *cacique* from the brink of death. Seven suns later, Coyomo and his father brought many gifts to Ipa's grandmother out of gratitude.

But it was at the annual harvesting of the prickly pear cactus fruit that Ipa looked forward to seeing Coyomo the most. People from many villages traveled to harvest the deep red and deliciously sweet tunas that grew abundantly in a region one day's journey from Ipa's village. Harvesting of the prickly pears was a time of great joy and merriment, especially for those eligible for marriage. Young adults participated in contests of running, kicking, or other feats of endurance. Men showed off their strength or dexterity, while women dressed in their finest clothes and held contests of their own. Occasionally girls and boys competed together, all in great fun. If a young man saw a certain girl that he wanted to marry, he would follow her home to her village and lay stalks of corn at her father's lodge. It was this way that men often found new wives from villages other than their own. Last autumn, after winning his foot-race against the other young men, Coyomo looked Ipa's way and smiled. And her heart was never the same.

For a moment Ipa forgot the turtle-men and became lost in thoughts of Coyomo and the chance that he would want to marry her. Was it truly possible? Or had he confused her name with her cousin's? After all, they both lived in the same lodge now. Xucate was beautiful beyond description, while Ipa was small. Besides, everyone knew that Xucate had shamelessly flirted with Coyomo at the last harvest games and since then bragged how she would marry him someday. Surely it was Xucate that Coyomo desired to marry, not Ipa.

Suddenly a new wave of anxiety moved over her. Coyomo was famous for his bravery. He alone had faced the black bear in the mountains and survived. Coyomo would stand up to the turtle-men and fight. If they were gods, they would strike him dead.

Ipa tried to force all thoughts of Coyomo from her mind, but her heart still felt sick. She tried to imagine what the turtle-men would look like. Ipa loved turtles and her favorite story was the legend of Turtle-Girl, which she had heard all her life. Ipa closed her eyes and could almost hear her grandmother's crackly voice recanting the story as the children snuggled into the warm buffalo hides beside a fire on a cold winter's night.

*Turtle-Girl was once a beautiful girl-child. All the gods loved her dearly and gave her special privileges,* the old woman would begin. *She drank from the Big Dipper and spoke with Grandfather Sun and Sister Moon. But one day Turtle-Girl grew very hungry and got into the Great Spirit's corn patch and stole some sacred corn. The Great Spirit banished her to the world beneath the ground. There Turtle-Girl met a tribe of people being held prisoner in a dark room with only one tiny hole in the wall. They looked human like her, but they were made of clay.*

*"I will set you free," Turtle-Girl proclaimed. Then she broke down the wall and led the clay people through a treacherous passageway up to Sacred Panther Mountain. When the sun touched their muddy faces, they became flesh and bone and called themselves The People. The Great Spirit was not pleased that his clay people had escaped, so he searched for Turtle-Girl to punish her.*

*Now, Turtle-Girl was terribly afraid, so she hid under a piece of round bark from a fallen cottonwood tree beside the Great River. When the Great Spirit saw the bark trembling, with legs and arms sticking out from it, he laughed and clapped his hands. The rounded piece of bark became attached to Turtle-Girl's back, and she was forced to crawl on all fours the rest of her life. She slid into the river to hide, but every year she crawls up on the bank to lay her eggs in the sand and cries great tears for her misdeeds. But The People loved Turtle-Girl and were grateful to her. They promised to never eat her flesh like the other animals in the river. And so it is today. You must never kill a turtle, and when you see one it will bring you good fortune.*

A smile crept to Ipa's lips as she touched the small turtle pendant hanging around her neck. Her father could not have chosen a better gift.

As Ipa opened her eyes and looked across the desert, a distant flash winked at her. She cupped a hand over her eyes and squinted. She saw a man running across the plain toward the foot of the mountain. The sun bounced off a pendant around his neck as he traveled at a steady pace along the trail.

Time passed too slowly. Silence smothered the air, save for the sound of mothers pulling their children closer and whispering words to calm their fears. Then one of the women grunted and pointed a finger callused from many years of grinding corn.

"That is my son running toward us."

The women quickly gathered their baskets and climbed down the mountain to meet the messenger.

"Word has come from the villages of the junction. The strangers do not want to harm us," he said as he leaned on a rock, catching his breath. "Quickly, return to the village and start preparing a feast for the strangers. They will be here by tomorrow evening."

A cry of relief rippled through the crowd as women thanked the Great Spirit. Ipa felt as if a boulder had been lifted from her shoulders, and suddenly she hugged Kadoh. Xucate threw her arms around Ipa and laughed with joy. Soon the air filled with women's prattle and cackles of glee as they hurriedly retraced their steps.

That night and the next day, the women worked swiftly. Girls ground corn all morning and fetched sweet water from the spring. Ipa's aunt placed several fresh sotol and agave cabbages into an earth oven to cook slowly. Xucate brought squash and beans from the roof and put them in calabashes of water to soak overnight. The young men scattered into the desert with their rabbit sticks and returned with limp, gray bodies carried in fiber nets. Some women ground dried buffalo meat and put it into pots of boiling water until it turned into a mush. Even the children worked, busily sweeping the earth with fresh juniper branches to make the air smell sweet.

Ipa's uncle and the older men of the village retired to the *kiva* to sing sacred songs and to pray, and to paint their faces and bodies with bright stripes of yellow and red ochre and white gypsum.

When the shadows grew longer and Ipa hurried back from her uncle's granary, she watched her friends and family bustling about, seeming too busy to worry about the strangers. She wondered if hers was the only heart that raced, and if hers were the only knees that trembled.

Suddenly she heard a scraping sound and looked up. As she watched the village crier climb on his rooftop, her heart pounded like a war drum.

"The strangers are coming," the crier shouted in a loud, clear voice. He repeated the words three more times until every person had stopped what he was doing and crawled onto his roof.

Ipa sat with her family on top of her uncle's house, watching a line in the desert grow closer.

"I see the great sacred deer they ride upon," whispered Kadoh.

"The men are as round as squash, and ugly," Xucate added, but Ipa knew it was not possible to see the men's faces.

As the strangers grew closer, whispers rippled over the rooftops. Never had Ipa seen such men, if indeed they were human.

First came other dark-skinned people like Ipa, carrying leaves on the ends of long sticks. They waved these slowly back and forth, creating a breeze for the white-skinned men.

"See, already they have taken slaves," Xucate whispered.

Two men in long brown robes led the procession. Though the desert sand was hot, no sandals covered their feet. They had removed the hair from the top of their skulls, leaving only fringes. The exposed circles of skin had been reddened by the sun.

"They will surely get sun sickness," Ipa's aunt whispered, then giggled.

As the train of men came closer, the laughter rose. Some men stood on the roofs, doubled over in laughter, pointing and clapping and making flute-like noises with their mouths.

The turtle-men did not seem to notice. They kept coming, sitting still on the backs of great, hoofed beasts that had no horns. Soon they were so close that Ipa could hear the squeak of the leather that they sat upon and the jingle of the lines that ran into the mouths of the sacred deer they rode. Everything about them seemed to shine or squeak or jingle. So close were they, that Ipa could have leaned over the roof and touched the tips of their pointed lances.

The turtle-men were not short and round, as Ipa had first thought. It was the padded leather they wore around their chests and backs that made them appear that way. Their legs looked too skinny for their round bodies, and seemed to have been painted. Shiny head coverings that curved up sharply on the ends flashed in the sun when the men turned their heads. Bushy hair covered the sun-reddened faces of the men.

Even though her heart was in her throat, Ipa joined in the laughter.

"Look at their sacred deer," Kadoh whispered. "Have you ever seen such beasts? Where are their antlers? And see how their tails swish like a woman's hair." He stared at the strange animals.

"They are foolish to wear so many clothes in the heat of the day," Ipa's aunt whispered. "They sweat like men in a sweat bath."

"Yes, and they smell like men in a sweat bath," Xucate added. She held her nose and made such a face that even Ipa could not stop from bursting into laughter.

Behind the mounted men walked many more brown-skinned people, carrying bundles on their shoulders. Two of them carried a strange object made of two pieces of wood tied together.

Ipa could not understand the words coming from the mouths of the strangers, but a man of the Abriache tribe on the Lesser River had accompanied them and served as an interpreter. His village spoke a dialect of Ipa's language, though he pronounced many of the words differently.

Ipa's father greeted them with the sign of peace by raising his hands to the sun, then placing them on his breast. He spoke to the Abriache guide, using his hands to make signs when the man did not understand the words.

"The strangers call themselves *españoles*," Ipa's father announced at last. "They have traveled the Lesser River for many suns, from the place where the macaws live. They are hungry and tired and want to rest their great sacred deer for a while."

"You are welcome to share all that we have, strangers," Ipa's uncle replied. "Take these things." He waved the village's sacred cane over the pile of goods in the middle of the plaza. Then he breathed on the leader's hand to show his respect.

The band of *españoles* listened carefully as the guide interpreted the words. Their leader, a man with black chin hair shaped into a point, shouted at his warriors and they climbed down from the giant animals. They stretched their arms and legs and removed their silver bonnets.

"Tell the *españoles* we will give them food and drink and a place to rest, and anything they need," Ipa's uncle said. He presented the leader with three large blue stones.

The *español* leader smiled and nodded, then he shouted to his warriors. The band of men pounced onto the pile of goods like hungry grasshoppers. They picked through the things and shoved and hit and fought over who would get bows and arrows and tanned hides. But they left the beautiful baskets, grinding stones, a good supply of yucca roots, and a prayer stick covered with majestic eagle feathers.

"These strangers do not know the value of things," Ipa's aunt whispered as she twisted the grains of corn off a cob into a basket. "Your father always gets a good trade for my baskets."

"And it took my husband many days to find the eagle's nest for those feathers," said another woman. "He still bears the scars of the mother eagle's claws when he stole away one of her chicks."

"I wonder if their hairs cover all of their bodies," Xucate said, making the women near her burst into giggles.

Ipa wanted to join in the laughter, but her heart still pounded in her chest. When her uncle motioned for her and Kadoh to join him, she discovered that her legs shook like a newborn fawn's.

"Little Niece, bring some of your medicine plants for the sacred deer of this young man. Its leg is swollen from a snakebite," her uncle said. "And Nephew, fetch some food for this young man."

Ipa and Kadoh stared at the young *español* standing next to their uncle under the cottonwood tree. He had not joined his companions fighting over the gifts, but remained beside a golden brown animal that hung its head and rested its weight off one hind leg. The *español* ran his hand over the animal's neck and spoke to it in a soft, gentle voice that seemed full of concern.

"Quickly, now," Ipa's uncle said, and gave Ka-doh a gentle push. Kadoh nodded. He ripped his feet from the ground and padded toward their aunt's lodge.

"My niece will bring great medicine for your sacred deer," Ipa's uncle said with a flourish of his feathered cane. "And my nephew will bring you food and drink for your stomach." He said all this in his own language to the Abriache guide. The guide spoke to the *español* with strange words that sounded rattly and soft, like the growl of a panther.

"*Muchas gracias,*" said the young stranger, his dark black eyes looking directly at Ipa. Though dust covered his face and his silver hat had pressed a red line across his brow, he was not unpleasant to look at. The nose was far larger than those of any of the men in her village, but the teeth were straight and white when he smiled. If only brown hair did not grow out of his face, perhaps it would be handsome underneath.

Ipa trotted to her grandmother's empty house, where she kept roots and leaves and berries and stems of medicine plants. She had treated humans for snakebite, but never an animal. Sometimes the medicine worked, sometimes all the prayers and chanting could not save the person, especially if it was a child.

By the time Ipa returned to the young man, the guide and her uncle were gone.

"*Ah, medicina,*" the young man said, smiling and rubbing his hands together.

Ipa tiptoed forward and cautiously laid a bundle of mesquite bean pods in front of the animal, then stepped back. The animal blew air from its nostrils and the soft white muzzle quivered. Suddenly it raised its lips and chomped down on the beans.

"*¡Bueno!*" the stranger shouted, then clapped his hands together.

Ipa laid her basket down and knelt beside the giant beast. She carefully mixed the crushed leaves of a *lantana* bush with buffalo fat to make a paste, then smeared it on the swollen leg. On top of this she patted a layer of red clay. She removed sacred corn pollen from her medicine pouch and sprinkled it on the sacred deer, then chanted a prayer to the Great Spirit.

The stranger watched her with wide, curious eyes.

"*Muchas gracias,*" he said at last, after Ipa had finished the healing ceremony. "*Me llamo Rodrigo Carlos de Castellanos.*" The words rolled off his tongue like water gurgling over stones in the river.

Ipa felt her face turning hot. Perhaps he did not like her ceremony. She had never treated a sick deer before and probably had done it all wrong. The stranger must have seen through her and was displeased.

"*Rodrigo,*" the man repeated, thumping his finger on his chest.

Ipa found it impossible to look into his piercing black eyes. She swallowed hard and glanced toward the plaza, where she saw Kadoh tiptoeing with a basket of food.

"*¿Como te llamas?*" the stranger asked in a softer voice, as if coaxing an animal into a snare.

Ipa began to tremble. Thoughts of gods with flashing eyes and hurling bolts of lightning swirled in her head. She wanted to turn and run, but to disobey her uncle's orders was impossible.

"*Ahh . . .*" He sighed and shook his head. Ipa felt his hand slip under her chin and force it up. She felt the warmth of his fingers and smelled the dust still clinging to the leather that covered them.

He smiled, showing most of his teeth. Ipa imitated him, thinking it would please him. He laughed and nodded.

"*¡Bueno!*" He patted her cheek.

Kadoh crept closer and timidly handed the man a gourd filled with sotol drink and a handful of flattened corn cakes and some roasted rabbit. The *español* devoured the food. He finished the sotol, then sighed heavily and leaned back against the trunk of the cottonwood tree.

"*Me llamo Rodrigo,*" he said, thumping his chest again.

"What did he say?" Kadoh whispered.

"Maybe he did not like the food," Ipa replied under her breath. "It was not very much. The real feast will be later tonight."

"Tell him that," Kadoh advised.

Ipa cleared her throat and spoke in her most persuasive voice. "Sir, I am sorry our food is so meager, but the women need time to make special dishes and bake agave bulbs in the earth ovens. The men of the village already sit in the council lodge busily painting their bodies and discussing the dances they will perform for our honored guests."

The stranger cocked his head to one side, then scratched his beard.

"I want to touch this sacred deer," Kadoh whispered. "It is so splendid."

"It might turn and devour you," Ipa replied. "I have never seen an animal so big, except for the black bear that our father brought home when I was very young."

The *español* saw Kadoh's wide eyes staring at the animal. He gently took Kadoh's hand and placed it on the shiny golden brown skin. The skin quivered and the animal snorted and stomped a hoof. Kadoh yelped and leaped back. The stranger laughed, so did Ipa, then Kadoh joined in.

Kadoh returned his small hand to the broad glistening neck and stroked it again. He ran his hand from the neck to the shoulders. This time the animal sighed and thrust its head into the pile of beans again, its ears twitching back and forth.

"Its skin is warm and soft," Kadoh whispered.

"*Caballo*," the young man said, patting the animal's neck. "*De Andalucía*." He stared into Ipa's blank face, then patted the animal's neck again. "*Caballo*."

Ipa and Kadoh glanced at each other. "What do you think he wants us to do?" Kadoh asked.

"I do not know," Ipa whispered. "But why take a chance on angering him? I think we should do as he does."

Kadoh nodded in agreement.

"*Caballo*." Kadoh and Ipa repeated the strange word in unison. She wondered if the word meant deer in the stranger's language, or maybe it meant wondrous or beautiful or maybe it was a pet name for the beast. She glanced up to see the man's dark eyes smiling at her.

"*¡Bueno!*" he said, grinning and clapping. "*¡Muy bueno!*"

Kadoh and Ipa exchanged glances again, then began clapping and smiling, too. "*Muy bueno*," they repeated.

The stranger doubled over in glee and clapped his hands together even louder.

This was a strange god indeed, Ipa thought. He appeared to be friendly and kind. She prayed that he would remain that way.

71

## Chapter Four

IPA WIPED a stream of perspiration from her temple and stepped back as her aunt, using two sticks as tongs, placed another hot stone from the fire into the water-filled calabash. Immediately the water churned and bubbled, then began to simmer. Her aunt dropped in a handful of rabbit meat cut into tiny chunks, some squash, and dried beans that had been soaked separately. Ipa stirred the stew idly while her eyes watched the *españoles* sitting in the pueblo plaza.

The men of her village had formed two lines and now danced forward, first two at a time, then four, then eight, until every man had danced around the fire. They had spent the day painting their bodies and dressing their heads in goose and turkey feathers. She recognized her uncle's tall, slender form at the front of the line, his feathered cane gripped in one hand and a rattling gourd in the other. Those not dancing sang songs and clapped their thighs with their hands or made flutelike noises with their mouths. The strangers laughed and clapped, even though the occasion was a solemn one. They had removed their leather turtle shells and quilted shirts padded with many layers of straw and cotton. These coverings were so thick that surely an enemy's arrow would not penetrate them. The *españoles* had kept on the thin cloth that stretched over their legs and the puffed-up pants that made their hips look as round as squash. They wore cloth shirts over their upper bodies, too. The strangers smelled awful, and Ipa had not seen one of them bathe in the river, even though they reeked of dust and sweat. Her own people bathed often during the warm seasons, using yucca roots for suds. Boys her own age even bathed in the icy waters during winter to test their endurance.

"Niece, no time for idleness." Her aunt's sharp tongue interrupted Ipa's daydream. "Run to the communal granary and fetch more soft corn. And you, Daughter, quickly go test the agave bulbs— they have been baking in the ground long enough."

Xucate looked up from where she knelt at the

first grinding stone, crushing dried kernels of corn with a rounded stone *mano*. Xucate always performed the first grinding of the dried corn, for her strength was great and she could break the flint-hard kernels easily. Ipa's aunt would perform the second grinding on the next stone, making the corn even finer. Ipa, whose arms were weak, would break the corn into a fine meal on the last grinding stone. Every day the women and girls ground the corn until their arms ached, then patted balls of cornmeal mush into flat corn cakes.

"But Mother," Xucate protested, "the strangers are eating all our food. If we give them the agave bulbs, from what will we make flour during the cold winter months?"

"Do not worry, child. Our kindness and generosity to strangers will be rewarded. We must show them that we are a peaceful people. What good is a basket full of food if we are dead and cannot eat it? Now hurry."

Ipa and her cousin walked together across the far end of the darkening plaza where Grandfather Sun's long golden fingers had dragged across the men's faces, leaving them in shadows. The flames of the central bonfire around which the men now danced grew brighter and cinders climbed into the sky like runaway rabbits with their tails on fire. The strange men laughed and clapped their hands together, pointing at the dancers. Most of them had been drinking sotol for a long time and now their great noses had turned red.

"Look, Little Cousin, that *español* is watching you," Xucate whispered as they paused at the place where steam rose from small holes in the ground and the earth felt hot. Xucate poked a sharp stick into a slot in the ground to test the bulbs for their doneness, then rose. "His wicked eyes are following every move you make."

Ipa glanced over her shoulder at the young man who called himself Rodrigo. He stood apart from the other strangers, beside his sick animal, stroking its neck and speaking softly. He caught Ipa's eyes a moment, nodded, and smiled lightly.

Xucate chuckled.

"He likes you, Cousin. Perhaps you should grind corn tonight outside our house. If you tell him you brought the rain once and that you know the secret of the medicine plants, maybe he will marry you this very night. Maybe now is your chance to get a husband." Xucate laughed and tossed her shiny hair over one shoulder.

Though the words were only spoken in jest, Ipa felt her cheeks turn hot. Suddenly she could not hold back the secret that had been bursting to get free from her heart.

"Do not be so sure that I will not find a husband. A brave warrior in the second village at the junction inquired about me just three suns ago."

Xucate's laughter stopped and her lips fell into a frown.

"Where did you hear such news?"

"My father told me."

"Then it must be so. Congratulations, Little Cousin." Xucate smiled and hugged Ipa fiercely. "The man is getting a fine bargain. No other girl your age knows medicine plants. Your father is the finest hunter and trader in all the villages, and your uncle is a grand *cacique* known for his wisdom. You are kindhearted and gentle natured like a doe. Yes, you will make a fine prize. Do you know the young man's name? Perhaps I have seen him at the harvest games." Xucate squeezed Ipa's hands in her own and her eyes twinkled.

Suddenly Ipa wished she had not spoken. Xucate's teasing tongue had suddenly turned sweet as yucca fruit.

"I ... I ... am not sure." Ipa staggered over her words.

"Come, come, you must tell me."

"It's only a rumor. It cannot be true. One as great as he would not want one so small and common as me. . . ."

"Then you *do* know his name?"

"I must go now." Ipa broke from her cousin's hands. "Besides, it is bad luck to speak of a marriage before it happens. The god of ill fortune will hear our wishes and work his mischief to prevent them from coming true. My marriage is not certain yet."

"That is true." Xucate began scraping the earth from the top of the oven, her strong arms lifting layers of rocks and hides as if they were nothing. "You must perform all the bridal tasks well enough to suit the man's family. Perhaps your weak arms will fail you." She jabbed a cooked agave bulb and placed it into her basket.

Ipa started to walk away, but Xucate's words stopped her.

"Little Cousin," Xucate said without looking up from her work. "I promise you I will find out his name. And I will learn why you are hiding the truth from me."

Ipa ran into the shadows of the night, glad to get away from Xucate's inquisition. She hated going into the granaries after dark, but she could not bear being around her cousin another moment.

Ipa groped her way to the cone-shaped structure made of woven willow branches. She stepped gingerly, for mice loved to nibble the grains and play in the darkness. But the mice did not bother her as much as the snakes that came to feast on the mice.

Ipa crept to the communal storage hut that belonged to the whole village. This corn was used for emergencies and when strangers visited. Her aunt's corn hut was closer to their house. Since Ipa's uncle was the *cacique,* he did not have to plant his own cornfield, or pull weeds, or harvest, or do any of the work. Neither was he allowed to hunt, for all his time was spent praying and making decisions for the survival of the village.

As Ipa swished the ground ahead of her with a stalk of green cane, she heard something rustle in the bushes. Her heart leaped into her throat.

"Go away, Brother Rattlesnake. I do not want to see your lovely skin tonight. I am in too much of a hurry to stop and admire your beauty." She spoke as her grandmother often had spoken. The villagers claimed that the old woman had been able to charm any animal with flattery. Ipa prayed the snakes were listening. "I know your patterns are lovely in the moonlight, but we have important guests. If you would be so kind as to slide away from my feet, I will be most grateful."

A bush rustled behind her. Ipa yelped and turned around. A gray fox stared at her, a squeaking mouse dangling from its mouth.

"Go ahead, Sister Fox," Ipa said with a laugh. "You may share our feast tonight. But save some mice for my family's dinner tomorrow."

Ipa chuckled as the fox turned on silent feet and loped away into the canyon.

*"Ah, perdón, señorita."* A voice behind her made Ipa yelp and spin around again. The young *español* who called himself Rodrigo stood a few paces from her, a smile breaking his face. He held a strange box

with a tiny fire inside. It cast eerie shadows and made everything it touched turn gold. Rodrigo held the light up high as Ipa lifted the door to the storage hut.

The musty odor of dried corn and mildew filled her nostrils. Even though her aunt checked their granary daily for moldy ears and though Ipa replaced the juniper branch inside the dark room often, the musty smell was always there. This granary held what they called flour corn. It was not as hard as the flint corn that the women commonly used. Soft corn was easier to grind and had a sweeter flavor, but it molded easily. Worst of all, mice could eat this corn easier than the stone-hard flint corn. Ipa pinched her nose shut and at the same time heard Rodrigo go into a fit of sneezing behind her.

"*¡Madre mía!*" he said, then followed her lead and pinched his own nose.

The light fell across the piles of corn. Mice squeaked and scurried in all directions, bumping into one another in their haste to get away from the light.

"*¡Los ratones!*" Rodrigo shouted. He stomped his heavy leather shoes, lifting one foot after another, as if he were dancing. He forgot to pinch his nose and broke into another fit of sneezing. Ipa could not stop herself from giggling.

"*Ah, bueno,*" Rodrigo said as he stopped dancing and pointed to her smiling face. "*Muy bonita.*" He traced the outline of a smile on her face.

Ipa felt her cheeks turning red. She turned away and, after touching the bundle of sacred feathers in the corner of the room and giving a quick prayer of thanks to the Corn Mother, she piled the ears into her basket.

Ipa wondered what Rodrigo was doing there, but as the Abriache guide had explained to them, the *españoles* had many strange rituals for their gods.

He talked all the while they walked back to the pueblo, as if she could understand his tongue, and he helped her carry the basket to the grinding stones. He watched the women mash swollen, soft kernels of flint corn that had been soaked in lime water to remove their hard shells. He seemed fascinated as they spread this *nixtamal* paste around ground meat, then covered it with a corn husk and placed it in hot coals. The women and girls giggled as he dipped his finger into bowls of *masa* and *frijoles* and tasted a strip of fresh cactus pad. Sometimes he smiled, sometimes he made an awful face. Ipa was glad when at last he bowed at the waist and left, for already the women were calling him "He-Who-Likes-Ipa-tah-chi."

Later that night the women presented their finest feast before the honored guests. The men and boys of the village sang and danced some more. A few of the strangers got up and danced, too; others laughed and slapped their legs. They all downed so-tol drink until their eyes glazed over, except for the two dressed in the long brown tunics. A few of the strangers got sick and ran to the bushes to vomit, and one of them passed out.

The next morning, the *españoles* prayed on their knees in front of the wooden cross that had been planted at the end of the pueblo on a small rise in the ground. With bowed heads, they mumbled soft words, then touched their heads and hearts and both shoulders with their right hands. The man they called Padre wore a brown robe that reached to the ground and was cinched at the waist with a rope. Around his neck a long string of beads twinkled in the morning sun. He made secret signals in the air. The *españoles,* and even some of the brown-skinned people who accompanied them, repeated his words in unison.

After the ceremony, the Abriache guide called the villagers to an assembly in the middle of the plaza. He stood beside the leader of the *españoles* and translated his words.

"The *maestro de campo* wants to know if you have seen these metals in your region," the guide said. Two of the *españoles* held up ugly rocks that had been broken apart.

"The metal will look like this after it has been taken from the stones," the guide continued. The *maestro de campo* held up a drinking vessel. It was almost the color of certain yellow cactus blooms, but very shiny. Then the padre lifted up the cross that hung around his neck. A beam of sunlight hit it and bounced back into Ipa's curious eyes.

When the leaders of Ipa's village told the strangers that they did not know of such metals, the *maestro de campo* showed great disappointment. Next, the guide showed them pieces of woven cloth of many wondrous colors and asked if anyone knew where to find more of it. The village elders nodded and quickly the *cacique* told the *españoles* that the Corn People to the north made such clothing out of cotton. This news greatly pleased the *español* leader, who, out of gratitude, gave Ipa's uncle a necklace made of colored beads of a kind they had never seen before.

After the *maestro de campo* had stepped aside, the padre spoke to them.

"Fray Hernandez says that the god of the *español* is more powerful than the Great Spirit or Panther Spirit," the guide announced in a loud voice. "If you repeat his sacred words, his god will protect you and you will receive great rewards. If you do not bow to their god, you will have great misfortune."

"What kind of rewards are we going to get?" Kadoh whispered to Ipa as they formed a line with the rest of the village. "I hope they will give us macaw feathers. I will make a beautiful bonnet for Rodrigo's sacred deer."

"I hope it is some of those beads like the padre wears around his neck," Xucate replied as she stared at the robed man.

"Yes," Ipa's aunt agreed. "Truly those beads are finer than any I've seen before. They are rounder than mountain-laurel seeds."

Soon the whole village buzzed with speculation and anticipation. They eagerly stood in front of the padre as he made magical signs in the air. They diligently and respectfully repeated the strange words the guide told them to, though they did not know what they meant, nor did they care, except that it pleased the robed man and the captain of the soldiers. But after the padre left, a wave of disappointment rippled through the crowd and anger wrinkled the brow of Ipa's aunt.

"Where are the great rewards?" she said with a grunt. "We gave them all our best possessions. They give us nothing but words."

"I told you we should not trust those strangers," Xucate said. "I will not go near one of them. They smell like a wolf's den. It would be better if you and Kadoh stay away from that tall stranger, Cousin."

"But we are taking care of his sacred deer," Kadoh insisted. "Rodrigo is kind to me and Big Sister."

"Kind until you displease him," the Old One said with a snort. "Look at their strange weapons—the tall spikes tipped with shiny points and hooks on one side. And see those long knives that they carry on their hips? I've seen the blades cut through the yucca roots and slice a squash in less than half the time our digging tools would take. But do you think those things were made to cut yucca roots? No, they are weapons of war made for killing men. Some of the *españoles* carry heavy bows that shoot short, thick arrows. Why, they are strung so tight, the men must use both their hands and their feet to load them." The Old One paused and pretended to draw an imaginary crossbow.

"Yes, the arrows thump like thunder when they hit an object," Ipa's aunt said, interrupting the Old One. "Have you watched the faces of our warriors as the arrows split gourds into many pieces? The village men say nothing, but I know they are imagining the pain of the arrow in their own chests."

Though it was the idle gossip of women, what they said became true, for as the days passed, the more the visitors displayed their talents, the more the men of Ipa's village whispered among themselves and acted like mice, scampering to stay out of the way. Everyone prayed to the Great Spirit that these *españoles* would soon leave. The *cacique* ordered his people to present more gifts every day, until no one had anything of value left and the food supply was shrinking.

But in spite of the Old One's warning, Ipa and Kadoh continued to visit Rodrigo and his sick *caballo*. Ipa continued to doctor the horse's swollen leg with *lantana* leaves and fed it mesquite beans until it was past the danger of dying. Rodrigo seemed amazed that the mesquite beans were so helpful. He acted as if he had never seen them before, though Ipa could not imagine any land so far away that mesquite did not grow there.

Kadoh loved the *caballo*. He gathered grass and weeds from the riverbanks and fed mesquite bean pods to the animal by hand, stroking its shiny neck and speaking to it respectfully. He even slept with it at night and brought water in a large calabash to cool it off in the heat of the day. He and Ipa's father built an open manger made of *tornillo* wood poles topped with straw and leaves and covered with a layer of adobe mud. It looked just like the *ramadas* the men built in the far cornfields to protect the workers from the hot sun. Kadoh even snitched some of the macaw feathers from their uncle's house and made a bonnet for the animal. Rodrigo laughed, but he didn't remove the bonnet from the *caballo*'s head. He called the animal Alegro, which Ipa understood to mean a fast runner.

Soon Alegro recovered and pranced about, its small, finely shaped head held high and its glorious tail arched. The long tail and mane of all the *caballos* were magnificent to see as the *españoles* rode them and played games. Never had anyone in the village seen such wondrous beasts, nor such talented men. Ipa thought that Rodrigo was the best of them all. He was able to ride like the wind, then swoop down and pick up a turkey buried in the sand with just its neck and head sticking up. Surely no other man, not even Coyomo, had such talents.

On the sixth day, Ipa and Kadoh sat in the hot sun next to Alegro's manger. As usual, Kadoh fanned the beautiful animal to keep away flies. Rodrigo sat on a flat rock, rolling up a dried corn husk filled with leaves of the *tobago* plant that grew wild along the river. The village elders ground the leaves and pressed them into a cane stick or into a clay pipe and only smoked on solemn occasions, but Rodrigo enjoyed it all the time. He lit the end of the husk on a hot coal and breathed in deeply.

As he slowly exhaled, Ipa studied his handsome face and warm brown eyes. He had trimmed his beard and mustache so that he looked much less like a bear than when he first arrived. Ipa and Kadoh had learned a few words of Rodrigo's language. He was very eager to learn words of their own language, though he could not pronounce them correctly and Ipa and Kadoh had to bite their tongues to keep from laughing.

"Ipa beautiful," he said in her own language, tinged with a heavy accent. He touched her face gently, and she smelled the *tobago* on his fingers.

*"Rodrigo muy hermoso,"* Ipa replied with a smile, hoping she was saying the right word for handsome.

Rodrigo laughed, then pulled her close and placed a feathery soft kiss on her forehead. Ipa felt heat rush to her cheeks. Kadoh put his hand over his mouth to stifle his giggles. Ipa wanted to say something else, but no appropriate words of *español* would come to her mind. She had only learned little things like the words for sun and sky and river and earth and buffalo. She pulled away and grabbed her basket of herbs, then ran to the roof of her grandmother's old adobe house.

Sitting there among the ears of drying flint corn, she watched Rodrigo joking with Kadoh and repairing his saddle. A while later, he put Kadoh on Alegro's broad back and led him along the riverbank. Even from that distance, Ipa heard the joyful squeals of her little brother and the hearty laughter of Rodrigo. She wondered what it would be like to marry an *español,* but that could never be. His *caballo* would soon be completely well and he would go away forever.

On the seventh day, the *maestro de campo* became restless, and the guide told Ipa's uncle that they were preparing to leave. They wanted bags of water and any dried buffalo meat the village could spare. Ipa's aunt fussed and hid all her meat except for a few strips, but her uncle warned that it might bring the wrath of the Great Spirit on them if they tried to deceive the strangers.

On the dawn of the eighth day, Kadoh threw his arms around the neck of Alegro and sadly said goodbye to the beautiful animal. Rodrigo hugged Kadoh as if they were brothers.

"I think you would like to go with him," Ipa whispered to Kadoh as Rodrigo saddled Alegro.

"Yes, I would love to travel over the land with him and Alegro. Perhaps he would let me ride every day."

Kadoh handed Rodrigo the bow that he had carried for years. It was the kind that the village men were famous for making, reinforced on the ends with buffalo horns, though it was worn from use. Their father had been working on a new one since his return nine days ago.

"*Muchas gracias, mi amigo,*" Rodrigo said. He removed a small knife with a broken handle from its sheath and handed it to Kadoh.

"*Muchas gracias, mi amigo,*" Kadoh mimicked, then hugged Rodrigo tightly.

Ipa handed Rodrigo a basket of *charqui,* dried beef from the buffalo, which the *español* called *cibolas.* She also gave him a bag of *pinole.*

Rodrigo removed a delicate silver crucifix from his neck and slipped it over Ipa's head. It clinked softly next to the turtle amulet that her father had given her.

"Give him something," Kadoh whispered to his sister. "Show him the kindness he has shown us."

"What do I have he would want besides food?" Ipa replied.

"Your turtle charm."

"But Father gave that to me as a token of his love and respect."

"You *must* give him something of value, Sister," Kadoh insisted.

Ipa slowly removed the small pearly shell carved into the shape of a turtle. She handed it to Rodrigo. He kissed the turtle and smiled as he slipped it around his neck.

*"Muchas gracias, bonita."*

Without hesitation, he grabbed her hand and pressed his lips to her fingers. His lips felt soft and warm, but the hair on his chin tickled and scratched. With a flourish, he swooped off his helmet and bent low at the waist. Kadoh imitated him, though he had no hat. Ipa didn't know if this was something only men did, so she only made a little bow.

*"Vaya con Dios,"* Rodrigo said after he had swung up onto Alegro.

"And may the Great Spirit go with you," Ipa replied softly. She and Kadoh watched Rodrigo join the line of mounted men, foot soldiers, and native servants.

"I will miss Rodrigo." Kadoh sighed.

"And I will miss our father," Ipa added. "He agreed to guide the *españoles* to the land of the Corn People. I wish he were not going. We did not get to see him very long."

"He did not finish my new bow." Kadoh sighed,

then quickly added, "But it is a great honor that the strangers asked our father to guide them. Father knows the languages of the people there."

"But our enemies lie in that direction, too," Ipa reminded him.

"Our father is brave. He is not afraid of any man."

Ipa nodded. Her own heart swelled with pride as she saw her father take the place of the Abriache guide at the front of the procession.

*"Vaya con Dios,"* Rodrigo shouted out as the line of mounted men passed by, followed by a longer line of servants on foot.

The rising cloud of dust stung Ipa's eyes, making them water. Amid the clack of hooves, the squeak of leather, and the clang of metal, she watched the strangers leave her village.

Ipa and Kadoh climbed up on their grandmother's roof and sat watching the departing men and beasts. Her heart felt empty as Rodrigo slowly faded away and became but a speck on the horizon. She heard Kadoh sniff and knew that his eyes were as wet as her own. She squeezed his brown shoulders, then stood up.

"We must return to our lives, Little Beetle. Rodrigo and Alegro are gone forever." Kadoh looked up into her face, his eyes rimmed in red. He drew in a long, deep breath, then nodded and climbed from the house.

Soon Ipa was in the desert digging more agave bulbs to replace those eaten by the *españoles,* and grinding more corn. By the end of the day, Rodrigo seemed more like a dream than reality. After all, the river had not changed, the sky and desert and mountains had not changed. Only the tiny silver crucifix around her neck reminded her that she had met the *español.*

Perhaps she would think about Rodrigo once in a while, late at night before falling asleep, but he was gone, never to return. Now, it was Coyomo, the Brave One, whom she must think about. The fruit of the prickly cactus was getting ripe. Soon its sweet smell would fill the air as peccaries grunted and snorted and smacked their greedy lips over the juicy red fruit, devouring thorns and all. And soon the families of many villages would gather on the plain to collect the tunas and to watch the young adults play games. If Coyomo was coming to her uncle's lodge with stalks of corn, it would be very soon. And if Coyomo did indeed choose her to be his bride, how could she ever face her cousin, Xucate, again?

# Chapter Five

THE HARVEST games arrived amid a flurry of boisterous young men with painted bodies wearing jingling copper bells and feathers. The girls likewise dressed in their finest deerskin capes and ponchos and skirts. They painted their chins and eyes. They combed one another's long hair and twisted it into elaborate styles, all the while giggling and joking about who would end up marrying which man.

While the young men ran races and played games of kicking sticks or balls, the girls played games of their own. As usual, Xucate outran all the other girls in the footrace, her hair flying behind her in the wind. She ground corn faster and filled her basket higher in the women's games, her strong arms rolling the *mano* like one possessed by a demon. In every contest she surpassed the other unmarried girls, winning the admiration of all the young men.

Ipa did well in the game of carrying hot rocks to the calabash for boiling water and the basket-weaving game, but she could not beat her strong cousin in anything else. Yet it was all in good fun; Ipa was happy for her cousin. Some of the elders said Xucate was showing too much pride in her success, more like a young warrior or an Apache woman. A truly proper woman would be humble and share her victory, they said. But Ipa did not complain about her cousin's vanity; if ever a girl had the right to feel boastful, surely it was beautiful Xucate.

Nor did Ipa say a word when Xucate cast hungry eyes toward Coyomo throughout the week. In spite of Xucate's promise, she had not found out that it was Coyomo who had inquired about Ipa. In her heart, Ipa knew that every race won, every feat accomplished by Xucate, made her own chances with Coyomo grow smaller.

Two evenings after the games had ended, when Coyomo brought stalks of blue corn and laid them in front of the *cacique*'s lodge, a stir arose inside. Xucate danced with joy, so sure was she that Coyomo had come to choose her.

"Coyomo watched me win the footrace," Xucate proclaimed loudly to her mother, who was twirling her fire stick over dry grass. "He knows my worth. He has come for me."

Many other young men laid stalks in front of the *cacique*'s house that evening, too. Some corn was yellow, some red, some black, according to each man's family. They were all meant for Xucate, but she tossed them aside without regret, thus letting the men know that she was not interested.

Inside Ipa's heart a fierce battle raged on. If Coyomo chose her, it would be the greatest honor of her life. Yet if he did, surely it would bring down the wrath of her cousin. Hadn't Xucate boasted of her desire for Coyomo and her sureness that he would choose her? Wouldn't Xucate's heart die of humiliation if Coyomo chose small, weak Ipa over one so beautiful and strong? Though Ipa's head told her to forget Coyomo, her heart would not let her.

That night both girls dressed in their finest clothes and wove feathers into their hair. Each girl took seeds of Coyomo's blue corn and a grinding rock and sat in front of the *cacique*'s house. Many other girls had received cornstalks, too, and were in front of their father's lodges, grinding corn as they waited for young men. Ipa's fingers trembled as she began grinding the blue corn.

"Why do you grind Coyomo's corn?" Xucate asked with a toss of her silky black hair. "He will not choose you, Cousin. You are too small and unimportant. Your father roams the country, while my father

94

stays and leads the people. Why don't you go back inside now and save yourself the pain of his rejection? Or take the corn of one of my other suitors?"

Ipa felt a jab of pain in her heart. Xucate's words, once as sweet as yucca flowers, now had turned rancid, but Ipa refused to let her tears fall. Perhaps Xucate was right, perhaps Coyomo would not even glance Ipa's way. Only once during the games had she noticed him looking at her. And when she smiled meekly, his face had remained stern and unsmiling. Perhaps her father had been teasing with her after all and Coyomo had never spoken to him about a wife.

A short while later, as Ipa was still cracking the hard blue grains under her hand stone, Xucate's voice exclaimed in an excited whisper.

"He is coming!"

The strings of copper bells around his knees jingled and the necklaces of blue stones and white bear teeth and pink coral clacked against his chest as he strode across the plaza to the *cacique*'s lodge. Ipa held her breath and tried to still her racing heart as he came closer. At last he stopped in front of her. Ipa's heart pounded in her chest and in her ears so loudly that she could hardly hear Coyomo's words.

"Stop grinding your corn and be my wife, Ipa-tah-chi," he said in a firm voice, full of confidence.

Ipa heard a little gasp come from Xucate's lips. She swallowed hard and her fingers trembled as they continued their job. Only the rasp of stone against corn filled the air. Ipa held her breath while she waited for Coyomo to repeat his words. She didn't want to appear overly anxious. Her grandmother had taught her that a girl must never let the suitor think she wants him.

*It is best to keep grinding the corn for three full nights,* the old woman had said one day while twisting Ipa's long black hair around her ears. *He will think he has gotten a great value if he must work hard to win your affections.*

Ipa knew her grandmother had been all-wise, but her heart told her that if she did not stop the grinding now, Coyomo would not bother to return the next night. Or he might turn and choose Xucate, who would not hesitate to accept his proposal.

Ipa stared at the ground and continued the grinding. She heard a whispery curse from her cousin, and then the sigh of Coyomo. He left on feet so silent Ipa did not know he was gone until her cousin's voice screeched into the air.

"You are a fool, Cousin! No other girl would turn down Coyomo, the Brave One. If you do not accept him, I shall leap out of your shadow and snatch him away." She threw her hand stone to the ground and ran sobbing into the darkness.

That night Ipa could not sleep. The next day she could not concentrate on her work. The day dragged on and on, until evening when she took down another ear of Coyomo's gift corn. The stars filled the sky when she saw his tall figure striding across the plaza. His village was two days' walk from hers. He must have camped out in the desert because of her refusal. A twinge of guilt touched her as he approached. But once again she glanced down and rolled the stone against the corn, trying to ignore his eloquent words.

"I will be a good husband," he said. "I will sink the strongest cottonwood limbs into the earth to build you a grand pit house. I will dig the floor deep to keep you cool in the hottest days of summer and warm in the coldest days of winter. I will place a sacred eagle feather under each corner post and keep a bundle of sacred feathers hanging from the ceiling for good fortune. I will bring you deer hides to make beautiful dresses, and blue stones and shells to string around your lovely neck. I will make you proud to be my wife. Of all the men in my village, I am the one who faced Brother Black Bear and brought him to his knees. I still carry his mark on my side."

He pointed a finger to a jagged scar running across his ribs on his right side. People in many villages had heard the story of Coyomo and the bear, the fiercest of all the animals.

Ipa's heart weakened, but her grandmother's words rang in her ears. *You must make him ask you three nights or he will not respect you. He will think you were an easy prize and therefore of little worth.*

Ipa swallowed hard and stared at his sandaled

feet while she continued to grind the corn. She heard his sigh of exasperation and thought she heard him curse under his breath. When he walked away, Ipa felt her heart fill with anguish. She quickly climbed to the roof of her uncle's house and flung herself there among the drying corn and willow baskets. She wept and could not sleep until just before Grandfather Sun peeked his rosy face above the distant mountains. Her aunt found her there just after dawn and woke her up. No other day in her life had seemed so long.

That night, Ipa's heart was heavy as she watched the stars rise and walk their path across the sky. The Old One once told her that the stars were the campfires of the departed ones. She wondered if her mother and grandmother were watching over her. Ipa had not slept all day, and keeping her eyes open was difficult. When all the fires had gone out in the lodges and night birds sang their sad songs, her aunt peeked her head out of the hole in the roof.

"Coyomo is not coming tonight, child," she whispered. "You waited too long. You angered him. Come inside and sleep or you will be no good at your work tomorrow."

But Ipa refused and continued grinding the corn until it was nothing more than a fine powder. Sister Moon had crept to the edge of the mountains and the night birds had quieted. Tears silently trickled down Ipa's cheeks while her aching arms pressed and rolled the stone across the cornmeal. She thought she heard Xucate's gleeful laughter from inside the house, but it must have been the screech of an owl. Then she thought of her grandmother's words.

*If he is not willing to visit you three nights in a row, then what kind of husband will he be? Three nights is but a drop in the Great River compared to a lifetime together.*

A snapping twig made Ipa jerk her head back. It could have been an armadillo thrashing through the brush in senseless night wanderings, or a badger turning over rocks to dig for ant eggs. She ground more slowly, her ears straining. But she heard nothing.

"He is not coming. Why do I wait?" she finally whispered aloud.

"Yes, why do you wait, Ipa-tah-chi? I have asked myself the same question."

Ipa drew in a sharp breath and looked up at Coyomo. The red-pink sky outlined his straight, tall figure with its broad shoulders. Though the shadows hid his face, Ipa saw the morning breeze stir the turkey feathers in his hair and the fringes of his breechcloth that hung to the knees of his sinewy legs.

Her heart raced as she quickly put three grains of blue corn she had been saving onto the stone mill. With renewed vigor she rolled the *mano* over the *metate*.

"Have I not promised you everything a man can

*99*

promise a bride?" He raised a hand to accentuate his question. "Why do you refuse me, Ipa-tah-chi? Does your heart belong to another man? Do you find me lacking?"

Ipa swallowed hard. She shrugged her shoulders and shook her head slightly.

"Then what more can I say to convince you that I will make the best husband for you? I've seen the way your eyes look at me and you've seen my eyes on you. It is meant to be. My friends tell me to find another, more beautiful, one whose father is more important. They tell me to choose Xucate, who is tall and strong and beautiful. But my foolish heart will not listen to them. It tells me to go with the girl with the lovely, gentle eyes.

"The first time I saw you, when I was but a boy of fifteen summers, I watched you work diligently beside your old grandmother to save my father's life. Never had I seen such gentleness and compassion in one so young. Your beautiful eyes have haunted me since that day. I thought those eyes were filled with love for me, but I must have been wrong. I am not a brave warrior, as everyone thinks, but a fool who should not be wasting another night of sleep for one who does not care for me." He spun on his heels and started to walk away. The crash of the grinding stone made him stop and turn.

"I will be honored to be your wife," Ipa whispered as she stood before him. The pale sunlight struck his face as she looked up into it. Coyomo's eyes glimmered and a smile touched his lips. He slipped his hand around hers and squeezed tightly. Ipa felt the warmth and strength flow into her own fingers. She smiled and looked at the ground, unable to bear the look of affection in his eyes. He removed a necklace of a single blue stone from his neck and placed it around hers.

"Until our marriage day, my wife-to-be," he whispered.

Ipa nodded. "Until our marriage day, my husband-to-be," she replied.

She watched his lean, powerful legs carry him swiftly across the plaza and toward the river, which was the fastest route back to his village. She knew she would see him again as soon as he had killed a deer to provide the skin for her wedding dress. And after that, she would not see him again until their wedding day.

As the smoke of early fires rose from the lodges and the birds broke into their morning songs, Ipa breathed in the fragrant air. No longer were her eyes tired and her body weak. She was filled with the strength of ten women as she returned to her uncle's house and announced that she was to be the wife of Coyomo, the Brave One.

# Chapter Six

THE WINTER passed slowly. With no fields of corn to worry about, it was a time for inside work and sleeping late. The men made arrowheads and stone tools and yucca-fiber fishing nets; the women wove baskets and sleeping mats and sandals. Men repaired sagging roofs and women smeared new layers of adobe mud over the outside walls. Girls kept a wary eye on the stock of corn, removing molded ears and rationing so that it would last until next harvest. Older boys sat in the round *kiva* listening respectfully as the elders told stories about ancestors and tales of brave deeds; they learned about the duties of men and prepared for initiations. On the winter's solstice each household replaced its bundle of sacred feathers and prayed for the sun to come back to earth.

When the season of blooming yucca flowers arrived and the Sun-Watcher saw the sun rising between two special mountains, it was time for planting corn. The men poked holes in the hard ground with sharpened sticks and dropped seed corn into each hole. The shaman danced and sang, waving his prayer stick over the earth. He caught many songbirds with snares made from human hair and released them over the fields, instructing them to carry his prayers to the Rain Spirit.

Ipa sat on a rock, listening to women laughing and chattering like a flock of crows. They were happy, not just because the tasty sweet yucca flowers were bountiful that season but because, far on the horizon, over the mountains, the dark clouds hovered and lightning flashed. The air felt cooler and the wind was stronger. All these signs of rain made their hearts light and happy.

"It is a good sign," Ipa's aunt said as she lay a deerskin under a thorny *cholla* bush and thrashed it with a stick until the berries fell onto the skin. "Rain on the morning of a girl's wedding means healthy children and a life of plenty."

"I pray that it arrives by tomorrow morning," Ipa said as she helped her aunt put the berries into a basket, "but if not, at least the cornfields will have good fortune."

Her aunt chuckled. "You are always the practical one, aren't you, child? You are so different from my own daughter, who dreams her days away wishing for things that cannot be. And when she cannot have what her heart desires, she pouts like a disappointed child."

Ipa glanced across the desert at Xucate knocking down a tall yucca stalk covered with creamy white blooms. She missed the companionship of her cousin, the laughter, the teasing, and the pride in each other's talents. But since the day of her engagement, Xucate's fiery anger was unquenchable.

Ipa still remembered the look in her cousin's eyes the morning of Coyomo's third visit. Ipa had gone back inside the house just as the others were waking up. When Ipa showed them the blue stone around her neck, Xucate scrambled up the ladder, pausing only long enough to shout down from the roof, "It is *I* who should have been his wife. *I* am the true daughter of the *cacique*. You are only here at the mercy of my father. Coyomo was to be *my* husband."

Ipa swallowed hard as she relived that moment of humiliation. Ipa had tried to soothe her cousin's wounds with kindness, but Xucate would have none of it.

The preparations for Ipa's marriage had begun the day after her engagement to Coyomo. Five days later, Coyomo returned with a deer carcass: a large buck with a fine pelt. It had been smothered, so that no blood was shed. He dropped the deer in front of the *cacique*'s house, announced that Ipa was to become his bride, and then left.

Without the help of anyone, Ipa hung the deer from a tree limb, then skinned, gutted, and cleaned it. Her hands turned red with the blood and it splattered on her face and legs. She carefully cut the flesh in portions, some to be eaten that night at the engagement feast, and others to be sliced into thin strips and hung over sticks to dry, for eating later. Every part of the deer was saved. She laid aside the antlers for use as awls for poking holes. The bones would make tools for digging yucca or agave roots or as spear tips. The sinew Ipa gave to her uncle to make bowstring, and the sticky glue from the hooves to hold the feathers to arrow shafts. The deer brains would be saved for the tanning of the hide.

All morning and night Ipa skinned, cut, and prepared the deer meat. The next day, after she finished scraping meat from the last bone, she fell into a deep exhaustion and had to be carried into the house and laid on her mat.

"Sleep, Little One," her aunt said. "Tonight we will feast in honor of your engagement." And feast they did, with dancing and singing and drinking.

Ipa could hardly remember it now, it seemed so

long ago. As soon as the feast was over, she began the long, difficult task of tanning the deerskin. From it would come her wedding ensemble.

Many times Ipa had watched her grandmother and aunt stake hides to the ground and tediously scrape the bits of meat and the hair from them. Then came the time to soak the skin in the brains of the deer to make it soft. Ipa had never done this before and she was unsure of herself. It was smelly and unpleasant, but she knew the long, hard work was necessary. Her wedding ensemble was not just for her own vanity; it was to prove to Coyomo's family that she knew the duties of women. No one could help her, not even her own mother, if she had been alive. And if Coyomo's family did not approve of her craftsmanship, they could call off the wedding.

Day after day Ipa worked the deerskin, beating any stiff parts of the hide until they were soft and pliable. She used the sharp tips of sotol leaves to make needles and *ixtle* fibers from yucca leaves to make thread to sew the pieces of skin together. She trimmed the upper seam with bits of rabbit fur, the bright gold parrot feathers given to her by her father, shells that he had brought from the people who lived by the great water, and the hard, red seeds of the mountain laurel tree.

During the days that the skin was soaking, Ipa sat under the cottonwood tree weaving baskets from supple willow branches and reeds or *nolina* leaves.

She twisted them and worked them around stiffer twigs the way her grandmother had taught her. As Ipa wove and twisted dark and light reeds into a geometric pattern, she thought of her grandmother and wished the old woman could be there to share her happiness. But it was not proper to think about the dead, so Ipa often had to force the memories away.

All winter long Ipa made or traded for special items to take with her to Coyomo's house. Clay pots did not travel well because they broke too easily, so she would only carry one with her. It had come from the pueblos of the Corn People to the north, who traded beautiful fine pots and cotton blankets for buffalo hides or deerskins. The soft, pliable skins of both deer and buffalo made by her village women brought the greatest price of anything they made. Even the *españoles* said they were the finest skins they had ever seen.

Ipa thought about the young stranger, Rodrigo, from time to time. He had been kind and not like the others who drank until they staggered and whose arms grabbed at every woman in the village who was foolish enough to go near them. And Rodrigo had shown great kindness toward his ailing *caballo,* and tenderness toward Kadoh. Ipa wondered how it might feel to touch his pale skin, his hair-covered face. But these thoughts came to her mostly at night, just before she drifted to sleep. During the days, her

*107*

life was filled with tedious chores and the long preparation of wedding items. During the day, her heart only had time to think of Coyomo. For as her aunt so often pointed out, Ipa was a practical girl. She would never see Rodrigo again, and the day of her marriage to Coyomo was drawing very near.

All morning long, while she gathered yucca flowers, Ipa's mind strayed to thoughts of her wedding. As each part of the day passed, her heart carried her through the steps of her marriage: *This time tomorrow I will be waking; this time tomorrow I will be bathing; this time tomorrow I will be drinking from the wedding gourd; this time tomorrow I will be the wife of Coyomo, the Brave One.* Her breath came shorter and her fingers trembled each time she thought of this last thing.

She completed the day's work without knowing what she did. That night, the first night of the full moon after the planting of the corn, Ipa and the women sneaked down to the river for the leaving-the-village ceremony. The women washed Ipa's long, thick hair with the suds of yucca roots, all the while giving her advice about living with a man. They told her about the trials of childbirth and gave her a small, soft deerskin pouch filled with herbs to help her in times when cramping pains became unbearable.

At midnight, Ipa ate six grains of blue corn and sprinkled corn pollen mixed with bright yellow cattail pollen in the six sacred directions—north, south, east, west, above, and below. She asked permission of her uncle to leave his lodge, then said farewell to her male friends and relatives, for her wedding would be made up of women and a few children. She carefully folded her wedding dress and filled her burden-basket with precious seed corn to give to Coyomo. She carried dried beef, *pinole, pinyon* nuts, and a cake of sweet yucca to give to her mother-in-law. But most importantly, she stuffed another basket with all the medicine plants she could fit inside.

With the village women and children loaded down with Ipa's baskets, gourds, and gifts for Coyomo's family, they began the trek to Sacred Panther Mountain. There, just before dawn, Ipa would bathe once again, this time in the sacred waters of the mountain pool, and dress in her wedding ensemble. Coyomo's family and friends would arrive soon after dawn. They would examine her handiwork and, if acceptable, Coyomo and Ipa would share a gourd of water from the sacred pool. Then Ipa would say good-bye to her aunt and friends and accompany Coyomo and his relatives back to his village, where her home would be for the rest of her life. It was a ceremony reserved for the sons and daughters of the *caciques*.

Ipa walked in silence beside her aunt across the moonlit plain. Coyotes yelped at each other far in the distance, and lizards and rodents scurried out of the procession's way. Ipa's heart was happy and sad at the same time. Marrying Coyomo was a great honor and he would be a good husband, but she would miss her small village, her aunt and uncle, her brother and her father, even Xucate. Her father had not yet returned from guiding the *españoles* to the land of the Corn People. Ipa had wanted to say good-bye to him. She could not shake away the strange feeling in the pit of her stomach that told her something terrible had happened to her father.

Ipa forced all negative thoughts from her mind and concentrated on each step. She tried to imagine how Coyomo would be dressed, and what gifts his family would bring to exchange for her gifts. The other women prattled on about Coyomo's family—his sisters and brothers, his father—telling stories they had heard. But Ipa told her tongue to remain still. She would find out about all these things soon enough.

Ipa's legs ached and the bottoms of her feet grew sore from the stones that constantly jabbed at holes in the heels of her yucca-fiber sandals. She had a new pair in her basket, but those would not be put on her feet until she dressed in her wedding clothes.

At last the sacred mountain's shadow fell across her face. It was really not a mountain as much as an eruption of rocks and earth in the middle of the desert. The sides of the mountain were solid, bare rock where nothing grew except in the dirt-filled crevices.

But on top of the formation, within its many shallow pits between boulders as large as houses, small tanks of water remained throughout the year. It was here that Turtle-Girl had led the clay people up from the underworld to the surface of the earth, where the sunlight turned them into humans. The turtles that lived in the pools here were sacred. The shells of turtles found dead here were made into rattles for the shaman.

Bits of loose rocks and gravel spewed down at Ipa's feet as she climbed up the rocky surface, but she did not mind. The last leg of the journey was here. By the time they reached the summit, the women and children huffed with exhaustion. Ipa paused at the top of the path.

To her left, the disappointing storm clouds drifted away. The rain had fallen only a few moments, and the drops had dried up almost as soon as they touched the parched sand. Now the sky was clear and the sinking moon's silver light shimmered on the still water of a pool cradled between red boulders. Soon Ipa would bathe in the sacred waters, and get on with a new life in a new village.

Ipa looked down as the last of the women climbed to the top. Below and far away tiny pinpoints of light marked the dying bonfires lit by the village men who had remained behind. This would be the last time she ever saw her little village sitting at the base of a crooked canyon beside the twisting river. Coyomo's village lay in a serene valley where the river ran tame and smooth, and there were no canyon walls to climb up or down. A great pain ripped at Ipa's heart and a tear slid down her cheek. Her grandmother's house, her uncle's house, and her beloved canyon would all become memories.

Ipa drew in a breath, deep and long enough to last a lifetime, then turned away. She walked to the sacred pool and to her future with Coyomo. His village would be her village from this moment on, and his life would be her life.

# Chapter Seven

THE *PINYON* torch cast eerie shadows across the stones and a stench of dust from the beginning of time filled the chamber. Across one wall a hunt was frozen in time, sticklike deer lying on the ground, sticklike men dancing in victory. But on another chamber wall, far removed from the other figures and of a darker red-brown paint, a panther poised to strike.

Ipa stooped low to keep from scraping her head until she arrived in the sacred chamber. She lifted the torch with its pungent fumes and stared at the panther. Her mind returned to the day of her village's massacre, the day her grandmother died and her brother Ximi was taken captive. She had prayed to the Great Panther Spirit for rain that morning. The rains had come, but at what sacrifice? Did she dare pray to the great panther again? If she wished for a long, happy life with Coyomo, would there be a price to pay?

Ipa's eyes began to blur and her lungs labored to breathe the sooty air. She dropped to her knees, removed sacred corn pollen from a pouch around her neck, and sprinkled it in the six sacred directions. She closed her eyes, and sang in a low voice:

*"Great Panther Spirit, bless my marriage and grant me healthy children and a strong back the rest of my days. May the corn rustle in the fields when I die."* It was the sacred chant that each mother passed down to her daughter.

Ipa drank from the marriage gourd. The bitter liquid bit her tongue and slipped down her throat to her heart, where it exploded and sent a wave of heat across her chest. The panther moved and the deer figures leaped to their feet. The happy cries of hunters filled the cave.

*"Great Panther Spirit, bless my marriage and grant me healthy children and a strong back the rest of my days. May the corn rustle in the fields when I die."* Ipa repeated the words three more times, then removed her old clothes and rolled them into a tight bundle to give to her aunt.

The morning wind met Ipa like a friendly dog

and licked away the beads of perspiration from her flushed face as she stepped out of the dark cave entrance. She handed her aunt the old clothes and walked to the sacred pool. The water felt icy cold to her feet and legs, but she remained quiet as her aunt lathered up the yucca root and slid it over her body. After a few moments, the first chill turned to delicious warmth and the sacred waters washed away the layers of dust and dirt. Ipa closed her eyes and followed the path of the sponge over her shoulders, down the curve of her spine, and over the firmness of her thighs. She crossed her arms over her small breasts as the foamy water slid over her shoulders, then she stretched them out so that the spongy roots could travel over every inch of her arms and fingers. Slowly, the first rosy glow of Grandfather Sun crept over the mountain and flooded her face with gold.

"The first season away from your village will be the hardest," her aunt said. "At first, your husband and his family will seem strange. But some things will not be different. The corn will grow the same. The squash vines will grow the same. The river's water will taste the same. Soon you will have children to love and care for. In time you will forget your aunt and uncle, and your little village. Coyomo will be the *cacique* of the second village on the junction soon, and you will have many important duties. You will forget us."

"No, I will never forget my village," Ipa protested. But her aunt laughed.

As the sacred waters washed away all her impurities, the breath of the wind blew across Ipa's body and a row of chill bumps rose over her arms. Never had she felt so pure and cleansed. The fragrance of reeds, juniper, and wildflowers near the pool wafted on the breeze and filled her lungs.

At last, Ipa stepped from the sacred pool onto a flat rock, carefully avoiding the dirt so that her feet would stay clean until she had placed on her newly woven yucca-fiber sandals. Her aunt slipped the new deerskin poncho trimmed with feathers and bits of rabbit fur over Ipa's head, then cinched the lacing on her skirt. In silence, she coiled Ipa's long, shiny hair to the back of her neck and braided a yellow parrot feather into it. She returned Coyomo's necklace of blue stone and the silver crucifix to her niece's neck. Ipa felt the softness of the deerskin pressing against her small breasts and hugging her narrow hips. Her aunt nodded and smiled, then placed her callused hands around Ipa's face and stroked the smooth skin.

"You are a beautiful bride," she said softly.

"Aunt, I feel spirits watching over me," Ipa whispered.

The older woman nodded. "It is the sacred waters that allow you to communicate with our ancestors. Come now, it is time to go to your husband-to-be."

As Ipa descended the trail from the sacred pool, the other women gave their compliments and good wishes. Even her cousin's eyes widened with awe, though she did not speak.

Kadoh and the other children who had come along waited at the end of the path near a high bluff that jutted out over the side of the mountain and gave a panoramic view of the land below. The campfires had gone out in her village, replaced by tiny lines of smoke streaming into the neverending sky.

Ipa sat on the rock, waiting for Coyomo's party to arrive. Soon she felt the warmth of Grandfather Sun on the back of her neck. A bead of perspiration trickled between her shoulder blades. All the women remained quiet, each lost in deep thoughts of her own wedding or of her wedding-to-be. Only the happy warble of a mockingbird and the rasp of grasshoppers scraping their hind legs broke the silence.

"There!" Kadoh suddenly shouted. "I see the wedding party."

Everyone rose and squinted. At last, Ipa saw the figures. They walked two abreast. Though she could not see their faces clearly, she knew that Coyomo would be the front man and beside him would be his mother.

She could see the dust of their feet rising in small clouds behind the party. Coyomo became larger and clearer. His deerskin breechcloth, decorated with bits of colored beads and feathers, hung almost to the ground. He wore his hair cut very short to form a skullcap the same as the men of her village wore. Three bright blue macaw feathers rose from the crown, complementing his blue stones and white bear-tooth necklace and earrings. She could hear the faint jingle of copper bells around his neck and on his feather-covered knee-bands.

Ipa heard Xucate take in a sharp breath. She, too, must be thinking how glorious Coyomo looked. Ipa knew she might never see her cousin again. She wanted to say good-bye in friendship. For a moment she thought of all the days of their youth that they had spent together climbing rocks and swimming in the river, laughing as sisters and sharing each other's hopes and dreams. All of a sudden, Ipa's heart swelled with the desire to hug Xucate and wash away the past season of mistrust and hatred that had arisen between them. She wanted to say that if she could start her life over again, she would run the other way when Coyomo brought the stalk of blue corn, that a sister's love was more important than being the wife of a *cacique*.

"Xucate . . . " she began, then hesitated as she struggled for the words to ease the pain in her cousin's heart. But all of the words she was prepared to say only sounded shallow and insincere. Ipa sighed. "Cousin, I wish you well." She pressed her hand against her cousin's cheek, stared into the black eyes filled with anguish and pain, then turned and started down the trail behind Kadoh and her aunt.

"What is it?" Ipa asked when she saw her aunt and brother stop near the bottom of the trail.

"Perhaps it is a bear," Xucate said from behind her. "Perhaps Coyomo, the Brave One, will slay it for your wedding feast." The words, meant to be spoken in jest, came out bitter.

"It's Apaches!" someone shouted, and Ipa's heart stopped. Could this happen to her again? Was the Great Panther Spirit playing some kind of cruel prank?

She pushed her aunt aside and stared at the plain. The wedding party was closer now and she could clearly distinguish Coyomo from the others. Coyomo was shouting at the men in his party, ordering them to bunch together and face the west, with the women behind them. At first Ipa could not see what they were looking at, then she heard a noise like distant thunder.

"A whirlwind?" Kadoh whispered as he came to stand beside her.

"I think not. It is moving too fast. The dust is too strange. And the noise is too loud."

"It must be a herd of antelope," Ipa's aunt whispered.

Ipa watched the cloud of dust moving across the desert closer to the wedding party, traveling fast like a herd of frightened buffalo. But it was not the

delicate hooves of antelope, nor was it the pounding hooves of angry buffalo. She saw a flash of silver,
then another, and heard shouting men.

"¡Caballos!" Kadoh shouted. "It is the españoles
riding their caballos."

Ipa swallowed, but her heart was in her throat
and would not go down. Her stomach fluttered and
her fingers trembled as she wrapped her arms
around her brother's shoulders and pulled him back
toward her.

"Why are they racing?" Kadoh asked. "Is Rodrigo with them?"

"I do not know," she replied in a dry whisper.

Behind Ipa the women of her village began
scrambling back up the mountain, except for Xucate,
who refused to move.

"What do the españoles want?" Xucate said in a
voice that trembled like the earth. "Is this their way
of celebrating a wedding?"

Kadoh nodded. "It must be that," he said with
hope in his voice. "It is a game like we saw them
play before."

But when the mounted men reached the wedding party, they did not stop and dismount, or show
any sign of laughter. They shouted and whirled *lazo*
ropes above their heads. With screams, the women
of Coyomo's wedding party dropped their baskets
and scrambled toward Sacred Panther Mountain.

The *españoles* pointed their strange metal sticks

into the air, making fire and smoke and thunder explode from the ends. A man near Coyomo charged toward a horse, shaking his spear. Suddenly he fell to the ground and grabbed his blood-covered side.

"Look, Sister!" Kadoh squealed in disbelief. "The strangers are killing Coyomo's people. Why?" His small body trembled with outrage.

Ipa felt the blood drain from her face. She did not want to see the horror unfolding, but she could not tear her eyes away. She watched Coyomo, his blue macaw feathers bobbing as he threw his spear at a mounted *español*. Even from the mountainside, Ipa heard the crack as the spear hit the thick leather shell around the *español*'s chest and fell harmless to the ground.

Five of the women from Coyomo's party reached the foot of the mountain trail, gasping for air.

"We are doomed!" one of them shrieked, and pushed Kadoh and Ipa aside in her haste. "Run back up the mountain!"

"I am going to fight," Kadoh suddenly shouted as he broke away from Ipa's arms and ran.

"No, Little Cousin," Xucate yelled. "You are too young to fight."

Kadoh refused to listen. He tore across the rocky desert toward the mounted warriors, with only a rabbit stick in his hand for a weapon. Ipa chased after her brother, trying to ignore her gasping lungs and the sharp pain in her side, but Kadoh's legs were strong and fast.

"Little Cousin, come back," Ipa heard Xucate calling from somewhere behind her. "It will be safe in the mountains!"

"No, I will fight like a man!" Kadoh shouted over his shoulder. He let loose the same piercing war cry that Ipa had often heard from their older brother.

Ipa heard Xucate's feet pounding beside her and glanced over her shoulder.

"Please help me catch him," Ipa called to Xucate. Her cousin increased her speed and her long legs devoured the ground in smooth, even strides.

*"Great Spirit, please save my little brother. Give Xucate's heels the wings of an eagle; give her heart the strength of a buffalo."* Ipa sent her silent prayer to the Great Spirit again and again as she ran.

Ahead, the dust and shouting intensified. The gleaming metal hats of the *españoles* and the slender legs of their mounts and the legs of Coyomo's warriors and their raised spears all blended together into one horrible storm of shouting and screaming and neighing of horses and the wailing of women. The dust was so thick Ipa could not see her brother but she heard Xucate's voice calling his name.

"Do you see Little Beetle?" Ipa shouted to her cousin, who had stopped in her tracks when the dust became too great to see.

"I saw him over there," Xucate called back.

The girls turned toward a shadowy boy in the dust storm, but before they reached him a horse blocked their view. When the horse stepped aside, they saw a child's body lying still on the ground.

"Little Brother!" Ipa shouted, then ran to his side.

Ipa knelt over Kadoh, then wiped the dust from his face. A stream of blood trickled from the side of his head. He groaned softly.

"He is still alive!" Ipa cried out in relief. "Cousin, help me carry him back to the mountain," Ipa begged.

Ipa and Xucate lifted Kadoh up. Still in a daze, he did not argue with them. They half ran, half staggered back toward Sacred Panther Mountain.

Ipa heard the thunder of hooves behind her, but she did not dare stop to look. Kadoh was a child of not quite nine summers and she was a mere girl of hardly fourteen summers with no weapon; surely the *españoles* would not bother with them.

Ipa felt her lungs aching, and her feet grew raw from the thorns and rocks that jabbed at the sides of her sandals. Another moment and her heart would surely burst, she thought. Soon her side throbbed with so much pain that she was forced to stop.

"I cannot go another step," Ipa cried out to Xucate, gasping for air. "Save yourself and my brother and leave me behind."

Without a word, Xucate lifted Kadoh into her

own arms and began running again. She did not seem to mind the load. Ipa silently thanked the Great Spirit for giving Xucate such strength. She struggled for air a moment, then picked her feet up and followed many paces behind her cousin.

The dust choked Ipa's mouth and lungs, but her feet continued to trot until she had almost reached the foot of Sacred Panther Mountain. Suddenly, she heard something whistling in the air and a sharp cry of pain from her cousin's lips. Xucate fell to the ground, bringing Kadoh down on top of her. Ipa stumbled over both of them and felt the hot sand splash into her face.

A mounted *español* jerked a *lazo* tightly around Xucate's chest, pinning her arms. She kicked and fought and screamed, but he only laughed and muttered words of his wicked language as he dismounted. Kadoh sat on the ground, his hand pressed to his bleeding head and his eyes staring blankly ahead. When the Spaniard shook Kadoh, the boy passed out and slumped over.

A second *español* rode up and with a flick of his hand, his rope slid around Ipa's shoulders. Ipa felt all her strength suddenly drain from her body. She tried to move but could not.

As the bearded man dismounted with great leathery squeaks and metallic clangs, Ipa tried to scoot away. He towered over his captives, his hands on his waist.

*"Indios,"* he said with a snarl and a look of disgust on his face.

Ipa remembered hearing the word from Rodrigo. It seemed like only yesterday that he had been so kind to her. Surely this *español* would show kindness, too. Ipa struggled to her knees. She cleared the dust from her throat and repeated the only words of the *español* language that she could remember at the moment.

*"Muchas gracias,"* she said softly.

Kadoh's eyes flickered open and he mumbled the words, too. *"Muchas gracias,"* he whispered, then closed his eyes again.

The Spaniard's black eyes grew large and round, then he slapped his knee and threw his head back and laughed a laugh so loud Ipa was sure the women in the mountains could hear. She knew they were watching her now—her aunt and most of the women from Coyomo's wedding procession. She wondered what they thought as they saw Ipa, the future bride of Coyomo, the Brave One, her wedding dress ruined and caked with dirt, now a slave of the *españoles.*

# Chapter Eight

AFTER THE Spaniard had bound Ipa's and Xucate's hands and walked away, Ipa looked across the desert. All around her men coughed from the dust in their lungs and groaned from their wounds. An old woman wailed relentlessly and chanted the sacred words of a death song for a warrior lying still at her feet. Ipa struggled to stand up but collapsed; her shaky legs were too weak from the desperate chase after Kadoh.

She looked behind her and saw that Kadoh was now lying on the ground very still, blood oozing from his head wound. A sickening feeling crept into her heart.

"Little Beetle!" Ipa whimpered. She walked on her knees closer to him. Her arms ached to hold him and wipe the dirt from his face, but she could not budge the tight rope that cut into her wrists.

"He still breathes," Xucate said in a raspy voice. Her once shiny hair was now caked with dirt and tangled into an ugly mat. She sat a few paces away, her feet digging into the sand and her eyes following a small, wiry Spaniard walking their way. "What does he want from us?"

Ipa tried to speak, but her tongue was too numb to form the words so she shook her head. Her beautiful golden parrot feathers fell to the ground only to be caught by a gust of hot wind that scattered them across the desert. Suddenly Ipa remembered her wedding and why she was there. Her red, stinging eyes frantically swept over the crowd of dusty villagers, horses, and Spaniards, searching for Coyomo's familiar face. But she could not find the blue macaw feathers and the wide shoulders of her husband-to-be. A sigh of relief slipped from her lips. He must have escaped to the mountain. He would soon rescue them with a band of angry warriors. She imagined him even now, running to her village to tell her uncle. The men would paint their faces and string their bows and gather their best arrows and set out into the desert to avenge Coyomo's people. They would strike at night while the Spaniards slept.

Loud shouting tore Ipa from her daydream. She

saw the Spaniards kicking and shoving the village men into a line. Suddenly brutish arms rudely jerked Ipa and Xucate to their feet.

The short, wiry Spaniard rattled his strange language in Ipa's face. When Ipa stared at him blankly, he squeezed her arm and shook her. Her legs trembled so that she was sure she would collapse again. Then he stood over Kadoh, prodding him with the toe of his boot.

"Leave him alone!" Xucate shouted, and kicked sand into the Spaniard's face. He pushed her to the ground and planted his boot into her side.

Ipa winced and waited for her cousin's cry of pain, but Xucate's lips remained tightly closed.

Ipa looked into the hair-covered face of her captor. She swallowed down a layer of dust and tried to calm her voice.

"My brother is hurt," she pleaded in her most sincere voice. "He needs help."

"*¿Qué?*" the man said as he cocked his head to one side.

"My brother—*hermano*," she repeated. Ipa nodded her head toward Kadoh.

The Spaniard nudged Kadoh's bare leg again. The boy moaned slightly but did not move.

"*Inútil,*" he said, then called over a brown-skinned man dressed in a deerskin breechcloth and moccasins.

"Pedro! *¡Aquí!*" the Spaniard shouted.

The man turned and walked toward them with long, graceful strides. Though he wore a black Spanish hat on his head, Ipa knew at once he was a Jumano, a hunting people who often came to her village to trade buffalo hides for colored stones and corn. The Jumano people had once lived on the river like Ipa's people, but they had abandoned their mud houses long ago and now roamed the plains and slept in buffalo-skin tipis, returning to the river only in the winter. The guide spoke the language of the *españoles,* but his tongue pronounced the words with a different accent.

"Why have they done this to us?" Xucate screeched into the emotionless tattooed face.

"They are taking all of you to the south—to work in a silver mine," the Jumano replied.

"Silver?" Ipa could not believe her ears. "The shiny substance that some people use for trinkets? But it is almost worthless. Why would the *españoles* want it?"

The guide did not gesture, nor change expressions.

"The Spaniards have many strange ways," he said. "Silver is sacred to their god. They value it more than corn or squash or beans. They dig it out of Earthmother's back and melt it into long bars."

"But why? I do not understand," Xucate suddenly shouted. "Why are we prisoners?"

"*Shh,* Cousin, do not shout," Ipa whispered. "It

129

will only make the Spaniards more angry. We must try to reason with them."

She turned to the Jumano guide called Pedro. "Please tell them we will give them all the corn and beans and squash that our village can spare," Ipa pleaded. "They are welcome to eat and drink and rest with us. We will give them baskets and pottery; buffalo skins and deerskins. I will give them my valuable medicine plants. We are a friendly people with no desire to fight. Please, tell the *españoles* they have made a mistake. I am sure they will understand."

"This was not a mistake," the Jumano said as he brushed the dirt from Kadoh's face and rubbed a leaf from his medicine pouch under the boy's nose.

"But this was a wedding party!" Xucate's voice rose. "They have defiled a sacred wedding ceremony! Tell them!"

But the Jumano guide did not move nor did he translate Ipa's or Xucate's words.

"It is pointless to tell them," he said at last, then turned his back and walked to another Spaniard who had called out his name.

"He is a traitor to his people," Xucate said, then turned her head and spat.

Ipa fought back tears of anguish and confusion. The Spaniard near her climbed back onto his horse. Kadoh had awakened and was sitting up now, pressing his hand to his head, but the Spaniard did not seem to care if Kadoh was still alive.

"Little Brother!" Ipa whispered as she saw the line of prisoners start to move. "Pretend that you are dead, and they will leave you behind. When it is safe, Aunt will come down and get you. Quickly, close your eyes and lie back down. Be very still."

But Kadoh did not obey his sister. He struggled to his feet.

"Where is Ximi?" he asked. "I saw him running across the desert just now. I must find him."

Ipa swallowed hard.

"Ximi is not here, Little Beetle," she said. "You know that. He is with the Apaches for four winters now."

"Kadoh's wound has given him the head-sickness, as warriors often suffer in battle," Xucate whispered in Ipa's ear. "He is lost forever."

An *español* with skin blacker than night and curly hair like a buffalo bound Kadoh's wrists snugly, then walked to the older woman who had been wailing. She turned her head and looked up into the black man's face. Tears from her red, swollen eyes had cut streaks through the dust on her cheeks, making her look hideous. Her shrieks and wails had subsided into soft sobs that shook her chest uncontrollably. A young woman who was with child tried to comfort her, but the older one continued to pull her hair and rock back and forth. Even when a mounted *español* poked her with his lance, the woman refused to move.

"Why are they not moving?" Ipa whispered to her cousin.

"Someone is dead beside them," Xucate said. "I can see his feet."

The captain of the Spaniards shouted a command. His men prodded the prisoners with spiked lances to make them move forward. Ipa and Xucate were near the end of the line with the women and children. Ipa strained her eyes to see over the heads of the men in front of her, once more looking for the blue macaw feathers in Coyomo's hair. If the Spaniards had arranged the men according to strength and valor, and Coyomo had not escaped, he would be at the front. But she saw only dusty heads bent low in shame.

The line of prisoners slowly passed by the two weeping women and the dead warrior. The black *español* tugged at the woman's arms, but she still refused to leave the body at her feet. The more the black man pulled, the louder she wailed and the more the pregnant woman beside her sobbed.

Suddenly the leader of the mounted *español* removed a coiled-up leather rope from his saddle and unfurled it with a loud pop. The first time it struck the air. When the old woman still did not move, he raised the leather high and snapped it toward her back. It ripped through her clothes like a knife.

Ipa heard a gasp from the prisoners and felt her

own heart stop as the old woman screamed in pain. But still she would not get up.

"Mother, he is dead. What good will it do for you to die, also?" the younger one pleaded, but to no avail.

"My life is of no value, now," the old woman sobbed. "I do not choose to live as a slave."

"The old one is brave," Xucate whispered under her breath. "I pray to the Great Spirit that she defies the white devil and spits in his eyes before she dies."

Ipa nodded, but her tongue would not speak. She watched the Jumano guide, Pedro, step between the Spaniard and the old woman just as the leather rope struck again. It bit into his flesh, leaving a red line across his chest, but he did not flinch. He spoke in his calm voice to the younger woman. She stood and joined the line of prisoners. Then he spoke in the Spanish language. The leader listened, then rolled up his whip and walked away, leaving the old woman slumped over the dead body.

In silence the group began marching again. They passed two more dead Otomoacas men lying on the ground. The wind gently stirred the fringes on their breechcloths and the turkey feathers in their hair. A dry tumbleweed passed over one of them, lodged for a moment, then broke free and bounced toward Sacred Panther Mountain. Ipa glanced over her shoulder at the fading mountain. She imagined the women of Coyomo's village slowly, cautiously climbing down the trail, then hurrying to the old woman. She imagined their cries of anguish and heartbreak when they saw the three dead warriors and the dust of the prisoners on the horizon. Ipa and the other women let their tears flow until the sacred mountain was small and Grandfather Sun was high overhead, but Xucate did not cry.

Ipa's stomach growled and churned, for she had not eaten anything all day but for the few grains of sacred corn the night before. Her throat ached with dryness and swallowing became as painful as the thorns in her feet.

When Grandfather Sun began to climb down his sky path, Ipa saw an arroyo sparcely lined with mesquite trees. A shout traveled the length of the line among the soldiers. They stopped their horses and dismounted in the thin shade of the feathery branches.

Groans and sighs of relief rippled through the band of prisoners as they collapsed to the ground, even though they had to rest in the sun. The young woman who was with child grimaced as she lowered herself to a boulder.

"I will not survive this journey," she said. "If my child is born, call her Daughter-of-Sadness and raise her for me."

Ipa did not know what to say to the woman, so she nodded.

"Sister, Ximi is thirsty," Kadoh said as they

leaned against the boulders. "I must find water for him."

"Ximi is not here, Little Beetle," she said, fighting back the fatigue and annoyance.

"Yes, he is. I saw him there behind the rocks now. He is very thirsty, Sister."

Ipa sighed. It was useless to argue with one who had head-sickness. "Close your eyes and rest, Little Brother. Ximi will be here soon with water. I will awaken you when he arrives."

Xucate snorted. "Lies, Cousin?"

"*Shh,* Xucate. He is confused. We must humor him until he gets well. It is not so much a lie."

"If you prefer to hear lies, then I shall tell you a lie now. Your husband-to-be is alive and plotting how to rescue us."

"How is that a lie? Do you doubt that he will come after us?"

"I *know* he is not coming. It is a lie I told you."

"But how do you know it is a lie?" Ipa felt her face turning hot. She knew it was her cousin's jealousy that made her speak this way, but still she did not want to hear such accusations about Coyomo, the Brave One.

"It is a lie because your husband-to-be is not alive." Xucate's eyes looked across the desert in the direction of the sacred mountain, which was now just a bump on the horizon.

"No, that is not true." Ipa had to force herself to breathe again.

"Ask the woman with child."

Ipa turned to the woman beside her.

"Mother warned him not to marry today," the woman said. "She saw a crow on her roof this morning. She said it could only mean something terrible would happen." The woman let out a sob, then she rolled her eyes wildly in all directions. "*Shh!* We must not talk about the dead."

"Dead?" Ipa felt as if a hand had slapped her face with a mighty blow. Tears welled up in her eyes and a lump like a sharp rock rose to her throat. Her voice trembled as she forced her next question.

"Then it is true? My husband-to-be is dead?"

The woman looked deeply into Ipa's damp eyes, then nodded.

"I am sorry, Sister-to-be. He was my brother. The old woman who would not leave is our mother."

Ipa felt hot tears spill down her dusty cheeks. "But he was the most valiant of them all. How is it possible?"

"The *españoles* pointed a stick at him. It spat fire and thunder and put a hole into his back while he was fighting another."

"I did not know it was he who was lying there," Ipa said softly to the air. "I did not see the blue macaw feathers in his hair."

Ipa imagined herself leaning over his still body,

her tears dribbling onto his cold cheek. She could almost smell the maleness of him, feel the roughness of his face, the strength of his neck. How many nights had she dreamed of being in his strong arms. Now it was over. There would be no strong arms, no loving heart, no special smiles and sweet words, no beautiful children, and no one to share her old age with and recall the days of her youth.

Ipa turned to Xucate, whose eyes remained dry. Ipa wrestled with an anger greater than she had ever felt before.

"Why did you not tell me, Cousin, so that I could pray for his spirit's journey? I thought you cared for him deeply."

Xucate shrugged, then pushed away from the boulder.

"Why should I care? He was not my husband-to-be."

Suddenly the anger tore through Ipa's heart. She tried to force her tongue to remain silent, but the words broke their bounds.

"Your heart is cruel beyond words, Cousin," Ipa said between clenched teeth. "You have hated me from the moment the Brave One chose me to be his bride. I tried to remain as your sister, but your heart was destroyed by jealousy."

Xucate swirled around and glared into Ipa's face. "It was I who should have been his bride. I am the daughter of the *cacique*. If he had chosen me, he would still be alive today."

"Why do you say that?" the woman with child asked.

"The shaman would have selected a different day for my wedding. The Spanish slavers would not have attacked on *my* wedding day. Everything is your fault, Ipa-tah-chi. You stole the Brave One from me, then you brought his death." Fury raged in her black eyes.

"And you denied me my duty of singing my husband-to-be's death song, of saying farewell, of steering his spirit to the celestial camping grounds," Ipa said. "You have gotten your revenge at last, Cousin. Now get out of my sight. You are no longer my sister."

Xucate's lips quivered, and for a moment Ipa thought she would cry. Suddenly she swirled around and ran to the other side of the boulders. Ipa thought she heard her cousin sobbing, but she did not care.

Ipa squeezed her eyes closed and drew up the image of the dead body of Coyomo. She felt a deep gaping wound in her heart and a pressure crushing her chest.

*"My eyes are as a broken vessel that spills water into the dry desert for naught,"* she began, whispering the wife's death chant under her breath. *"My heart is a festering wound within my chest. My life is not worth living without you, my husband. May your spirit make*

*the long journey to the dark region with the sun to guide you and the wind in your face. I will never forget you, Brave One. Never."*

And when Ipa had finished the chant for Coyomo, she began another chant for the loss of a sister, and this time her eyes flowed like rain.

A hiss and crack interrupted Ipa's chant. She saw the black leather rope with tentacles on the end strike the ground and spit up gravel and dust. The Spaniard's muscles rippled as his powerful arm wielded the whip, aiming it as precisely as an arrow. He snapped it again, and it landed at Ipa's feet. Quickly the women rose and joined the men, who were already standing.

All night they trudged across the rocky desert. Ipa's mouth became as dry as the earth beneath her feet. Her sandals offered little protection from the sharp rocks, nettles, and cactus needles. She wanted to stop, to drop to the ground and let the crows pick the flesh from her bones. But if anyone fell or tried to break away from the line, the whip lashed into his back, leaving long red gashes.

The next day, when the noonday heat rose in clear ripples above the desert, they crossed a ford in the Lesser River, far to the south of her village. Never in her life had water tasted so sweet, Ipa thought as she dropped to her knees and buried her face in the green water. Her hands were still tied behind her back, so she drank like an animal. She pushed her face deeper, until the water covered her head, then brought it out and shook it.

Kadoh sat beside her, staring at the sierras.

"You must drink, Little Brother, and refresh your body."

"Is Ximi drinking the water?" he asked, not taking his eyes from the distant mountains. "Are we downwind from the deer? Will we have a bountiful hunt today?"

Ipa closed her eyes and drew in a long, deep breath. Her arms longed to hold Kadoh and comfort him.

"Ximi wants you to drink. It will make you strong for the hunt."

Whether Kadoh believed her lie or not, Ipa did not know, but he slowly leaned over and lapped at the water like a panther.

The *españoles* removed the saddles from the backs of their horses and let the animals graze on the grass along the river. The men removed their padded vests and, after eating, stretched out on the ground under the shade of cottonwood trees.

Ipa was exhausted and should have slept soundly, but her heart was too heavy. The sobs of women and the grunts and whines of Kadoh kept her awake. Once she heard the whispers of an *español* and the protests of one of the women. He put his hand over the woman's mouth and dragged her behind a boulder. Soon her protests became whimpers.

Ipa squeezed her eyes shut and buried her face against Kadoh's back.

Ipa's stomach awoke before her eyes. It rolled and twisted and screamed, but all she had for it was water. She thought of the wedding food in her burden-basket, but her hands were still tied. She looked around for the woman with child but did not see her.

"Where is the woman with child?"

"Over there." One of the women pointed to a pile of stones, marking a grave. "Her child came while you slept. It was an untimely birth. The baby died shortly after the mother."

The slavers had unbound the hands of two women to help in the birthing and the burial. Since they had not tried to escape, the soldiers loosened all the women's hands. Ipa's wrists were swollen and raw from the rope burns, and her arms felt as if they had been wrenched from their sockets.

That evening, the Spaniards distributed a handful of *pinole* to each prisoner, then sat under the trees and ate strips of dried beef and corn cakes. When most of the Spaniards had fallen asleep, Xucate whispered into Ipa's ear.

"I am starving, Cousin. You have corn in your burden-basket. Share it with me and Kadoh."

"It is seed corn for my husband-to-be's family," Ipa protested. "It is the best in our village. It would be a great waste to eat it."

*141*

"Your husband-to-be's family is dead," Xucate hissed. "And we are alive. The corn belongs to the living."

The eyes of the other women and children stared at her hungrily.

"If I give food to you, then I must give it to everyone," Ipa said. Though Xucate cast an angry glance at her, Ipa removed her basket and distributed grains of flint-hard corn. She gave away most of the *pinole* and *pinyon* nuts, but held back the sweet yucca cake for Kadoh.

When the worst heat of the day was gone, the *españoles* filled their water bags and mounted their horses. With a collective groan, the prisoners rose and began to march. They spoke very little among themselves, for fear of the ever-present whip. They marched all evening and through the night until the hottest part of the next day, resting often in the shade of boulders or at an occasional spring. Ipa handed out the rest of her corn, except for six grains of blue corn left over from the stalks that Coyomo had laid in front of her uncle's lodge. Those she hid in her deerskin pouch.

Near the end of the third day, when Ipa was sure she would not be able to go another step, they met another band of mounted Spaniards leading a group of weary captives. Their line stretched all the way to the horizon. From the clothing and body tattoos, Ipa knew that some belonged to the Tobosos tribe along the Lesser River to the south of the junction. Their tribe often traded macaw or parrot feathers to her father for blue stones or corn. They spoke a tongue that was strange, and they wore hardly any clothes. The men cropped their hair evenly all over. As in her group, most of the prisoners were men and boys. There were very few women. Their ribs showed through their brown skin and their faces were etched with deep frowns. At the shout of the mounted soldiers, they dropped to the desert, their lean, gaunt faces covered with expressions of exhaustion and hopelessness.

"I wonder when we will look like that," Xucate said to no one in particular. She was surprised to hear a man's voice answer.

"You will never lose your beauty, even in death."

Ipa and Xucate turned to see the Jumano guide, Pedro, looking at them, straddled across the back of a horse. Of all the native peoples who accompanied the Spaniards, he was the only one allowed to ride beside them.

"Why do you associate with those less-than-human Spaniards?" Xucate asked him, tossing her hair to one side.

A slight smile crossed his lips. "If I did not translate and interfere, how do you think they would treat our people?"

"Ha! It cannot get any worse than this." Xucate

put her hands on her hips and glared up into his pockmarked face.

For a reply, he snorted and chuckled to himself.

"Pedro." Ipa ignored her cousin's angry hiss and stepped closer to the horse. "You say we are going to work for the Spaniards in a place to the south. That the men will have to dig inside Earthmother's back."

"Yes, that is true."

"But why do they want children? My brother is only beginning his ninth summer. He is too small to carry heavy loads or dig into the hard earth."

"The Spaniards cherish the young boys most of all. They teach them how to speak their language and then take them as translators on long *entradas,* expeditions into the northern lands. The young ones learn fast and do not cause any trouble. They are well cared for."

"Is that how you came to be a slave of the *españoles?*" Xucate said, her dark eyes flashing at the guide. "Were you taken as a boy and trained to be obedient, as some men train their pack dogs to respond to commands? Shall I call you Pack-Dog from now on? I spit on dogs." Xucate spat over her shoulder.

Pedro's face turned crimson, then he jerked the reins and spun his horse around.

"Do not be so rude to him, Cousin," Ipa said. "I think he could be a friend. He is not cruel, and he seems to care about Kadoh."

"Pack-Dog!" Xucate shouted at the Jumano's back, ignoring Ipa.

The next three days Ipa's feet continued to walk and her heart continued to beat. She expected death to overtake her and accepted it, but it did not come. Others in the line dropped. If they did not respond to the whip, the slavers left them there in the desert for the crows and buzzards. No one buried them; no one sang their death song. The Spaniards gave their captives just enough *pinole* and water to stay alive, but not enough for strength.

On the sixth day, after passing through a dry salt flat, Pedro spoke to the *español* leader on behalf of the prisoners. He spoke his words low and evenly, without emotion, pointing first to the weary prisoners, then to the desert. After a moment, the Jumano stood in front of the captives.

"You may go into the desert and gather roots and berries and cactus," he said. "The women can build a fire to cook whatever they find." His black eyes glanced at Xucate, and Ipa thought she saw a smile.

The people shouted with joy and scrambled toward a clump of yucca plants and a patch of cactus. The men and women tore at the ground with sticks and stones and their bare hands. They ate plants raw that they usually only ate cooked, and chewed on cactus leaves for juice. The slavers laughed and pointed, as if they were watching a happy rain dance.

One of the mounted men chased the women and girls like a boy playing with rabbits.

"If one of those Spaniards touches me, I will slit his throat," Xucate hissed.

"Do you have a knife?" Ipa asked as she scraped needles off a cactus pad and gave it to Kadoh.

"I have this yucca point. It is as sharp as a knife. It would blind a man easily. When the black guard is asleep, I am going to escape."

Ipa nodded, but secretly she hoped that her cousin would not run away and leave her and Kadoh behind. A while later, after the women had started fires and were roasting bulbs, Pedro returned. Around his saddle the limp gray bodies of several rabbits hung loosely. He dropped them at Xucate's feet.

"Here, master," he said. "Your obedient Pack-Dog has brought you food."

Never had food tasted so sweet to Ipa, and for the first time in six days, she fell into a deep, almost peaceful sleep.

By the eighth day, the people's hunger had returned. Though Ipa sometimes saw Pedro slipping bits of dried meat to Xucate, her cousin did not choose to share her food.

That morning, they came to a small village on the Lesser River. Most of the people of the village had fled, leaving behind the old and sick ones. The slavers raided the granaries and houses, then distributed corn and beans and dried meat to the hungry captives. Ipa felt sorry for the villagers who stood by helplessly watching their supplies being devoured. Guilt washed over her, but still she shoved the food down her throat and stuffed her baskets as if she would never have food again.

On the tenth day, the slavers began acting strangely. They kept their eyes upon the horizon and sent the black guard and Pedro ahead of them on foot to scout the countryside.

"What is wrong?" Xucate asked Pedro when he returned.

"We are entering the land of the *chichimeca*. They will kill not only the Spaniards, but anyone who dares to cross their lands. *Chichimeca* is the name that Spaniards call any people who act bravely and refuse to bow down to their god."

"Then I am praying in my heart for the *chichimeca* to come," Xucate said. "If I must die in order for the Spaniards to die, then let it be."

The next morning, the *chichimeca* attacked, viciously killing two Spaniards and three of the prisoners. Several men received wounds and cried out in pain, until Ipa's heart filled with compassion for them.

She removed medicine plants from her basket.

"Where are you going?" Xucate asked.

"I cannot stand by and see men suffer like that. I must help them."

"Even the Spaniards?"

"Yes. I will treat all the men."

"But they are vile and despicable. They killed your husband-to-be. How can you think of such a thing?" Xucate grabbed Ipa's arm and tried to pull her back.

"They are men. They feel pain like any other," Ipa said as she jerked free from her cousin and walked to the Jumano guide and explained that she knew medicine plants.

Pedro took her to the Spanish leader, who had a deep gash in his arm from an arrow that had missed its mark and cut through his skin. She washed the wound and sprinkled powdered root on it, then applied a layer of cactus pulp. He watched her with curious, amazed eyes, then smiled and nodded his head. He took her to his other men and let her apply her medicine until most of her plants had been used up. That evening he let her go into the desert and gather more roots and leaves and berries to treat the prisoners.

The Spanish leader handed her a small bundle of dried beef and gave her extra water. When Ipa returned to the women, she shared her rewards. Xucate no longer complained about Ipa's kindness to the strangers.

For three more days and nights they marched, sleeping only briefly, all eyes watching for sign of the *chichimeca*. The desert had turned rugged and mountainous. Ipa imagined an enemy hiding behind every boulder and gathered herbs along the way in anticipation of another battle. But the *chichimeca* did not strike again.

On the fourteenth day, Ipa could feel her ribs pressing against her taut skin. She marveled how any one of the survivors of this long journey could be of use to the slavers. One of every three people had dropped by the wayside, and those who survived were so low-spirited that they prayed for death.

On the fifteenth day, the mounted slavers stopped at the top of a hill. They shouted and cheered and waved their arms in the air. Shortly afterward, Ipa and Xucate dragged their weary bodies to the crest of the hill. Below, they saw a village, small and dirty, nestled at the foot of a stark gray mountain. In the center of the village the white walls of a fantastic stone building glistened in the sun. Behind it strange animals grazed in areas closed off by walls of stone or wood.

Most of the slavers rode down to the village, shouting and whooping like excited boys in a footrace.

"We are here," Xucate said quietly.

"Yes, at last," Ipa said. She felt her heart pound a little faster. Below was the world of the *españoles*. There would be food and drink and a place to sleep, perhaps, but whether it would be better or worse than death, she could not say.

# Chapter Nine

WHEN THE slavers reached the village, they whooped and shouted and rode their horses around in circles before dismounting and allowing the weary animals to sink their noses into a stone water trough. The prisoners did not get such excellent treatment. Weak, and almost delirious from hunger and exhaustion, the survivors staggered into the plaza in front of a building with thick white walls. They crumpled to the ground. For a long time they sat in the draining heat, their heads resting on their knees.

At last Ipa heard the sound of men arguing in the rolling language of her captors. She lifted her head slightly and peered through her filthy, tangled hair at the captain of the slavers talking to two bearded men in long brown garments that almost touched the ground. Their bare feet peeked out from under the hems. They looked very much like the padres who had visited her village the previous autumn. The older one, whose hair was streaked with gray, was shorter than the captain and his belly hung over a rope tied at his waist. The younger robed man stood a full head above the captain. He was reed thin, with long bony hands dangling from the ends of the baggy sleeves of his brown robe. His fringe of black hair shone like a raven's wing. Silver crosses on the ends of long bead necklaces twinkled in the sunlight.

The older padre's face turned crimson as his tongue rolled and he jabbed his finger toward the prisoners.

"What is he saying?" Xucate asked as she lifted her head.

"I do not know their language," Ipa replied sharply. She had not quite forgiven her cousin for her cruelty. She would not have spoken to Xucate at all during the journey, except that Xucate had watched over Kadoh as if he were her own brother and bestowed on him the only kindness she seemed to possess.

"I heard you speak in their tongue to the captain," Xucate insisted.

"Only a few words, and truly I know not what they mean," Ipa replied.

"The old one is angry. What does it mean?"

Ipa shook her head. "I do not know."

"Sister, Ximi is thirsty." Kadoh lifted his head slightly, his dark eyes blank. "Can we drink from those stone pits over there where the *caballos* are drinking?"

The horses had finished drinking, their bellies stretched large and round. Now they stood in a walled-in corral eating bundles of dried grass. Their heavy saddles had been removed and they looked content. Ipa nodded to her brother.

"Go drink. If the water is good enough for their beasts of burden, truly it will be good enough for their slaves."

Kadoh struggled to his feet, steadying himself a moment before creeping to the water. Ipa thought she could hear his sigh of relief as he sank his cupped hand into the liquid and raised it to his mouth. Ipa tried to run her tongue over her cracked lips, but it was too swollen to move. She tried to swallow, but her throat was parched and dry.

Xucate elbowed Ipa and nodded toward Kadoh. "There is water. Shall we join him?"

Ipa rose and walked without hesitation toward the water trough. Other prisoners saw Kadoh and stood. Some began to trot, and soon a horde of men stampeded over the girls, pushing them aside. They shoved Kadoh away and fought as their hands reached into the water.

A whip cracked and a man screamed as it bit into his flesh. The prisoners scrambled back to the plaza, where two slavers flogged them without mercy.

The padres stopped their arguing outside the great white house long enough to watch the prisoners jostling at the water trough. The gray-haired one rushed to the nearest slaver. He wrenched the whip from the soldier's hand and threw it to the ground. The younger padre disappeared inside the white house but quickly returned with a gourd dipper and a round wooden vessel that had a thin carrying handle. He filled this vessel with water and walked on his bare feet toward the prisoners huddling in the dust.

*"Los indios pobres. Los niños miserables,"* he muttered as he offered the water-filled gourd to the first man. The prisoner drank hesitantly at first, then grabbed the gourd and gulped the liquid down. The tall man moved through the crowd until his wooden vessel was empty, then he returned to the trough and filled it again. The older padre hurried inside the white building and returned with a loaf of bread much like those Ipa's aunt made from ground mesquite beans and acorn flour, but much larger and rounder. And the smell was different. He tore off chunks and handed them to the prisoners. When

they did not respond, he spoke in the Jumano language.

"Food," he said. "Food."

Even though Jumano was a language Ipa knew well, the old man's accent was thick and the words were hard to understand. He made eating motions with his hands and finally pushed a piece of bread into his own mouth and chewed it noisily.

"Good. Food," he said as he rubbed his stomach and smiled. Seeing that he did not die, the prisoners began eating.

When everyone had eaten food and drunk water, the older padre vanished inside the white building but soon returned carrying a small vessel. He walked among the prisoners, sprinkling clear liquid onto their heads and mumbling words softly and making magical signs in the air with a piece of silver that looked like the pendant Rodrigo had given Ipa, only much larger. The tall, thin padre followed beside him, with what looked like layers of thin white bark. He used a turkey feather to make strange marks on the sheets.

"Perhaps the old one is the village medicine man," Kadoh said. "He is sprinkling mesquite juice to help make us well."

Ipa glanced at her little brother. The gash on his head had healed, but his eyes still looked as if they saw the shadows of warriors who were not there.

The gray-haired one paused in front of Ipa and Xucate. Ipa stared into his strange eyes the color of a crisp, cool winter sky. Her knees began to tremble as he lifted the delicate vessel over her head.

Ipa squeezed her eyes tightly shut, expecting to feel a hiss or burn as the medicine dotted her head, but instead she felt only cool water dribbling through her hair like crawling insects.

*"In nomine Patris, et Filii, et Spiritus Sancti. Amen,"* his voice chanted.

The strange words and silver crucifix reminded her of Rodrigo. She thought of Rodrigo's kindness and smiling face and remembered the words he had taught her.

*"Muchas gracias,"* Ipa said.

The old man's blue eyes opened wide, then a smile broke across his rosy-colored face. He saw the tiny silver cross around her neck and clasped his hands together.

*"¡Cielos!"* he exclaimed, then quickly called the leader of the slavers over. For several minutes they babbled in their rattling tongue. The slaver pointed to the gash in his arm, then pointed to Ipa's medicine basket.

"He is telling the old one that you treated the wounded men," Xucate whispered. "Maybe he wants to take your medicine plants."

Ipa pulled her medicine basket closer to her

chest. She would give him her blue stone, or her silver cross, but she would never part with her medicine plants without a fight.

Suddenly the old man turned to Ipa and smiled sweetly. He took her face in his hands. His fingers were cracked and callused on the tips like those of men who work in the cornfields.

"I name you Angelita," he said slowly in the language of the Jumano people, "for you have been sent by God and you have the face of an angel." The tall one scribbled marks rapidly with the turkey quill.

Although Ipa understood the language, she did not know what "angel" meant. Perhaps he thought her face was hideous like a demon's. "Angelita," he repeated as he patted her head softly.

Ipa heard Xucate snicker under her breath.

"He thinks you are a little girl," she whispered. "Maybe you will not have to do any hard work. Perhaps you can pretend you are an imbecile."

Ipa felt her face turn hot. "He is only being kind," she said under her breath. "These two *españoles* are different from the others. Would you insult the one who gives you water and food?"

"But they are Spaniards, all the same. How can you defend them? Spaniards killed your beloved husband-to-be."

Ipa felt heat flash to her cheeks again. At that moment her hatred for her own cousin was stronger than her hatred for the Spaniards in front of her.

"It is for me to decide who I will forgive and who I will not," she said with an angry snarl.

"If you do not care to avenge the Dead One's honor, than I shall. I shall spit on this old Spaniard's face," Xucate hissed. And so she did. When he raised the vessel to sprinkle the water, Xucate knocked it from his hand. The gurgling water formed a dark spot in the sand where it fell.

The old man gasped, then snatched up the sacred vessel. He flayed his arms in outrage, but he did not try to sprinkle Xucate again. He moved on to Kadoh, who looked but did not seem to see.

After the prisoners had been sprinkled, the slavers shoved them into a line. A heavy man, who wore a flowing cape and ruffled white collar, rode into the plaza on a magnificent white horse that pranced sideways and shook its head impatiently.

"*Ahh,*" Kadoh whispered. "That is the most beautiful *caballo* I have ever seen. Look at his tail. It shimmers like new corn tassels."

The big Spaniard dismounted and walked slowly down the line of prisoners. Ipa could not take her eyes off his huge nose. It reminded her of an armadillo's snout. And the hair on his chin had been trimmed into a point. In his left hand he carried a small leather-covered stick. Whenever he tapped the head of a prisoner, two soldiers roughly jerked that man from the line and put him into a separate crowd of men. Occasionally the big man grunted his disapproval, dismissing a sickly man as if he were an inferior animal caught in a trap, too small and worthless to keep. The ones that he dismissed were led by the two padres to the steps of the white building.

All the time the big Spaniard strutted, the Jumano guide, Pedro, stood motionless nearby. The black hat on his head hid most of his face in a shadow and covered any emotion he might have displayed. At last the Spaniard stopped in front of Kadoh. He rubbed his pointed chin, then spoke to Kadoh.

"Señor Diestro wants to know how many summers you have," Pedro translated.

"I am almost in my ninth summer. I already go with the men to the cornfields," Kadoh said. "I am big for my age. And very strong and brave. My uncle is the *cacique*. My father is captain of the hunters. My brother is the greatest of the warriors. He fought the Apaches."

Ipa wanted to scream at Kadoh for his foolishness. *Now is not the time for bragging, Little Brother,* she thought. *Better if you pretend to be sickly.*

"You are but a child, small and weak," the Jumano faithfully translated the words of the laughing Spaniard.

"No." Kadoh shook his head fiercely. "I am not weak. I have killed rabbits with my club. And I have speared fish in the river many times. My uncle says I will be *cacique* when I am a man."

The Jumano's lips turned up slightly at the corner as he translated, the only display of emotion in his stone face. The big Spaniard laughed, then put his hand on Kadoh's shoulder. The guards pulled him away to join the other men.

"Little Beetle!" Ipa shouted, and ran to her brother.

"Please do not let them take him to the mine," she pleaded as she wrapped her arms around Kadoh. "Remember, you told me that boys would be taught to speak the Spanish language and become translators. You said children are treated well." When Ipa saw no response in the black eyes, she lowered her voice to a whisper. "He has head-sickness from a wound. He is afraid of the dark. He will never survive."

The Jumano glanced at Xucate, who had also put a hand on Kadoh's shoulder. She did not speak, but her eyes met his.

"I will tell him," Pedro said after a long quietness. He spoke to the big Spaniard and the padres, gesturing toward Kadoh. In a moment he returned.

"Fray Ignatio says that if the boy has head-sickness, he is no good to him. He will never be able to learn the language. Your brother will be sent to the silver mine. He will carry water to the workers."

A sob burst from Ipa's lips as one of the soldiers ripped Kadoh from her arms. "He is still a child!" she cried.

"Then he will become a man fast, or he will die a child," Pedro replied dryly. He started to turn away, but his gaze fell on the silver crucifix hanging around Ipa's neck. His black eyes met hers a moment. "I see you already worship the Spaniards' god. Either you are wise beyond your years or you are a fool," he said in a low voice, then walked away.

The big Spaniard strutted in front of the ragged men. He shouted words, gesturing and pointing toward the mountains as he spoke.

"His name is Juan Diestro." Pedro translated for the prisoners, who stood in silence, their faces drawn. "He is overseer of the silver mine. He needs the strongest men to dig ore from the earth's belly in Big Mountain over there." He waved his arm across the desert toward the gray mountain. "As subjects of the viceroy of New Spain, you will adhere to all Spanish laws. Your people must pay tribute and taxes to Señor Antonio Sánchez, the *corregidor* of your villages and lands. You will also pay tribute to the Holy Church. In return, you will be protected from harm."

"But how can we pay tribute when our hands are empty?" one of the men, who had the appearance of a *cacique,* asked. "Everything we have is in our villages."

"If you cannot pay in silver or gold or corn, you will be allowed to pay by working. Señor Diestro has obtained the right to use your labor in his silver mine. You will be paid money for your work, which you in

160

turn will use to pay your tributes to Señor Sánchez and to buy food, clothes, and a place to live."

Ipa saw the men lower their heads. So they had been captured and made slaves of the *españoles* without the honor of fighting, without the glory of dying in battle. Ipa felt their shame and hung her head, too.

"The women, children, and some of the men will work in the mission, growing food and tending livestock for the Spaniards and the miners. The old one is called Fray Bernardo; the tall one is Fray Ignatio. They are Franciscan friars on a mission for their god. Obey them and you will survive."

"And how long will we have to work?" the *cacique* asked. "Our cornfields will go untended and our wives and children will starve if we do not return by next planting season."

Pedro glanced at Juan Diestro as if to translate the question, then decided against it. The older friar, Fray Bernardo, saw Pedro's hesitation and stepped up.

"I will explain to them," he said in a cheerful voice. He spoke to them in a choppy version of the Jumano language, though at times he mixed in the words of other tribes, making strange combinations. If Ipa had not been so tired and weak-hearted, she would have laughed.

"Your servitude will last one year and shall occur every four years," the plump man explained. "You will toil in the mine six days of the week. Of course, you shall not work on Sunday, for that day is holy and you will attend mass and pray to Jesucristo." He quickly crossed himself. "Every miner must chisel out a *quintal*—one and a quarter tons of ore per day. This you will carry in sacks on your backs from your small tunnels to one larger tunnel, where it will be hauled off by donkey cart. If you cannot meet your quota, then you will work longer than one year until it is met, or you may be asked to work on Sunday, though I do not like that alternative myself."

The men murmured and the smell of fear filled the air.

"With your earnings, you must buy food, tools, and candles. At the end of the year, you will be allowed to return to your villages, but you must come here again in four years."

"If you are still alive," Xucate whispered.

"It is no less than slavery," said the woman next to Ipa.

After the friar had finished his speech, Juan Diestro mounted his prancing white stallion and steered him to the front of the stone steps where the women, children, and a few men stood. He paused in front of Xucate, his eyes gleaming. He ran his tongue over his narrow lips before speaking to the guide.

"He wants to know your name and how many summers you have known," Pedro translated.

For a reply Xucate spat at the ground.

"Man-killer!" she shrieked at Diestro. "Your

warriors killed our people. I will never be your slave." She spat into the white stallion's beautiful face. It neighed and reared high.

Whether or not Pedro translated correctly, Ipa could not say, but Juan Diestro suddenly raised his hand and brought it down hard across Xucate's face. He grabbed her arm and jabbed his spurs into the horse's sides, making it run fast in a circle around the plaza. Ipa watched in horror as Xucate's bare feet dragged on the hard ground. Tears stained the tall girl's dusty cheeks, but she did not cry out in pain.

Pedro pressed his lips together and his black eyes glanced at Ipa as if to say, *There, see what I mean*. For an instant his hands clenched into fists, but before anyone noticed, he let them open again.

Juan Diestro returned to the white steps and dropped Xucate. She climbed to her feet, though they were bloody with cuts and scrapes. Her eyes glared back at his face. Diestro snorted and swung his stallion around. He gave the command and the soldiers prodded the men chosen to become miners.

Ipa watched them, both the brave and the cowardly, the young and the old, shuffle in a single line toward the mountains. Kadoh turned his head, confusion on his face.

"Little Beetle!" she cried, and started to run for him. The Jumano grabbed her arm.

"Do not be a fool," he whispered.

Ipa felt a sharp lump rise to her throat as she

watched her brother being swallowed up in the shuffling feet and dust. He looked so small and confused. She thought she heard him shout "Ximi!" and she could not stop the tears from sliding down her cheeks.

Ipa wanted to stay outside and watch the men until they disappeared, but Fray Bernardo and Fray Ignatio opened the heavy wooden doors that led into the white stone building. They herded the newcomers inside.

"This is the mission Nuestra Señora de la Clemencia," Fray Bernardo explained in his strange accent. "You will live here. You will be given food, clothing, and rooms in exchange for labor. In addition to the communal field, each family will be allowed a small plot of land to grow its own vegetables. From this day forth you are all Christians and will obey the laws of Jesucristo, our Savior. The men among you will work in the fields or tend the livestock or help build the rest of the mission. The women will learn to weave wool or cast pottery or sew. The products will be shipped to Mexico City or Vera Cruz and on to Spain. You are our children, and like any father, we will treat you firmly but with love. Now, come inside and receive our blessings. Tomorrow you will begin your first catechisms."

The brown-skinned people who already lived at the mission looked on with only mildly curious eyes, as if they had seen this many times before. Instead of deerskin or buffalo-skin clothing, they wore white cotton tunics tied with colorful sashes. As they entered the mission, some of them knelt and kissed the hems of the friars' robes and made the magic sign over their hearts and shoulders.

Ipa looked at Xucate. Ants and flies crawled on her bleeding feet, but she did not cry. They exchanged glances in silence, then Ipa put her arm around her cousin and helped her limp through the open door of the chapel. Ipa's heart pounded as she stepped inside. She could not help but think that she was going into a dark pit that led to the bowels of the earth and the horrors of the underworld.

## Chapter Ten

*I*PA AWAKENED to the sound of a rooster crowing outside her window. For a moment she did not open her eyes. She pretended that she was in her uncle's lodge on a cold spring morning, snuggled into a buffalo hide. A warm sensation crept over her as she stretched her legs.

Ipa opened her eyes and saw the adobe walls, the rough-hewn wooden beams, and the tiny square window letting in a cold, gray dawn. She smelled the wax of last night's candles and the straw inside the mattress beneath her. Then she heard the morning bells, the ones she had heard every morning for the past year.

A wave of loneliness swept over her as she realized where she was. She drew her legs up under her chin and squeezed her eyes shut. She tried to go back to sleep, but the rattle of clay pots across the room and the shuffle of feet outside the window would not let her.

Cold air bit into Ipa's arms and legs as she rose and slipped a yellowed cotton dress over her head, cinching it at the waist with a cotton cord. Over this she pulled a wool poncho. After brushing her long hair and twisting it into a knot on top of her head, she slid her feet into her sandals, then hurried to a mat in the corner of the room.

"Wake up, Cousin," she whispered, shaking Xucate's shoulders.

"Leave me alone," Xucate growled as she slapped Ipa's hand away.

The clang of metal striking metal floated across the misty plaza that stretched between the chapel and the quarters where the *indios* lived.

"Listen, Cousin—the morning bells are ringing. You will be late for Sunday mass again. You know Fray Bernardo will be displeased. He says Jesucristo will be unhappy if we do not pray to him every day."

The bells rang out again; loud, resonating peals that reached every corner of the mission. From a crudely built wooden table, Ipa grabbed two strings of beads made from hard seeds and bits of colored glass. She draped one around her hand and lay the other one beside her cousin. As usual, Xucate had slept in the same deerskin dress that she had worn on the day of her capture a year ago, even though the friars frowned on it. They insisted the women wear the soft white cotton cloth made on the mission looms or the itchy wool gathered from the merino sheep that grazed the hillsides.

But every night before snuffing out the candle flame, Xucate removed the white cotton dress and slipped into her deerskin tunic, which she kept hidden in a corner. Even on the coldest night, she slept on a floor mat rather than the wooden cot.

"I will go back someday," Xucate swore each night before she closed her eyes. But each morning she would still be there. Ipa had long ago given up trying to make Xucate change her disobedient ways.

"Quickly, Cousin, take your *rosario*," Ipa insisted. "You must get up."

Xucate pushed the beads away and turned her back on Ipa.

"I do not care about the Spaniards' god. He has brought only pain and heartache to our people. I spit on Jesucristo." She spat over her left shoulder. "I also spit on Juan Diestro, that son of demons."

Ipa quickly crossed herself as she rose to her feet.

"At least that is one thing we agree on. I despise the overseer of the silver mine, like every other woman in the mission. He is not only cruel to the men and boys, but his eyes rove over the women as if he were studying his next meal."

"You are the lucky one, Ipa," Xucate said. "You look younger than your fifteen years. Diestro's lecherous eyes skip over you."

Ipa nodded. It was true she was still small for her age. Even though her stomach never was empty, as it had been most of her life, she had still not grown as tall as her cousin. And Juan Diestro preferred the more mature girls, like Xucate, whose beauty was more breathtaking than ever now that she was sixteen years old.

The woman who shared the room with Ipa and Xucate had finished nursing her baby and sat it on the floor while she combed her hair. The woman, Lucia, came from a village far to the south of Ipa's home. Her husband had died in the mine not long ago. The friars forbade all *indios* to speak in native languages, so when Lucia and Ipa spoke, it was in the tongue of their Spanish captors. The baby had been born a few days after Ipa's arrival. Now it toddled across the dirt floor, cooing at its mother as she hastily slipped on her yucca-fiber sandals.

Ipa glanced at her sleepy cousin one more time as she closed the heavy wooden door with black nailheads shaped like flowers. She joined a dozen other people who walked in silence across the foggy plaza toward the chapel with its steep bell tower. When Ipa had first arrived, the bells frightened her. They sounded too much like the wind wailing through a hole in the canyon, the hole that her grandmother had told her held evil spirits. For this reason, more than any, Ipa obeyed the friars in their dull brown robes and bare feet. One day, she woke exceptionally early and slipped outside. She saw Fray Bernardo go into the tower room and followed him. Through the open door, she spied him pulling a rope dangling from the top of the tower. Even though she watched his arms jerk the rope, the sudden clang of the bells startled her. But from that day forward, she knew the bells were the voices of humans, not demons.

Ipa had learned many things since her arrival. She learned that the Spaniards came from the land where the sun rose, that their god had three names, and that they called everyone except themselves *indios,* whether they be the Buffalo People from the flat plains or the Corn People who lived in adobe cities to the west. Every six moons, the slavers returned with more *indios,* to replace those buried in the overflowing cemetery. Some of the men helped the friars build more stone rooms onto the mission, or worked in the cornfields, but most of them were sent to the silver mine.

Ipa quickened her step. Lately there had been so many *indios* that the chapel filled up quickly and some had to stand outside for the mass. On Sundays, the men from the silver mine came to the mission. It was the only day of rest for them. Often, many of them were too tired to come and remained in over-crowded *barrios* located on the far side of town, closer to the mine and outside the comfort and security of the mission walls.

Sunday was the only day that Ipa got to see Kadoh. When the weather was good, they sat in the *patio* garden after mass, feeding the birds, or walked to the stables and petted the horses, for Kadoh still loved these animals. Ipa would give him corn cakes smeared with the red jam of prickly pear fruit, or beans and wild onions, or whatever special treat she could find. He rarely spoke. His empty eyes would stare at her as if she were a stranger. Most often he would simply thank her and say that Ximi would enjoy the food.

Ipa squeezed between two women and entered the chapel through the heavy wooden side doors that were thicker than her arm. As always, the smell of candles and musty incense filled the air. In the front pews sat the Spaniards dressed in their finest clothes. Juan Diestro's stiff, white, ruffled collar made it difficult for him to bow his head, and his wife, a pale, sickly-looking woman with large black eyes, always looked as if her mind and soul were in another place. As was her custom, she wore a somber black dress of many layers and a lacy black *mantilla* over her head.

Behind the Spaniards sat the mission *indios* in their sandal-covered feet and white cotton clothes. And behind them, the miners, most still wearing the

*171*

deerskin breechcloths of their villages. Instead of beaded *rosarios,* many of them carried simple knotted cotton strings. Ipa's eyes scoured the faces of the miners, drawn and sad, their arms and legs marked with scars, but she could not find Kadoh's face among the crowd. Ipa sighed in frustration. Now she would worry all day why he had not come.

Fray Bernardo kissed the altar, then stood on a wooden platform behind a long table covered with a white cloth embroidered with gold thread. He made the sign of the cross with his hands and in a singsong voice spoke words that were like Spanish, but not the same.

"*In nomine Patris, et Filii, et Spiritus Sancti.*"

"*Amen,*" the people replied in unison.

"*Dominus vobiscum,*" Fray Bernardo said.

"*Et cum spiritu tuo,*" the people replied.

As the mass continued, Ipa murmured the words that the padres had taught her in unison with the other *indios,* but her eyes strayed to the walls of the chapel. Fray Ignatio had taught two men how to paint bright red, yellow, and blue stripes around the base and top of the walls. They had placed flower designs in each corner. High up on both walls, the pale beams of the rising sun struck colored glass inside small, rounded windows and cast colorful patterns on the walls.

Ipa's gaze wandered to her left, where a lifelike statue of Jesucristo nestled in an alcove. A crown of thorns pressed into his bleeding head and hideous red wounds gaped in his wrists and feet. His eyes rolled upward in agony. Ipa did not like to look at it, for it reminded her of Coyomo lying still on the desert floor, a bleeding hole in his back.

She preferred to look at the statue of Maria Regina on the opposite wall. The dark, kind eyes always seemed to be so full of love and pain as she held the baby Jesucristo in her arms. Ipa often sneaked into the chapel just to stare at the statue. She had never seen such beautiful clothes, a blue *manta* trimmed in gold over a pink robe and a white *mantilla,* and on her head a golden crown.

But even grander than the statues was the painting on the wall behind the altar. It depicted men and women in wondrous costumes of every color of the rainbow, standing near a river lined with green trees and lush flowers. A golden-haired god, dressed in white with large, feathered wings, hovered in the air. The *indios* said the winged god was the Rain Spirit, and often the men prayed to him when they planted the crops. Once Ipa asked Fray Bernardo if his homeland, España, looked like that.

"Ah, yes," he had sighed. "España is the most beautiful place on earth." Then he had gotten a faraway look in his blue eyes. It was always that way when he spoke of España.

"Then why do you stay here, Padre? Why do you not return to your home village?"

The old man had smiled and patted the top of Ipa's head.

"Because it is God's will. He has sent me here to save the souls of all your people."

"Won't you ever go back?"

"When my work is done here, I will move on to another mission and another people. And after that, another. There is so much work to be done. I shall die in this strange land someday."

Ipa's mind roamed as the mass continued. She imagined Fray Bernardo in a rocky grave with a simple wooden cross on top, like the ones that the friars made for the Spaniards when they died.

By the time the mass was over, the sun had risen and the fog had lifted. Even though the spring nights were still cold, the days were hot. Most of the men worked in the fields clearing rocks and boulders, digging the soil with strange plows pulled by oxen. Sometimes the oxen pulled two-wheeled carts whose wheels were taller than a man. Work in the fields kept the men busy from sunrise to sunset, with a break for lunch and a siesta, to avoid the noonday heat. But on evenings and Sundays they could work in their own small gardens, where they raised chile peppers or onions or beans or squash. Some of them raised the strange plants the friars had brought with them called melons. Once a week they came together and bought and sold and traded with one another. It was a happy time, like the time of harvest in her village.

Ipa returned to her room with a weary heart, for one of the miners had told her that Kadoh was sick. Xucate was gone, but she had started a fire in the corner hearth and ground enough cornmeal to make the day's supply of *tortillas*. Ipa never knew when to expect kindness from Xucate. Sometimes her tongue was as bitter as green cactus pears, sometimes sweet like yucca flowers. Ipa often saw Xucate staring at the mountains, in the direction of their village, her eyes turned black with hatred.

Suddenly Ipa wished her cousin were still in the room. She wanted to talk about Kadoh. Even though Xucate was often bitter and harsh, she truly loved Kadoh like a brother. And after all, she was the only one in the mission from Ipa's village. They had drunk the same river water and played in the same cornfields as children. If for no other reason than that, Ipa had at last forgiven her cousin for her cruelty and jealousy.

"Should I go to the *barrio* to visit my brother, Kadoh?" Ipa asked the widow, Lucia, as she mashed beans into a brown paste.

"No, no," the woman said, clucking her tongue and shaking her head. "It is a dangerous thing for a girl to do alone. The overcrowded shacks reek with the stench of human filth."

"Yes, I know. I go there sometimes with Fray Ignatio to help administer medicine to injured miners who are too sick to come to the infirmary. I ride in the back of his donkey cart. Hundreds of hungry eyes stare at me from beneath weary brows. Those dark alleys and stinking shacks—it is like going into the depths of Hades."

"*Si, si,* I have seen you going there," the widow said as she formed cornmeal mush into balls, then rapidly patted them into flat *tortillas.* "The friars are fortunate to have one so skilled with medicine plants, Angelita. All the *indios* know your medicine is powerful and your heart is kind. From the day you arrived you have helped the friars heal the sick. Even the Spaniards trust your knowledge. I don't think the miners would ever harm you. After all, they do not live in the *barrio* by free choice. But still, in my worst nightmares, I am living there."

All during breakfast, Ipa could not stop thinking about her brother, so afterward she sought out Fray Bernardo. He stood inside the granary, surveying the corn supply and complaining, as he often did, about the fact that his beloved wheat plants would not grow well in the rocky soil of the desert. His wheat had to be shipped all the way from Mexico City, along with other strange grains and products. He had tried again and again to make the wheat grow, but it was hopeless, so he ate corn cakes like the *indios.*

"Padre . . ." Ipa cleared her throat.

Fray Bernardo's blue eyes twinkled as he turned to her.

"What is it, Angelita?"

"I wish to speak about my brother Kadoh. He is only nine summers old. . . . No, it would be almost ten summers by now."

"Ah, that is whom you visit with every Sunday in the *patio*. I often wondered."

"Yes. He took a strong blow to the head the day we were captured and has not been himself since. Sometimes he doesn't know who I am. He speaks of our older brother as if he sees him daily, but our older brother was taken slave by the Apaches many years ago."

"Ah . . . *dementia*. The poor child."

"He did not come to mass today. One of the miners said he is sick. I am worried about him."

"And what do you want of me?"

"Juan Diestro uses Kadoh in the silver mine. He should be in your classroom learning to read and write like other boys. Or at the least, please let him have a less strenuous job—in the fields, or watching animals. He loves horses more than anything alive. He would be wonderful with them."

"A child in the mine . . . But surely he is not strong enough to carry the two hundred pounds of ore on his back?"

"No. Juan Diestro sends Kadoh down into the

tunnels ahead of the others to check the bracing timbers and to carry water. My brother is small and can get into tight places."

"Ah . . . I see." Fray Bernardo rubbed his chin. "Juan Diestro is in charge of the mine workers and I am in charge of the field laborers and livestock tenders. I provide for their souls and Diestro provides for their bodies. But still, the silver mine is no place for a child. How can he send a child down into the narrow, twisting ratholes that go deep into the earth where the air is too dusty to breathe? Too many die."

"Perhaps we can steal Kadoh away one night. I hear that many miners run away. That is why the slavers must go out and capture more *indios* so often."

"Yes, many do escape, but those who reach the desert and do not die from heat or starvation or snakebites are killed by the savage *chichimeca*," Fray Bernardo said. "Those who are recaptured live to regret it. They are flogged until their backs look like the jagged sierras."

Ipa swallowed hard. She had heard many stories of the horrors of the mine. Every time she saw Kadoh his eyes turned wild when he spoke of the evil "ratholes." Every woman in the mission knew a man working there and cried at night for his soul.

"I could hide my brother in my room. Perhaps Juan Diestro would not miss him."

Fray Bernardo leaned back on his walking stick.

"Not miss him? You are so innocent, Angelita. Juan Diestro counts his miners as a shepherd counts his sheep. He knows each man's walk and limp and number of tattoos on his skin. He would know your brother was gone, and he would come looking here."

"Please, Padre. Kadoh is only a child, and sickly. He hates those dark, narrow tunnels. He has always been afraid of the dark. It is driving him insane. If he does not get out soon, I fear he will take his own life."

"Many *indios* have done so already, even though I have taught them it is a sin. Getting silver ore for the crown is very costly, I'm afraid." He heaved a sigh that rattled his body. "I have written petitions to the viceroy of New Spain complaining of the treatment of the poor miners—especially the floggings and the iron shackles. I have written to the king and to the sovereign pontiff himself, the Pope. But nothing must interrupt the flow of silver into the royal coffers. And to think all these riches are only pilfered away on foolish wars. It is abominable." He struck the ground with his stick, then sighed again. "Come, let us pray for your brother."

"Will you speak to Juan Diestro?"

"Yes, I will speak to him tonight. But I must be careful. It is his silver that lines the coffers of our church."

Ipa's heart swelled with hope, and all day she

worked hard gathering medicine plants and pounding their roots and stems into powder for use in the infirmary where she worked every day. It helped to take her mind off her brother.

That evening, after vespers, Ipa saw Fray Bernardo speaking to Juan Diestro near the wooden confession booth with its black velvet curtain. Diestro's stiff, ruffled collar was always white, no matter how dusty the weather. His head appeared to be sitting on a fancy platter and reminded Ipa of the story of Salome and John the Baptist. The two men argued, with first Juan Diestro shaking his head, then Fray Bernardo doing the same. Diestro strutted on his cloth-covered legs, holding up his hand in protest to Fray Bernardo's words.

Ipa held her breath as she waited inside the opened side door that led to the courtyard. She heard footsteps behind her and out of the corner of her eyes she saw her cousin approaching.

"Why are they arguing?" Xucate whispered in the language of her people.

"They argue over Kadoh. Fray Bernardo wants him out of the mine, but Juan Diestro refuses."

"Diestro has the fangs of a snake for a heart," Xucate whispered, then spat over her shoulder. Her eyes filled with hatred as she glared at him.

At last the two men stopped arguing. Diestro swooped out the front door in a flurry of capes and ruffles and swishing velvet pantaloons. Fray Bernardo scurried over to Ipa, his face flushed crimson and beads of perspiration on his bald head.

"A small victory," he said in a husky voice.

Ipa's heart fluttered. "Kadoh is being set free?"

"Señor Diestro says he will let your brother come live with you shortly, after he has time to train another boy. He says Kadoh is not reliable anymore; that his mind is gone."

Ipa swallowed hard at the news but forced a smile. "At least my brother will be safe with me."

"*Gracias al cielo.*" Fray Bernardo looked toward the sky and pressed his hands together.

"*Muchas gracias,* Padre." Ipa flexed her knees and kissed the hem of the brown habit.

"Light an extra candle for Kadoh tonight," he whispered as he patted her hand. "And why were you not at mass this morning?" he asked, turning to Xucate.

She shrugged. "I said my prayers to the Great Spirit. I have no need of Jesucristo." Her Spanish was poor, for she hated to speak it.

Fray Bernardo clamped his mouth tightly shut, then turned and walked down the stone path that led to the cloister.

Ipa turned to Xucate. "Did you hear, Cousin? Little Brother will be freed very soon. Is that not wonderful news?"

But Xucate's lips did not smile. Her eyes glared at the back of Juan Diestro as he swung onto his beautiful prancing white horse and rode to the end of the town where his large house sat away from all others. She spat over her shoulder again.

"His promise is as empty as the wind," Xucate said. "Kadoh will not last another month in the mine. And he knows it."

# Chapter Eleven

A COOL AUTUMN wind swept across the plaza and rattled gourds dangling from an abandoned *ramada* in the middle of the cornfield, where workers took refuge from the noontime heat. In the distance, goats bleated and their leader's bell clanked as they worked their way down the rocky hillside. In a small valley between mountains, a herd of lean cattle with long horns grazed lazily and pigs grunted in the *patio*.

Ipa removed her multicolored *serape* from her shoulders before lighting a candle and placing it in front of the statue of Maria. She whispered a prayer for Kadoh, crossed herself, and rose. As she looked into the kind eyes of the statue, she sighed. She could not understand why Maria did not answer her prayers for Kadoh's safe return. Ipa had prepared an extra bed for her brother, made from quilted cotton stuffed with straw, and eagerly awaited their happy reunion. Spring had turned into summer, and the summer had passed, but still Kadoh had not been released from the mine. And even worse, he had stopped attending Sunday mass.

The stone path felt cool on Ipa's feet as she padded from the chapel to the infirmary at the far end of the mission. On passing by the weaving workshop, she heard the busy chatter of women as they combed wool from the merino sheep that roamed the hillsides. A young woman sat at one of the spinning wheels lost in her own world of daydreams. Three others sat behind large looms, meticulously weaving the wool threads into intricate patterns. Ipa still marveled at the itchy wool cloth. It was thicker and longer lasting than the light cotton cloth that the Corn People made and traded throughout the land. And once the threads had been dyed with reds, yellows, blues, and greens from berries, roots, or crushed insect bodies, the finished blankets and *serapes* were beautiful.

Ipa glanced into the pottery workshop as she tiptoed by, hoping to see her cousin, but as usual, Xucate had managed to avoid working indoors.

"I will never use their looms and their potter's

wheel and their sewing needles," Xucate often told Ipa. "I hate being inside the dark rooms that smell like sheep wool or wet clay. I must have fresh air to breathe. I must work with the sun on my back and the green corn at my feet and the wind in my hair. I will never, never learn the ways of the Spaniards."

Ipa loved the earthy smell of red potter's clay and took great pleasure in shaping bowls and vessels. But, although she had learned the Spanish techniques rapidly, Fray Ignatio wanted to use her talents in the infirmary.

While other girls and women worked together, laughing and chatting, Ipa worked alone with her medicine plants. She gathered roots of the *guayacan* for men's fevers and the roots of *ocotillo* for swellings. She pounded the roots into powder to be mixed with a paste of cactus pulp and placed on men's wounds. She plucked leaves of the purple sage bush to make medicine tea and the stinky leaves of *lantana* bushes for snakebites. When she made the sick or injured miners drink the tea, she made the sign of the cross over them and prayed to Maria and Jesucristo. But she also secretly sprinkled cornmeal in the six sacred directions and blew on their wounds as she asked the Great Spirit to take their pain away. She had to be very careful, for the friars frowned on the old religion of her people. More than once they had accused an old, stubborn shaman of *hechizeria* — sorcery. Finally he had been stoned to death. Most sick *indios* came to the friars and, after receiving a blessing and the touch of Fray Bernardo's hand or after confessing their sins, left happy and well. Only those who were very ill or hurt came to the infirmary.

As Ipa stood in front of the ornately carved wooden door, she heard the low groan of someone in pain and the wail of a sick infant. These were the sounds she had grown accustomed to. The infirmary always had patients to care for. Usually they were miners with mangled bodies and crushed bones from some creaky wall in the silver mine caving in; sometimes the patient was a miner near death from exhaustion or whip lashings. Sometimes it was a field worker who had been bitten by a rattlesnake.

Lately many patients were Spanish *soldados* who had been attacked by vicious *chichimeca*. The soldiers were garrisoned in a far corner of the mission until a permanent *presidio* could be built on a nearby hill. They protected the mule caravans loaded with silver on their journey to Vera Cruz and the caravans that brought supplies to the Spaniards and to the mission from Mexico City.

Ipa's heart wept for the dying Spaniards who held her hand like frightened children. They spoke of their homeland, parents, wives, and children. They called her Little Angel and thanked her for her medicine. When Ipa looked into the eyes of the *soldados,* she often thought about Rodrigo, the young adventurer who had been so kind to her and Kadoh.

She wondered what had happened to him and if he would remember her should they meet by chance one day.

When Ipa tended the miners, her heart ached with pain. For in each tired face she imagined the face of her brother. In each body scarred from the whip and iron leggings and marked with scrapes and abrasions from the narrow walls of the tunnels, she imagined the small body of Kadoh. He had lived past eleven summers now. In their village he would be training for the sacred initiation ceremonies of manhood. He would be talking in the *kiva* with the elders, dreaming of his first deer hunt, learning the sacred dances of warriors. His smooth, young face should be proudly carrying the tattoo of his first deer slaying, not the ugly scars of the Spaniard's whip. Ipa had not seen her brother after the day of Diestro's false promise many months ago. She did not even know if he was still alive, though some of the miners told her he was more insane than ever.

As Ipa opened the great wooden door to the infirmary, the stringent odor of crushed mesquite beans and fever weed hanging from poles tingled her nostrils. She saw Fray Ignatio outlined by the yellow light of a candle. He was stooped over a bed at the far end of the room. Ipa crossed herself and said a quick prayer for the soul of whoever it might be.

"Angelita, bring me a wet cloth and a cup of fever tea," Fray Ignatio said as he looked up.

"Another miner?" she asked softly as she saw the leg irons on the floor beside the bed.

He nodded. "Another cave-in. This one may lose his leg."

*At least this man's nightmare in the mine will have ended,* Ipa thought, but she said nothing. She hurried to the large wooden bucket on a worktable at one end of the infirmary. It was near empty. She would have to walk to the well in the center of the plaza and fill it again soon. She poured water onto a cotton cloth and filled a drinking gourd with a smelly, greenish liquid from a clay jug.

Ipa hurried to the bed and handed the cloth and the gourd to the priest. As he turned to take it, the candlelight fell across the miner's face.

"Kadoh!" she said with a gasp.

"You know this young man?"

Ipa nodded, unable to find her voice for a moment. "He is my brother." Her words trembled like the leaves on a cottonwood tree. "He was supposed to leave the mine and come live with me this past spring."

"I am sorry," Fray Ignatio said, turning his large brown eyes upward. The dark circles beneath them indicated that he had not slept all night. A wave of gratitude swept over Ipa for a moment, but then anger struck her heart. She felt her face turn hot.

"If my brother dies, I will kill Juan Diestro," she said calmly.

"*Shh,* Angelita, it is a sin to seek revenge. The Holy Word says to love thine enemies, child."

Ipa bowed her head shamefully and stared at the friar's long, bony fingers gently pressing the wet cloth to Kadoh's flushed face. It was then that she realized why the water bucket was so low. Fray Ignatio must have been up all night pressing wet rags to Kadoh's head and burning-hot body.

The friar tried to get Kadoh to drink the fever tea, but the boy's lips would not move.

"See if he will drink for you. His body needs medicine to help fight the fever."

Ipa knelt beside the cot and took Kadoh's hand. The pads of his fingers and thumb felt hard and callused.

"It is Ipa-tah-chi, your sister," Ipa said in the language of her people. "You must drink, Little Beetle."

She felt the weakest of twitches in Kadoh's hand.

"Please drink. Ximi wants you to drink."

She felt terrible for the lie, but Kadoh cracked his eyelids open and allowed Fray Ignatio to put the gourd to his lips again. This time Kadoh raised his head slightly and swallowed the liquid down in awkward, choking gulps.

Ipa cupped her brother's face in her hands and looked into the pain-filled eyes.

"Sister, is that you?" he asked.

She swallowed hard and smiled.

"Yes, Little Beetle."

"My leg hurts. The timber holding the wall collapsed. I did not have time to repair it. Juan Diestro will be angry. He will withhold my supper and flog me with his wicked whip. I must go back and repair the bracing." Kadoh tried to lift his body from the bed.

"No, no, stay here and rest." Ipa gently pressed down on his shoulders.

"No time to rest. I must go down into that hole. That hateful, demon-filled hole. It waits for me like a bear in a cave. Narrow and black. No air to breathe."

"What is the child saying? Is he delirious?" Fray Ignatio asked, for he had never learned the languages of the *indios* as well as Fray Bernardo.

Ipa nodded and fought back the tears. "He thinks he is inside the mine shaft. I curse Juan Diestro and his wicked soldiers." She turned her head aside and spat onto the stone floor.

Fray Ignatio parted his lips as if to protest but instead placed a hand on her arm. "Come with me a moment, Angelita," he whispered.

Ipa rose and followed him to the water bucket.

"Your brother's foot is crushed. If he lives, he will never be able to walk like a normal man. All we can do is keep him in bed and pray. Now, go watch over him and keep him still. Do not let him get up. I must go help with the matins, but I will return later with food."

Ipa watched the stooped shoulders of the friar as he walked out of the infirmary in determined strides. She had never felt comfortable in his presence. His tall, bony frame, pitted cheeks, and hollow eye sockets reminded her too much of a coyote. He did not have as much patience with the *indios* as Fray Bernardo. Many times Ipa saw the plump, gray-haired older padre sitting in the middle of the plaza playing toss-the-stick games with children so he could learn their language better. The gloomy Fray Ignatio preferred to stay inside his dim cloister filled with dark, carved furniture from Spain. Well into the night, until his candle burned low, he would scribble furiously in his journal.

Back at Kadoh's bedside, Ipa held his hand. He drank some water, muttered words about whips and stones and hunger, then closed his eyes and fell into a restless sleep.

Carefully Ipa lifted the thin blanket from Kadoh's body and forced herself to look at the mangled foot. It was caked with dried black blood and already the flesh had turned purple. Bands of red circled his ankles from the iron leggings. Ipa felt hot tears sliding down her cheeks and forced down a hard lump.

"I swear, Little Brother, you will never have to

work in the mine again," she whispered to his sleeping face.

Perhaps she was evil for thinking the thoughts
she had in her mind, but as she looked at her
brother's scarred body, all she could think was that
maybe losing a foot was only a small sacrifice to pay
for freedom from Juan Diestro.

# Chapter Twelve

By noon, Kadoh's fever was down. Ipa took the time to eat some corn *tortillas* and beans and made Kadoh drink a mug of broth. She also attended the other sick in the hospital. Most of them suffered from heat exhaustion, or from Juan Diestro's whip. One man had the deep gashes of a mule's hoof on his chest.

When the vesper bells softly rang, Ipa heard the heavy door creak. She looked up to see her cousin slipping into the infirmary.

"I heard about Kadoh," Xucate whispered as she stood over the bed, a look of disgust on her face. "If I were a man, Diestro would be dead now."

"*Shh,* Cousin, the Spanish *soldados* over there will hear you."

"Don't worry about them. They do not understand our language." Xucate cast a glance across the room to the other beds, then sat on a stool and pulled the wet cloth from Ipa's hand.

"Let me watch over Kadoh while you go to your precious vespers," she said. "You know I hate those foolish Spanish prayers."

"Thank you, Cousin," Ipa whispered, but Xucate waved her away.

Long shadows streaked across the plaza as Ipa joined the *indios* walking to the chapel, weary from a long day's work.

The community had burgeoned as more men came to work in the mine and in the mission fields. A small town had popped up, filled with mule caravan servants, merchants selling goods to miners, and soldiers in the garrison. Where once all of them could easily fit into the small chapel, now the mass had to be held outside in the open *patio,* especially for holy day festivals, which came often.

Ipa watched Fray Bernardo in his dull brown robe, a huge silver cross in the hand that motioned in the air. Ipa crossed herself and repeated the words of the Te Deum.

"*Te Deum laudamus . . . ,*" the chorus rose into the stifling-hot evening air. After it was over, they recited the Lord's Prayer. The soft murmurs rising from the lips of the congregation reminded her of the place on the Great River where the water tumbled over stones after a sudden rain.

Ipa closed her eyes and thought about her village. The deer would be moving through the canyon now, and the young hunters would be dancing the dance of the hunt. For days their feet would pound the earth as they slapped their hands on their legs and chanted the song of the hunt. One of them would slip the skin and antlers of a deer on his head and lead the hunters on a joyful mock hunt. They would slay him with false arrows and knives and bring him home to the women. The girls and women would dance, too, their high voices echoing down the canyon.

"*Buenas tardes, señorita,*" a voice said after the last words of the final benediction had drifted over the crowd and everyone rose to their feet.

Ipa turned and looked into the face of a young Spaniard. A startled sound escaped from her lips.

"Señor Rodrigo! What are you doing here?" she asked in Spanish.

"*Ah, bueno, bueno.* I see you have learned my language. And very well indeed. You are even more lovely than I remember, *señorita.*"

It felt strange for Ipa to finally understand the words that rolled off his tongue so smoothly. Before they had seemed like music, now they made her blush. She smiled slightly and glanced down. Rodrigo laughed lightly.

"I see you are still the same, but now you are a woman. How many years do you have?"

"I have sixteen summers."

"Ah . . . *muy bueno.* And what are you doing here so far from your charming little village on del Norte?"

Ipa felt the heat creep up her neck and burn her cheeks. "Do you not know?"

Rodrigo shook his head slowly, a puzzled look in his dark eyes.

"We were brought here as slaves."

"Slaves? Now, now, surely that is an exaggeration, my pretty one. The padres brought you here to save your soul. So you can have a better life. The last time I saw you, you were a skinny thing with a lovely face. Now you are healthy and fit. It would not be so in your own village, would it? Your lands were dry and the corn was scarce the last time I saw you. You might have starved by now if you had not come here. No?"

Ipa looked toward the distant sierras. The Lesser River, the one the padres called Rio Conchos, followed the curve of the mountains and at its end, where it joined Rio del Norte, her village lay two days' journey up the river. It was true what Rodrigo said. The corn often failed two years in a row during droughts and many of the weak ones—the very old and the very young—would die. She raised her eyes to meet his.

"Some would say that death in my humble village is better than being a slave here."

Rodrigo tilted his head to one side and clucked his tongue.

"You say that now with a full stomach. Your answer would be different if you were starving. Come, let us eat together. I have many questions. Where is that little brother of yours? I have thought of him often on the long weary trail. I think Alegro grew quite fond of those mesquite beans."

Ipa glanced toward the hospital.

"I will show you how well my little brother is prospering under this better life you speak of. Come, follow me."

Ipa led Rodrigo to the infirmary. He stood over Kadoh, his lips parted in shock. Xucate cast an angry glance at Ipa and opened her mouth as if to protest, then got up and left without speaking. Rodrigo did not seem to even notice her. He quickly sank to his knees beside the bed.

*"Madre de Dios,"* he said, quickly crossing himself. "Poor Kadoh." He lifted the thin blanket and flinched at the sight of the foot. "I should have taken him with me to tend my horse. Now his young life is ruined." Rodrigo's eyes grew moist as if it were his own brother on the cot. "I could have prevented all

this. And I have to give you sad news about your father, too."

Ipa felt her heart stop and the blood rush from her head.

"My father is dead?"

Rodrigo nodded slowly. "He died when an epidemic spread among the pueblo dwellers. I think your people call it the spotted sickness. I am sorry. He was a good, brave man who helped us through many perils."

Ipa dropped to her knees, making the sign of the cross without thinking. She stared at the flickering candle for a moment, remembering the last time she had seen her father, so happy and honored to be the guide for the strangers. Tears filled her eyes and slowly slid down her cheeks as she whispered the sacred father death song of her people.

A heavy sigh made her look up. Rodrigo put his elbows on the bed and pressed his hands to his forehead.

"Death follows us everywhere we go," he said, his eyes squeezed shut. "Gentle brown people with simple hearts die when they touch us."

"You must not blame yourself, Rodrigo," Ipa said softly, and touched his arm. "Why are you here at the mission anyway?"

Rodrigo opened his eyes. "I have grown weary of the life of an adventurer. Always riding, searching for one thing after another. There is no gold in the mountains. There are no great cities left to conquer like the grand *conquistadores* did. My grandfather rode with Cortés; my father knew Coronado. But all we found was the desert and simple people. And death. I am tired of it all." He heaved a ragged sigh. "So tired."

Ipa studied his face. He was leaner now, browned by the sun until he was as dark as she, and tiny cracks radiated from his eyes. His once neatly trimmed beard had grown longer and wilder, and his hair hung almost to his shoulders in dirty, tangled ringlets. The lips once so quick to form a smile now looked thin and taut.

He placed his hand on top of hers.

"I see you are still wearing the silver cross I gave you. Are you a Christian now?"

Ipa nodded.

Rodrigo fished a chain from his neck and lifted up the tiny carved turtle Ipa had given him. Instantly his eyes returned to the way she had remembered them, and a smile swept across his face.

"This little talisman you gave me saved my life once in the land of the pueblos. A shaman threw a magic pebble at me. It hit the little turtle and bounced right back into his face. You should have seen the shock in his eyes. I became *muy importante* after that." Rodrigo's familiar laugh filled Ipa's heart

*199*

with joy for a moment and reminded her of the village granary and the squealing mice that had made Rodrigo dance like a madman.

"I am glad to see you again, Señor Rodrigo," Ipa said.

"And you cannot know how glad I am to see you again." He pulled Ipa's fingers to his lips and held them there for several seconds before releasing her hand. He stood up. "But now I must report back to the *maestro de campo*. I will visit Kadoh in the morning after matins. *Hasta luego, preciosa*."

Ipa watched Rodrigo until he had vanished around the corner. From the town *cantina* outside the mission walls she heard rowdy laughter and knew that the soldiers were drinking. She hoped that Rodrigo was not going to join them.

Ipa sat back down beside her brother and continued her vigil until late that night when Xucate entered the hospital, carrying a woven reed mat under her arm. Everyone in the mission was asleep and all was silent save for the distant cry of the coyote and the laughter of drunken soldiers.

"I see your Spaniard found you, Cousin," Xucate said as she unrolled the mat beside the bed, then sat on a stool. "Here is a sleeping mat for you."

"He is not my Spaniard," Ipa said angrily. "And he did not come looking for me. He is here on business." Ipa sat on the mat reluctantly, but it felt wonderful to stretch her legs out.

"Ha! I saw the way his eyes looked at you. He has been carrying a hidden passion for you all this time. Maybe you should marry him. You are more Spanish than *indio* anyway. Look at you in your white cotton dress and Spanish hairstyle. It is a wonder you remember how to speak to me in our native language anymore. I imagine you have forgotten the smell of the Great River and the sound of rushing wind in the canyon and the rustle of the corn."

Ipa wanted to scream at her insolent cousin, but she dared not disturb Kadoh. She stretched out on the mat and turned her back.

"You are wrong, Xucate," Ipa said. "I have not forgotten."

Ipa slept a restless sleep until just before dawn, when Xucate woke her up and left. Not long afterward, Kadoh rolled over and opened his eyes. Ipa dipped a bowl of soup for him.

"Sister." His voice sounded strained and hoarse like the voices of her people after the rain dance. "I cannot go down into that dark rathole again." His dark eyes stared into space and his lips stretched taut as if he were watching some repulsive act.

"Hush, hush," Ipa whispered. "You must eat something." She lifted a spoonful of soup to his lips, but he pushed it away.

"I will not return to that darkness where death abides," he whispered, his eyes rolling from side to side. "The poor miners, God save them. They chisel the stone until their arms almost fall off. They crawl on their knees through twisting, dusty, narrow tunnels pushing or dragging bags of ore as heavy as a deer. Already there is a second mountain nearby made of the discarded ore. The men climb up and down the endless ladders, barely able to keep their balance. Many fall to their deaths. And Diestro— *El Diablo*"—Kadoh's lips turned down in a snarl— "that man shall die soon. And may it be by the biting tips of his own whip."

Ipa had seen the same fiery look of hatred in Kadoh's eyes when he spoke of avenging the Apaches. She tried to put the broth to his lips again, but he jerked away and knocked the spoon to the stone floor.

"Away, away. Spirit go away. It was not my fault you were stolen by Apaches, Brother. Away. Leave me alone." Kadoh pawed the air, then rolled onto his side and pulled his knees toward his chin and tried to form a ball like a sleeping dog.

Ipa sighed and pulled the blanket over his narrow shoulders. She forced herself to look at his foot. The flesh had turned black, but the swelling had gone down. She refreshed the poultice on his wounds, then crushed mountain laurel seeds for a potion to deaden the pain, being careful not to give him too much, for that would cause death.

Rodrigo did not attend the morning prayers nor

did he visit Kadoh that morning as promised. Ipa tried to hide her disappointment and pulled her *mantilla* high to conceal her sad face from Fray Bernardo.

After breakfast, Juan Diestro himself stomped into the infirmary, his boots jingling with heavy spurs. Fray Bernardo shuffled behind him, his hands tucked inside his baggy brown sleeves, taking four short steps for every one of the tall overseer's. Diestro stopped at the foot of Kadoh's bed.

"Lift the blanket," he demanded. Ipa followed his order in silence. When he saw the mangled foot, he snorted like a wild peccary and cursed. "He is of no use to me now. Do with him as you please, Padre. Throw him to the carrion birds, for all I care. Now I will have to train another boy. And I also require another servant girl."

Ipa shuddered as the overseer's cold black eyes swept over her.

"She will do," he said.

"But Señor Diestro, she is our little angel," Fray Bernardo protested. "She knows herbs and medicines very well. She tends the sick better than anyone else, and as you can see she is too small to be of much help. You need a girl of great strength and endurance."

"Do as you wish. But she must be comely."

A wave of relief swept over Ipa as she exhaled slowly. At last her puny size had served her well.

203

Juan Diestro turned on his heels. Ipa heard the tap and clink as he walked down the stone path that led from the infirmary to the plaza.

Fray Bernardo's face turned dark as if a rain cloud had passed over it. He began pacing the floor, rubbing his chin. In a moment Fray Ignatio entered through the side door. The two men whispered, paced a few moments, then nodded.

That night as Ipa lay on the floor mat next to Kadoh's bed, she heard soft footsteps above her.

"Ipa-tah-chi?" It was the voice of her cousin, Xucate, but it sounded strained and small, like a frightened child's. "Have you heard the news?"

Ipa did not want to look at Xucate's face because of their argument about Rodrigo the night before. Ipa shrugged her shoulders and remained silent.

"The good padres have given me to Juan Diestro. I am to be the servant of the devil."

Ipa sat up. "But why?"

"You know why, Little Cousin. Because I refused to let the good friars sprinkle the water on my head. Because I refused to bow to their statue of Maria or to speak the words they tried to teach me. Because I spat out the body of Jesucristo they put in my mouth. They are glad to be rid of me."

"No, it is not true. They only chose you because you are strong and beautiful."

"Ha!"

"What happened to Juan Diestro's other servant girl?"

"Fray Ignatio said she died of the spotted sickness. But I do not believe him. I think Juan Diestro beat her to death for disobeying. If the spotted sickness were among us, we would all be dying."

Ipa nodded. This white man's disease often ravaged the land wherever the Spaniards traveled and had killed her own father. But there had not been a case in the mission for over a year. Both Ipa and Xucate had become ill then but had survived. Sometimes entire villages perished. Those who lived never got the sickness again and were forced to wait on the sick ones and bury the dead. Ipa shuddered at the thought of touching dead people, the thing that she disliked the most about her work in the hospital. She prayed that the sickness would not come to the mission again during her lifetime.

Ipa heard Xucate unfurling a reed mat on the other side of Kadoh's bed. How strange that she had chosen to sleep in this cold, damp room filled with sickness rather than in the comfortable room with the widow and her child.

A long, heavy silence filled the air.

"I will miss you, Xucate," Ipa whispered in the darkness at last. Whether or not her cousin believed her, Ipa did not know, for Xucate did not reply.

The next morning when Ipa woke up, Xucate was gone. Though her cousin had always been a cactus thorn in her thumb, Ipa's heart felt heavy. After all, they not only shared the same grandfather but had breathed the same air and tasted the same river water. They had watched the same eagles soar over the canyons and felt the same wind blow in their faces. They both had mourned the death of Coyomo, the Brave One. Whether Ipa wanted to admit it or not, she was closer to Xucate than to any other.

# Chapter Thirteen

AN ANGRY wind whistled through the bell tower and around the mission walls, chilling Ipa to the bones. She pulled her wool *serape* closer around her shoulders as she hurriedly gathered herbs and vegetables from Fray Bernardo's *patio* garden.

Across the *patio,* near the cloister, a woman that everyone called Fat Maria stooped over a beehive-shaped oven, removing a long-handled paddle covered with loaves of bread. The tantalizing aroma filled Ipa's nostrils and reminded her stomach that she had not taken a break from work all morning. The distant line of low, blue-black clouds told her that an early winter storm was approaching and the tender vegetables had to be brought in.

On the other side of the garden, Rodrigo rapidly pulled cabbages and peppers indiscriminately, not bothering to separate the good from the bad. Ipa shook her head, but she had long ago stopped trying to teach Rodrigo about plants. He was intelligent and wise in most ways, but he had no interest in anything that grew in the ground. He only came to the garden to visit Ipa, and she cherished the hours they spent together talking about Rodrigo's adventures, his family, his hopes and dreams.

Rodrigo suddenly stood and sniffed the air.

"Ah, do I smell wheat bread?" He turned around. "Maria, your bread smells like the food of the gods. And I am starving for nourishment." He lay down his basket of vegetables and strolled toward the short, plump woman.

"No, *señor*," she said, and swatted his hand as he tried to take one of the loaves. "These are for the All Saints celebration today."

"Surely the good friars will not miss half a loaf. Angelita and I have worked so hard trying to save the vegetables for them. Shouldn't we be rewarded?" He twisted his eyebrows and took the expression of a lost child.

Maria stubbornly shook her head as she carefully placed the hot loaves into a basket. When she turned toward the kitchen, Rodrigo blocked her path, waving a handful of onions under her nose.

"Wouldn't you like some fresh onions for your husband?" Rodrigo asked. He put the onions close to his nose and breathed deeply. "Ah, special onions like the ones grown in Spain. Sweet and fragrant. Far better than those little wild ones you always use." He lowered his voice. "They will make your husband strong, like a wild stallion." Rodrigo raised one eyebrow and held the onions out.

Maria glanced toward the cloister, then grabbed the onions and slipped them under the fresh loaves. She quickly broke a loaf of bread in two and handed him one half.

"*Gracias,* Maria," Rodrigo said as he bowed and kissed her hand. Maria giggled and swatted at him before scurrying off to the kitchen.

"Angelita, you are working too hard. Let us stop and eat," Rodrigo called out as he stomped across the garden, unconcerned that his feet trampled the parsley.

"I have no time to stop," Ipa said. "Can you not see the sky?"

Rodrigo glanced toward the north, then shrugged. He tore off a hunk of warm bread and placed it in Ipa's hand. "Eat, *mi corazón.* No wonder you have no fat on your bones. How often is it that you get to eat wheat bread?"

Ipa sighed and laid her basket down. She had

learned that it was useless arguing with Rodrigo. She chewed the food slowly, savoring the strange flavor. She really did not care for the taste of wheat, but she did not want to hurt Rodrigo's feelings. Since wheat would not grow in this region, it had to be shipped from Mexico City, a long, difficult journey. Often by the time the wheat reached the mission, it was spoiled or filled with weevils. The friars treated their wheat as if it were silver.

Rodrigo laughed and rolled his eyes in an exaggerated manner as he ate the tender bread. Ipa ate a few bites, then put the rest away in her pocket.

"I will save this for Kadoh."

Rodrigo stopped laughing. "How is your brother today?"

"Better. He took a few steps this morning using that cane you carved for him from juniper wood."

"Good. After we finish here, I will visit him and help him with his walking."

Ipa placed her hand on Rodrigo's sleeve. "You are too kind. If it were not for your visits and encouragement, I think Kadoh would have died from a broken heart by now. You have become like an older brother to him."

"Kadoh's heart is strong and brave. He will survive."

"If only his head would get well, too."

Rodrigo nodded and sighed, but said nothing. Ipa knew he was thinking about Kadoh's spells of insanity. Though the boy usually remembered where he was, sometimes he lapsed into shouting matches with his own shadow or insisted that Ximi was in the room.

Rodrigo continued eating in silence for several moments, then paused and looked over Ipa's head.

"Angelita, is that not your cousin?"

Ipa turned and saw a girl creeping along the *patio* wall like a hungry, frightened coyote. A surge of joy rushed through Ipa's heart as she hurried toward the tall girl. She had missed Xucate more than she thought possible, for even an argument with one from her village was better than pleasant prattle with a stranger. The first few weeks after her departure, Xucate had attended Sunday mass, even though she did not believe in Jesucristo and refused to repeat the sacred words. She only came to speak to Ipa of the horrors of working for Juan Diestro and Diestro's wife, who had a jealous nature. But Xucate had missed the last two Sundays.

"Cousin, I am so glad to see you." Ipa threw her arms around Xucate.

The tall girl pulled back and raised her *mantilla* higher to cover all of her face except for one eye.

"I need your medicine plants," Xucate whispered.

Ipa's smile fell at the sound of her cousin's raspy voice.

"Are you sick? What kind of medicine do you need?"

"Something for this." She let the *mantilla* drop.

Ipa drew in air and held it as she stared at the puffy red flesh on Xucate's cheek, her blackened eyes, and a busted lip. Ipa swallowed hard.

"What happened?"

"I swear I will kill him if he touches me again." Xucate flinched with pain as she moved her swollen lips.

"Juan Diestro beat you?"

Xucate managed a laugh. "If the beatings were all he did, it would not be so unbearable."

"Tell Fray Bernardo about this. He will protect you."

"Ha! The friars are afraid of Diestro. He has many connections in Mexico City. His brother is *alcalde* of the town. They dare not make him angry."

"Then what about Diestro's wife? What does she say?"

A smile crept to Xucate's lips. "She is the one who orders the beatings. It is her way of punishing Diestro. He avoids me when my face is damaged. But never mind. Quickly, Cousin, fetch the medicine."

Ipa rushed into the infirmary and gathered powdered roots and leaves and berries.

"God go with you, Cousin," Ipa whispered as she pressed them into Xucate's hands.

Xucate stared at Ipa a moment, then hugged her tightly.

"Thank you, Cousin. You are the only one in this forsaken place that I can trust, so I will tell you my secret. I am going to run away. Will you come with me? You and Kadoh. Let us get away from this Spanish horror." Tears slid down her swollen, bruised cheeks and over the dried blood and torn lips.

"I cannot leave. Kadoh is still too sick to travel. Besides, how will you find your way back to our village?"

"I speak to Pedro, the Jumano guide, often. He has traveled the way many times. He told me a way back that the Spaniards will not know. They always follow the river. Pedro's way is faster."

"But surely more treacherous."

"Yes, but I am a desperate woman and desperate women act in treacherous ways. Come with me, Cousin. Three of us can survive better than one." Xucate squeezed Ipa's arms. Ipa glanced over her shoulder at Rodrigo, who sat on a tree stump, watching them. Ipa shook her head slowly.

"I cannot go with you."

Xucate released her grip, then stepped back. She touched the colored sash tied around Ipa's cotton dress.

"*Angelita*. You answer to their name like a dog comes to its master. You even speak their language as if you were born in their land by the sun. I would not be surprised if you marry one of those Spanish lizards. Perhaps the one who gave you the silver cross." She glanced over Ipa's shoulder at Rodrigo.

"Not all Spaniards are cruel like Juan Diestro. Rodrigo is kind and cares about Kadoh."

Xucate's eyes turned black.

"I see where your heart is, Cousin. But I warn you, the Spaniards are not a gentle breed. They take what they want, when they want." A sudden burst of pain made her put her hand to her cheek and grimace. "Good-bye, Ipa-tah-chi, my cousin. May the corn rustle in your fields when you die."

"Good-bye, Cousin. *Vaya con Dios.*"

Cold air blasted Ipa's face and made her shiver as she watched Xucate slip along the *patio* wall and vanish around the corner. Perhaps she was making the worst mistake of her life by not going with her.

# Chapter Fourteen

SPRING ARRIVED with thunder and lightning and driving rain, turning the desert into a lush vista of green grasses, waving *ocotillos,* and flowering cactus. The day before Easter, Ipa stood on a hillside gathering bouquets of wildflowers for the sunrise ceremony. The Easter pageant was the most colorful festival of the year, and the most sacred. The mission women had spent weeks sewing beads and feathers to costumes for the Holy Week processions and for the dances. Boys gathered juniper boughs from the mountains for the chapel door.

Ipa had not heard from Xucate since the day in the *patio* garden. She hoped that her cousin had escaped and was safe in their little village by the river. Often Ipa imagined the surprised looks on the faces of her aunt and uncle when their daughter stepped onto the roof and announced her arrival. No doubt at first they had thought she was a ghost and Xucate had to explain her absence and escape. Surely the village had feasted and men had danced the sacred dances as when warriors return from battle. Perhaps they had etched a tattoo of honor on her cheek for having outwitted the Spanish slavers. Xucate must have found a husband by now, probably the son of a *cacique* in one of the villages at the junction. At last Xucate would be free and happy. Her strong legs would walk the canyon trail, her strong back would carry a cradleboard for her firstborn as the sweet winds of home caressed her face.

Ipa sighed. She wondered if she would ever have a husband herself. She was approaching her seventeenth summer, far beyond the proper marrying age. Of all the young men who worked the fields, none interested her. They came from different villages, with different customs.

Strangely enough, she felt closer to Rodrigo than to the *indios*. Of all the Spaniards she had met, Rodrigo was the kindest. He never lashed out at her or the other *indios,* and there was always a quick smile on his lips. As soon as Kadoh was able to walk with the help of his juniper cane, Rodrigo had placed him in charge of tending his horse again. Before long,

Kadoh had learned much about the care of horses.

Ipa smiled to herself as she thought of Rodrigo teasing Kadoh, lifting him onto the horse, teaching him how to ride and praising his quick progress. By law, no *indio* was allowed to ride horses, only soldiers and *Dons*. But Rodrigo made an exception for Kadoh, and no one protested. If Rodrigo had not come along, surely Kadoh would have lost his will to live. On the ground, walking in a clumsy gait and enduring the taunting of others, Kadoh never smiled. But on top of a horse, he became a man.

On Easter morning, just before dawn, one of the Spaniards stripped himself naked save for a piece of wool swaddling wrapped around his loin. The man bore a heavy wooden cross on his back as he led a procession toward a hill overlooking the mission. The look of pain in his eyes was indeed real, as was the thin line of blood trickling down his back where the cross bit into his flesh. Ipa was not surprised to see Rodrigo's kind eyes weeping, but even the roughest *soldado* trembled with emotion. They wailed and beat their chests in an awful way. Many of the *indios* sobbed, too, more out of imitation than understanding. Ipa might have been moved to tears if the man carrying the cross had been anyone except who it was—Juan Diestro. All the while he labored with his burden and grimaced in agony, Ipa could not help but think of all the pain he had caused her little brother, her cousin, and others.

From deep inside the chapel, the new organ blasted. It had arrived from Mexico City the previous month and was Fray Ignatio's proudest possession. From the front steps of the chapel, a choir of men and boys, who had been practicing for many months, raised their voices in unison, singing songs in Latin. The rhythm of the music and the blending of male voices reminded Ipa of chanting before a hunt.

Cymbals, flutes, trumpets, and drums filled the air with music as the colorful procession of feathered men slowly climbed the hill behind the Spaniards. Girls tossed flower petals by the handful in the path of "Jesucristo." Later in the day the *indios* would perform the same dances they had danced in their villages for sacred ceremonies—the becoming-a-woman dance, the rain dance, the budding-of-corn dance.

The drum pounded louder as Juan Diestro staggered with the heavy cross. Twice he fell and others rushed to help him up, but he pushed them away. Ipa wondered if the good friars would nail Diestro's hands to the cross and let him hang, but they did not go that far. When men lifted the cross from Diestro's back, he collapsed with fatigue. Tears streamed down his face and he flailed his naked back with a small whip. Other Spaniards followed suit until the wailing and sound of flagellation made Ipa sick. Ipa wished that Xucate were there to see Diestro suffering. It would have pleased her.

One of the *indio* farmers, a former *cacique* in his village, slew a lamb, removed its liver, and smeared the blood over Diestro's body. The crowd cheered too jubilantly, Ipa thought, and she wondered if they were imagining it to be the liver of Juan Diestro, as she was.

After they had returned to the mission, Ipa noticed that Rodrigo was still weeping along with the others. Seeing his kind eyes so sad touched her heart, even though she did not understand his sorrow.

At the elaborate mass, celebrated outside to an overflowing crowd, the padres walked among the Spaniards, pressing small white wafers into their open mouths and speaking the sacred words.

*"Corpus Christi,"* Fray Ignatio said softly.

*"Amen,"* the Spaniards replied.

While Fray Ignatio tended the Spaniards, Fray Bernardo walked among the *indios.* Ipa watched her brother limp forward awkwardly, his head bowed. She thought how his chance to be a great hunter had been destroyed by the Spaniards. She thought of Coyomo lying on the desert sand, his lifeblood trickling from his wounds like those of Jesucristo. She had not met another as brave as Coyomo and often thought of how her life might have been as his wife. She thought about the sound of water rushing through the reeds, of women pounding clothes beside the river, of the laughter of children chasing away crows in the cornfields. She remembered the touch of her grandmother's old, gnarled hands. Suddenly Ipa's heart ached with desire to see her village. A tear slid down her cheek.

"See, they are like simple children," she heard Fray Bernardo say to the captain of the soldiers standing beside him. "They weep at the death of our Savior. You cannot tell me that these are savages."

"They weep now, but tomorrow they may steal from you or stab you in the back. You must never let your guard down, Padre. In the south the *indios* are stealing the horses and sheep and cows from missions daily. It is a wonder that any of the friars can survive."

"Ah, but not my children," Fray Bernardo said, shaking his head. "My children are innocent as babes. They would never harm one of us. It is not in their nature." He stopped in front of Ipa. "Look at this face. It is the face of an angel. *Corpus Christi,*" he whispered as he held out a wafer.

"*Amen,*" Ipa replied, and opened her mouth. She let the wafer rest on her tongue a moment. Never had she known of anyone who ate the body of his god. Perhaps the liver of an animal killed in the hunt to gain its prowess, or the spleen of an enemy to capture his courage. But the thought of devouring the body of Jesucristo made a row of chill bumps rise on her arm. She wanted to spit it out, as always, but she chewed it and swallowed it down to please the friars.

During the weeks after the Easter pageant, Ipa's

work increased many times over. When the mule train arrived, as it did every two years, it brought with it new Spanish soldiers with a new disease. An outbreak of fever killed many *indios,* and Ipa was thankful that the friars trusted her to ride a donkey into the mountains to gather more medicine plants.

After the epidemic passed, Fray Bernardo told Ipa she could have a plot of land near his herb garden to grow her medicine plants so she would not have to go so far. Ipa hoed and pulled weeds early every morning before going to the infirmary. Rodrigo usually joined her, kneeling beside her as he talked, showing no concern for what others might say. He lifted heavy stones and buckets of water and pushed the awkward wheelbarrow that Ipa hated to use.

"I received a letter from my uncle," Rodrigo said one morning, a month after Easter, while Ipa tilled the soil with a three-pronged tool.

"The uncle who lives in Mexico City?"

"Yes. He has found a position for me in the civil building. An old man will be retiring in a few months and my uncle used his influence and money to procure it for me. Of course, I must first go and meet the officials. They will decide if I am suitable. But that is only a trifle."

Ipa felt a jab of pain as if someone had wrenched her heart from her chest. She swallowed down a sharp lump and forced a smile.

"That is wonderful news, Rodrigo. I know you

want to return to Mexico City. You have lingered here far too long already." She tried to make her voice sound happy.

"Mexico City is very beautiful," Rodrigo said. "There are green trees everywhere and lovely flowers all year round. The fruits and vegetables grow as big as a man's head. Not like this dry, desolate place." He waved his hand toward the desert.

The sun had just risen and a cool morning breeze lifted Ipa's hair. The smell of blooming sage drifted into Ipa's heart and made her think of the river and the adobe pit houses of her people. She could think of no place on earth that could be more beautiful than that, but she did not tell Rodrigo her thoughts. She knew that the Spaniards called her homelands *El Despoblado* — the Uninhabited Land.

"I am ready to leave this place," Rodrigo continued. "It is time I took a wife and settled down."

Ipa felt the blood drain from her face, and for a moment she could not breathe. At last she drew in a deep breath.

"Of course, Rodrigo. I did not expect you to stay here forever."

"Angelita, *querida*." Rodrigo took her hand into his own and pressed it tenderly to his cheek. "Dearest Angelita, you do not understand. I want you to go with me to Mexico City and be my wife."

Ipa drew in a sharp breath and dropped the tilling fork. She stared into his eyes, then picked the tool up again and began striking the soil vigorously.

"What about my brother? Is there a place for an insane boy with a crippled leg in Mexico City? I have heard that Mexico City is in the middle of a lake, that people live on floating islands. Kadoh might step off his island and drown. He cannot swim with his crippled leg." Ipa heaved a sigh. "And what about the infirmary? The padres depend on my medicine. The miners in the *barrio,* the women in the mission—how can I leave them? Oh, Rodrigo, could we not marry and live here? The town is growing larger. Maybe someday it will be as grand as Mexico City."

Rodrigo tilted his head back and laughed. "My little angel, no city can ever be as grand as Mexico City." He took her hand and turned it over, tracing the vein from her wrist to the tip of her fingers before softly kissing it.

"I do not want to live without you, Angelita, but I am dying here in this forsaken desert. I have already stayed too long. I must seize this opportunity while I can."

Ipa felt as if a blanket were smothering her face. The heat was suddenly unbearable. She stood and started to run, but Rodrigo grabbed her hand and pulled her back to his side.

"I am leaving for Mexico City today to meet the government officers and to find a place to live," he said. "I will return in two months to finish business here. Give me your decision then, Angelita. I pray it will be yes." He spun on his heels, then strode off to the stables. Ipa watched him load his horse with baggage and then hug Kadoh.

As Rodrigo's horse plodded toward the southern trail, Ipa's heart pounded. She wanted to run after him, to scream for him to stay, but her trembling legs would not move nor would her voice shout. How could she be sure he would return? Perhaps he would find a Spanish girl with fair skin, dressed in layered skirts sticking out from her body. Surely any woman would realize how wonderful Rodrigo was, so kind, and considerate, and full of love. Ipa glanced down at her hands, still soiled with dirt from the garden.

"I am a fool," she whispered to the air. By the time Rodrigo's horse became but a speck on the horizon, Ipa knew what her answer would be when he returned.

IPA COUNTED the days by watching the phases of the moon. It had waxed and waned two times since Rodrigo's departure and was approaching another fullness. She wrestled day and night with her dilemma. It was Kadoh that worried her more than anything. How could a crippled boy with head-sickness survive in a city so far away from the mountains and desert? She could not imagine a place where trees grew all around and where it rained almost every day. The thought of so much water frightened her. Maybe Kadoh would go completely insane.

Ipa tried to tell Kadoh about going to live with Rodrigo, but he did not understand. Some days he searched the stables and horse pasture calling Rodrigo's name. Other days he pretended to be a great warrior riding beside Ximi. At first the friars were sympathetic to Kadoh's condition, but as time passed they grew more annoyed at his antics. When he rode a donkey through the herb garden, shaking his cane at them and calling them Apaches, they lost their patience and threatened to put him in the stockade.

"Please come soon, Rodrigo," Ipa prayed every night. At last the full moon rose, round and golden like a ripe melon. Ipa washed and dried her white cotton dress and tied it with a red-and-yellow sash that she had made from scraps of wool. That night she tied her hair into a bun the way Juan Diestro's wife wore hers, and put the silver crucifix and Coyomo's blue stone around her neck. She sat in her room, anticipating Rodrigo's knock at the door. She waited and waited, then slipped into a deep sleep.

About midnight, she awoke to a dull banging on the heavy door.

"Rodrigo!" she said, leaping to her feet.

When Ipa pulled the door open, she saw not the handsome figure of Rodrigo but the short squat body of Fray Bernardo. His lantern cast a golden light over his rosy face.

"You are needed in the infirmary," he whispered. "Come quickly."

Ipa didn't bother to put on her yucca-fiber sandals. Her bare feet padded over the slick gray stones that led to the low building attached to the far end of the mission. Inside, a candelabra cast horrendous shadows on the wall. She heard a moan in the far corner of the room and saw someone moving.

Ipa hurried to the last bed, far removed from the others. She saw blood, some black bruises, and a face as pale as death. Then she saw a belly swollen with child. The woman spoke and Ipa recognized the voice. It belonged to her cousin Xucate.

# Chapter Fifteen

IPA DROPPED to her knees beside the bed, staring at Xucate's bleeding lips and swollen eyes. Blood had dried black under her broken nails. Ipa did not question her cousin. She quickly mixed a cup of *agarita* leaf tea to lower her fever. As she cleaned the wounds, anger for Juan Diestro boiled in Ipa's heart and tears filled her eyes. All those nights she had imagined her cousin free and happy had been illusions. Xucate had stopped coming to Sunday mass not because she had escaped but because of her shame.

Fray Bernardo left, pulling closed the black curtain that separated this bed from the others. It was the dying bed, where those with broken bodies breathed their last breath. Ipa gently pressed a wet cloth to her cousin's head and dabbed at the blood clinging to her lips. She watched Xucate's head toss from side to side and her legs jerk as she kicked at invisible demons.

At dawn, Xucate woke with a shout. She sat up, eyes wildly searching for the enemy of her dreams.

*"Shh, shh,"* Ipa whispered, herself roused from a nightmare. "You are safe now."

"No, I will never be safe as long as that demon-man is alive. Who brought me here?"

"I think it was the Jumano guide, Pedro. I saw him in the shadows when I came into the infirmary last night." Ipa tried not to stare at her cousin's belly. From the looks of it, the child would be born within a month.

"What do you stare at, Little Cousin? Are you surprised to see me like this? Did you think Juan Diestro would keep his hands off me? Now we know what happened to his other servant girls, don't we?"

Ipa dropped her gaze to the floor. She had forgotten how bitter Xucate's tongue could be. She did not love Xucate like a sister, but she would never wish this on any woman, no matter how proud and selfish.

"I'm sorry," Ipa replied.

"Sorrow will not change the size of my belly."

"Do you want some bread and soup?" Ipa held up a piece of bread baked the day before for a special visit from important guests at the mission.

"I hate the Spaniards' wheat bread." Xucate pushed the food away.

"But you must eat."

"For what reason?"

"To keep your strength."

"So I can deliver the white devil's child? I would rather die than bear his demon-child. If you are my friend, bring me a knife from the kitchen. Help me cut this monster out of my stomach."

Ipa drew in a sharp breath.

"No, Cousin. It is a mortal sin to kill. And I am not allowed to take knives from the kitchen. Fat Maria watches the utensils like a hawk circling over a rabbit hole."

"But the padres trust you." Xucate lowered her voice to a harsh whisper. "You come and go as you please. I've seen you on the hillsides, gathering medicine plants. You are as Spanish as they are. Why, I suppose you have married that Spaniard by now."

Ipa felt heat pricking her neck. "Rodrigo is in Mexico City on business. But when he comes back we will marry."

"Ha! You are fortunate he did not plant his seed inside you before he deserted you."

"Rodrigo did not desert me. He is due to come back for me any day."

"He will not return for you. All Spaniards are liars. The bearded demon Diestro came for me the first night I arrived and did not stop until my belly was too big. Then his wife cursed me and kicked me and threw me out and demanded another to take my place. And the good padres will no doubt oblige her."

A sudden wave of pain coursed through Xucate. She gritted her teeth and threw her head back against the wall. She gripped the side of the bed until her knuckles turned pale.

"Is the child coming?" Ipa asked, laying her hand on Xucate's stomach. She thought she felt a kick.

Xucate shook her head but could not speak until the pain passed and she had relaxed.

"No, I am not in labor yet. The pain is from Diestro's boot. But the child will come soon, before the next moon. I must destroy it so there will be one less Spaniard in the world." Xucate grabbed Ipa's arm and jerked her forward with amazing strength. "You must help me, Cousin."

"No! I will not kill an innocent baby."

"It is not a true child. It is a Spaniard."

Ipa shook her head, trying to free herself from her cousin's grasp.

"You are insane, Xucate."

"Then at least help me escape back to our people. I will need food and water and a knife for protection. I have very little time. In the name of our grandfather and our people, please help me, Little Cousin." Xucate squeezed Ipa's arm until it throbbed with pain. Her dark eyes grew wild. "Come with me. Let us return to our village together."

"I cannot leave my brother here."

"We can bring him with us. I hear he has become an expert with the Spaniards' horses. He can steal three of them, and we will be back in our village before the moon wanes."

"Kadoh will not steal. The padres have taught us it is a mortal sin to steal."

"Kadoh owes his life to me!" Xucate spat the words out. "I saved him from the Apache woman's tomahawk. He *must* help me!"

Another wave of pain blanched Xucate's face, and she released her grip. Ipa stepped back.

"I will bring you food and water. But I cannot bring you a knife to kill an innocent baby."

"All right, then. Bring me the knife, and I swear I will not kill the child with it," Xucate said between teeth clenched in pain. "I swear by the Great Spirit."

Xucate waved Ipa away, then rolled onto her side and pulled her legs as far up as her stomach would allow.

All day Ipa performed her chores without thinking. One part of her head spun with thoughts of escape, of returning to her village. But another part of her head watched the road for the first sign of Rodrigo. At lunch she slipped into the chapel and knelt before the statue of Maria. She clasped her hands together and prayed for a sign, but the sight of the baby Jesucristo only made her think of Xucate.

During siesta, when everyone napped to avoid the hottest part of the day, Ipa sneaked into the refectory to get some corn *tortillas,* a goatskin bag filled with water, and some strips of dried beef. She saw a carving knife beside a slab of beef, and when Fat Maria turned her back, Ipa grabbed it. In the desert, she dug the roots of a plant that women used to deaden the pain of childbirth. She pounded them into a powder and put it inside a small buckskin pouch. As an afterthought, she took Xucate's old deerskin clothes, which had remained hidden since Xucate had become Diestro's servant.

After vespers, Ipa took a bowl of warm soup to Xucate. The tall girl drank it down and even ate the wheat bread this time.

"I will need all the strength I can gather," she explained. She took the food and water. Her eyes brightened when she saw the deerskin clothes.

"My old dress! Oh, how I have longed to feel deerskin next to my skin instead of the Spaniards' scratchy wool." But when Xucate tried on the skirt, it would not fit over her belly and the strings would not lace. She cursed and slipped the deerskin poncho over the white cotton dress.

"This will have to do. I will make another skirt

when I am rid of this child. And the knife?" She turned to Ipa.

Ipa sighed. Slowly she withdrew the knife. Her fingers trembled as she handed it to Xucate.

"Remember your promise. You swore you would not kill the baby with this knife."

"Yes, yes. I will keep my word," Xucate said as she clumsily climbed off the bed. "Are you coming with me?"

"No, I must stay with Kadoh."

"That is no reason to stay. You know Kadoh will come with me. You refuse because you are waiting for the Spaniard. Fool! He will not marry you." Xucate thrust the knife under the basket of food, then crept to the infirmary door and stepped into the blackness.

"Where will you go?" Ipa asked.

"I will go to Sacred Panther Mountain for the birth of the child. Then I will go home to our village."

"Watch over Kadoh. Do not let him get lost in the desert."

"I will treat him as if he were my own brother."

Ipa looked at the bruised face. She thought of the girl once so carefree, once so strong, who won every footrace, who ground corn faster and laughed louder than any other girl in the village. If Xucate had married Coyomo, their children would have been perfect. Xucate turned to go.

"Xucate, wait." Ipa quickly removed the blue stone that Coyomo had given her as an engagement gift. She slipped it around Xucate's neck. "It should have been yours."

Ipa saw Xucate's throat move as she swallowed hard.

"May the corn rustle in your fields when you die," Xucate whispered, then turned and ran on silent feet until the night swallowed her up.

Ipa returned to her room and tried to sleep, but sleep would not come. She thought she heard hooves in the night, but it could have been anyone.

Just before dawn, Ipa jumped from her bed and blinked. The mission bells pealed furiously. She hurried to the window and saw *indios* and Spaniards scurrying across the plaza. Then she saw Fray Bernardo and Fray Ignatio on the chapel steps, pacing and twisting their hands. Ipa ran out the door and joined the throng.

"Juan Diestro has been murdered in his sleep!" Ipa heard the whispers all around her on every pair of lips. "His body was mutilated, cut to pieces, and a kitchen knife was still in his heart when they found him."

Ipa's knees shook uncontrollably and she had to grasp the stone wall enclosing the *patio*. The others gathered in front of the steps, murmuring like a flock of doves, until Fray Bernardo raised his hands.

"Juan Diestro has been murdered!" he shouted.

"The captain of the garrison wants to quesion all of you. If you know anything about this ful deed, speak to me now and save yourself a floggig or imprisonment."

Ipa felt the blood drain from her face wh she saw Fat Maria step forward. Ipa thought she rd the words "missing kitchen knife," but the pounding in her eardrums drowned out the so around her. Then Fat Maria and Fray Bern turned toward her. The cook's plump brown fir pointed accusingly.

A host of eyes turned and stared at Ipa. She f hands reaching for her. With a whimper, she brol away and ran toward the stables.

"Little Brother!" she cried as she entered th corral. The horses squealed and scattered. "Kadoh!"

But her brother did not reply.

Ipa pushed the rumps of the horses aside and worked her way to the open-ended building where the friars kept the oxcarts and garden tools and fodder for the livestock.

"Kadoh!" she shouted again.

"Kadoh is not here," a man's voice said behind her. "He ran away last night with Juan Diestro's stallion and one of my best Andalusian mares."

Ipa spun around only to bump into a sturdy soldier. He grabbed her hair and pulled her against his doublet. The smell of it made her sick. She kicked and bit his hand, but it did no good. He squeezed her neck until she thought the life would ooze out of her. He head felt light, and she knew she was going to fain But before she passed out, she saw the brown robes the padres, and then the shiny metal breast-plate the captain of the guards. The last thing she hear s she plunged into dark nothingness was his an oice.

rrest her for the murder of Juan Diestro!"

## Chapter Sixteen

IPA AWAKENED to the smell of dust and mold. At first she could see nothing, then gradually the room became clear: a pile of dirty straw, a filthy bucket that reeked of human excrement, and iron bars on a small window. She sat up and rubbed her throat.

Ipa was not sure how long she sat, staring at a mouse nibbling on seeds in the hay, when she heard heavy boots approaching. She crouched into the corner and stared at the wooden door.

The heavy crossbar squeaked as a hand lifted it from its slot. Fray Bernardo's whisper floated in the air.

"She has been accused of murdering Juan Diestro. I think the child is innocent, but the captain will have his way, in the end. He must punish someone for the deed to set an example for the other *indios*. They are on the verge of insurrection this very day, were they not so weak from working in the mine. If she confesses, perhaps she will be spared. If not, there is no hope for the child. Talk to her."

Ipa squinted at the candlelight as a man stepped into the doorway. For a moment she could not see his face, only shadows and the glimmer of a silver cross on his neck. Then Fray Bernardo gently closed the door and held the light closer to the stranger's face.

"Ah, my little dove, what have you done?" Rodrigo's voice echoed through the stagnant air and sent a rush of joy over Ipa's tired body. She whimpered as she climbed to her feet and flung herself into his outstretched arms. She pressed her cheek to his doublet, smelling the dust of his long journey and a hint of wine.

"I know nothing about Juan Diestro's death." The words gushed from her lips. "I was asleep all night. I woke to the bells sounding the alarm. I am just as ignorant of what happened as anyone in the mission."

"But he was stabbed with a stolen kitchen knife. A knife that Fat Maria saw you handling that very evening," Fray Bernardo said.

"Tell us the truth, Angelita," Rodrigo said softly.

Ipa swallowed hard as she searched the dark eyes above her. He was a Spaniard whose parents had been born in a land across an ocean that she had never seen nor could even imagine the depth and breadth of. His kindred soldiers had murdered and raped and pillaged the peoples of New Spain for longer than two lifetimes. Yet, she could not make herself hate him. He had shown great kindness to her, and that was the only thought in her mind. She sighed a final time, then drew in a deep breath.

"Yes, I stole the kitchen knife. But I did not kill Juan Diestro."

"Foolish child," Fray Bernardo moaned. "Whatever possessed you to steal? You know the penalty for theft."

"I needed the knife for an important chore."

"Lies, only lies." Fray Bernardo shook his head. "You are protecting someone, aren't you? We know that your brother stole Juan Diestro's horse and a mare and ran away. Was it Kadoh who killed Señor Diestro?"

"No!" Ipa shouted. "Kadoh is just a simple-minded boy. He hated Diestro, but so did every other miner in the *barrio*."

"Then it was your cousin, Xucate, wasn't it?" Rodrigo said softly. "Why do you protect her, Angelita? She was always a troublemaker."

Ipa crumpled to the floor and hid her face in her hands for a moment. Then she turned her face toward Rodrigo and seized his hand.

"Please do not judge Xucate. She had good cause to run away. She needed the knife for survival in the desert. She did not want to stay here for the birth of her child."

"She was with child?" Rodrigo's face registered his shock. He glanced at Fray Bernardo, who nodded.

"Juan Diestro violated her many times," Ipa continued. "That is why she hated him so. She needed the knife for the journey. I also gave her food and water. I knew she was running away, but I cannot believe she murdered the overseer. You must believe me." Her thin fingers twisted Rodrigo's sleeve.

Rodrigo pulled Ipa from the floor, then pressed his cheek to her forehead.

"Do you know where Xucate has gone?"

Ipa stared at the door's iron nailheads shaped like flowers. They reminded her of the flowers that grew on top of Sacred Panther Mountain. Xucate would follow the path the Jumano guide had told her about and then go to the caves of the sacred mountain and wait for the child to be born. The time of birth was growing nearer. Perhaps Xucate would not even make it to the sacred mountain. Kadoh would be of no help to her. He might leave her alone in the desert while he chased visions of Ximi and phantom deer.

"I do not know where she will go," Ipa lied. "All I know is that she was ashamed and will not return to our village in her condition."

"But surely you know where she will go to hide. She must have told you her plans before she left," Fray Bernardo insisted.

Ipa looked into the faces of the two men who had been most kind to her. She wanted to trust them, but they were Spaniards and it was a Spaniard who had destroyed Xucate's life. The birth of her first child, a time for a woman to be proud and full of love, would be a time of heartache and hatred. Xucate, who should have had any husband she chose, would give birth alone in the desert, full of shame.

Slowly Ipa shook her head. "She told me nothing," she lied.

Fray Bernardo lifted the candle closer. "Dear child, if you want to save your life you must tell us where Xucate has gone. If it is your brother you worry about, I will explain to the captain of the garrison that the boy is not right in the head. I will make him promise not to harm the boy. But Xucate must pay for her crime. Someone must die to avenge Juan Diestro's death. Do not let it be you, child." He suddenly stopped speaking and turned. "*Shh,* someone is coming. Rodrigo, leave quickly."

Rodrigo pressed Ipa's hands in his own and kissed her fingers.

"I will come back again when it is safe. Please do not sacrifice yourself for Xucate. She is not worth it."

Ipa watched Rodrigo leave. She had to bite her tongue at his remark. Xucate was strong willed and proud, it was true, but no woman deserved what had happened to Xucate. But how could Rodrigo or any man understand?

The captain arrived and immediately Fray Bernardo told him that Xucate was the murderer. Ipa felt nauseated at the ease with which the padre betrayed Xucate, but in her heart she knew he was doing it for her sake. The captain questioned Ipa again and again, trying to break her spirit, but she continued to swear her innocence and would not give them a hint as to where Xucate might have gone.

"All your gallant efforts at protecting her will be to no avail," the captain said. "And you will die for your silence. Tell me where she is hiding and I will spare you."

But Ipa refused to speak. His strikes to her face only made her more determined. That night, as she lay crumpled on the straw, Fray Bernardo and the captain came one more time. The good padre held a bowl of stew, the captain held a whip.

"You have a choice," the captain snarled. "Food or the whip."

Ipa closed her eyes and pulled her knees up to her chin, bracing for the whipping.

"For the sake of our blessed mother Maria, she is but a child," Fray Bernardo insisted. "Let her eat; show her kindness. She is innocent. I cannot stand by and let you harm her."

The captain ran his fingers over the sleek leather whip as if stroking a beloved pet.

"I have been told that this girl practices *hechizeria* — sorcery. She chants and prays to her heathen god and concocts secret potions to cure the sick."

"No, Angelita is not a *hechizera!*" Fray Bernardo glanced around the room, as if the word itself might conjure up a devil. "She is a good Christian, with a pure heart. She cares for the sick out of Christian charity. You are wrong, señor."

The captain shrugged. "Perhaps you are right, Fray Bernardo, but the *alcalde* wants to know who killed his brother. He insists on finding the truth of the matter. Who am I to withhold important information? Perhaps he will come to the conclusion that you find the sorcery of the *indios* more powerful than the healing love of our Heavenly Father."

Fray Bernardo's face turned the color of ashes, and his hand flew to the crucifix around his neck.

"*¡Dios!*" he cried out and quickly crossed himself.

A thin smile slid across the captain's lips. "I will leave her alone for now, Padre. Let her contemplate her situation and dream of the joys of being stoned

243

as a witch. In the morning I will return." He glanced at the bowl of stew in the padre's trembling hands. He struck it with the butt end of the whip, knocking it to the floor. "Let the animal starve."

Ipa tried to fight back her tears, but could not stop them from flowing down her cheeks. Fray Bernardo's sad eyes glanced at her a final time before he closed the door and lowered the bar.

Ipa stared at the patch of stars twinkling through the cell window and tried to think of the sacred mountain. She imagined Xucate in the cave, delivering her baby and suddenly feeling love and affection for it. Perhaps Xucate would take it to the village and raise it. Ipa's aunt would be overjoyed to see her first grandchild and the return of her daughter. Ipa imagined Kadoh returning to the village a triumphant hero, with two valuable horses and the skill to ride them like a Spaniard. He would teach the men and boys to ride. And since he had chosen wisely, a mare and a stallion, the village would someday have its own herd. The men of her village would put on their war paint and stand up to the Spaniards.

Ipa turned her eyes to the inside of the tiny cell. She wondered if she was the first woman to be held there. The jail was new; the *presidio* was still under construction half a league from the mission, on a hill that gave them a view of the valleys. The *indios* of the region did not care for the silver from the mine, but they wanted the livestock. And the *chichimeca* were notoriously fierce. Of all the *indios* in the region, they alone had refused to bow down to the cross of Jesucristo. Perhaps they would take pity on Xucate and Kadoh and give them safe passage across the desert.

With these thoughts in her head, Ipa drifted into a restless sleep and began to dream.

She dreamed of the canyon and the village of her birth. The square houses squatted along the river and corn was drying on the flat roofs. The setting sun cast gold and red and orange lights against the adobe walls of her father's lodge. She saw him and her stoop-shouldered grandmother, her mother, her brothers, her aunt, and her uncle, the village chief. She saw Coyomo, the Brave One, shaking his spear; and she saw her cousin, Xucate, standing on the rooftop, her strong arms and legs braced against a wind that rose and fell like the breathing of a sleeping panther.

She was smiling in her dream, for when she awoke her lips were parted. For a moment she did not open her eyes, for she wanted to feel the wind on her face and smell the river once again.

But a donkey brayed under her window, so she opened her eyes. And with their opening, everything was gone—her father's house, her mother and grandmother, her brothers, her aunt and uncle, Coyomo, and Xucate standing on the roof—all gone to dust.

Ipa saw a pale light from under the cell door. She heard the thud of the crossbar being lifted. She stood, grasping the tiny silver crucifix in her fingers as she whispered the Lord's Prayer. She prayed that if this was the time for her death, it would be swift and painless.

The door creaked open and a shaft of yellow light cut into the dark room.

"Angelita," a voice whispered.

A wave of relief swept over Ipa.

"Rodrigo, is it you?"

"Yes. Come quickly."

Ipa did not hesitate. She hurried through the door and followed Rodrigo down the narrow corridor. He snuffed out his candle and dropped it to the floor. In silence they trotted to the stables, where a saddled horse and donkey waited. Rodrigo helped Ipa onto the donkey, then swung into the saddle of his horse.

They had reached the edge of the town before Rodrigo spoke.

"I could not stand by and watch you die for a crime you did not commit. The captain is looking for blood, any blood as long as it is *indio* blood."

"You are risking your life by helping me, Rodrigo. Return before it's too late. If they see you helping me escape, it's surely death for treason."

Rodrigo nodded. "You are right, but we must not speak. The night air carries our words too easily."

In the distance a coyote howled, and Ipa noticed that the moon was high, shedding its pale beams over the desert in front of them.

On top of a hill Rodrigo stopped.

"This is as far as I dare go. No one will miss the donkey except Fray Bernardo, and he will not say anything. Go back to your people, Angelita." He gave her a buckskin bag filled with food and a gourd filled with water.

Ipa felt the sting of anguish prick her heart as she placed the bag over her shoulder. The lump in her throat would not allow her to speak. She swallowed again and again before the words would come out.

"And what about us? What about Mexico City? You have not yet asked me what my answer is."

"Ah, Little One . . . " Rodrigo leaned on the saddle and glanced toward the mission before turning back to her. "It is not safe for me to be seen with you for a while. I must pretend ignorance and go about my daily business until this incident is forgotten. As far as the captain is concerned, I am just visiting Fray Bernardo and Fray Ignatio on business."

*Then Xucate was right,* Ipa whispered to herself.

"Do not look so sad, *mi corazón.* When everything is forgotten, I will come to your little village by the river and take you back to Mexico City to be my wife."

"But how will you find me?"

"Do not worry. The path to your village is an easy one down the Rio Conchos to *La Junta*. I have made the trip before. You will be waiting for me, won't you? You won't marry some important old *cacique*, will you?" He slid his gloved fingers under Ipa's chin and forced her to look into his eyes. She swallowed hard.

"I will wait," she said. "But will you come?"

Rodrigo allowed himself the luxury of laughing lightly. He pulled Ipa's hand close to his lips and kissed the slender fingers.

"Of course I will come for you—within the year. I have already found the perfect house for us in Mexico City. It is on Hidalgo Street, across from a beautiful little shrine dedicated to Our Lady of Guadeloupe. There is a water fountain in the plaza and a fantastic garden so you can plant all the herbs and flowers your heart desires."

Ipa felt hot tears sliding down her cheeks. Her heart told her to scream and rant like a madwoman; it told her to throw her arms around him and beg for him to take her with him.

"I will wait for you," she said quietly.

Rodrigo pulled her hand to his heart. Ipa felt the strong beat through the quilted doublet. He leaned over and kissed her lips softly. "*Vaya con Dios,* Angelita."

"Go with God, too," she whispered, then watched him swing his horse around and ride down

248

the hill. Tears blurred the white mission walls and the rustling cornfields and the campfires from the *barrio* at the foot of Big Mountain. She should be glad to have her freedom at last—no more praying on hard, cold floors three times a day, no more taking orders from gloomy Fray Ignatio, no more heckling from the garrison soldiers, or cold glares from the Spanish wives.

A sharp lump rose to her throat. She knew she would miss old Fray Bernardo and her garden and helping the sick more than anything else in the mission. She wondered how the sick ones would manage without her.

Ipa let the tears fall for a few moments more, until Rodrigo was gone from sight. She wiped her nose on her sleeve and turned the little burro around. All that below was behind her now. It was the world of the Spaniards. Getting back to her village safely was now all that she must think of.

Ipa took a deep breath and looked toward the lonely desert. As far as her eyes could see the ground was barren, spotted with pointed yucca and sotol and waving *ocotillo* plants. In the distance the jagged sierras protruded into the sky like the black teeth of a demon. Her village lay on the other side of the mountains, many days away. The donkey's back was uncomfortable and the little beast was unruly. It would be a long, arduous journey.

As Ipa jammed her heels into the donkey's sides

she prayed that she would remember how to survive in the desert. Maybe she had been away too many years, and would forget which plants were nourishing and which were poisonous. Perhaps she would forget the way home and get hopelessly lost in the desert or the mountains, to be killed by a panther or wolf.

But more than this, she wondered if the village of her people would take her back. She glanced at her white cotton dress and the black Spanish hat that Rodrigo had insisted she wear for protection from the sun. With her hair twisted up in the way of the Spanish women, she hardly looked like an *indio*. Would her people recognize her and welcome her home?

Ipa crossed herself and prayed to Jesucristo and to Maria and to the Heavenly Father. For many miles she fingered the beads of her *rosario* and repeated prayers. When she had finished, she glanced up at the moon. A coyote howled very near and something rustled the tall grass.

Quickly Ipa lifted her hands to the mountains and prayed to the Great Spirit and then to Turtle-Girl and the Panther Spirit. After all, she was a practical girl.

# *Chapter Seventeen*

*T*HE DONKEY'S sides felt wet against Ipa's bare legs, but she saw Sacred Panther Mountain in the distance and would not let the little beast rest. Her aching muscles and raw, chapped legs reminded her of her weary journey for the past nine days. She had slept only briefly during the hottest part of the day, lying in the shade of any shrub or rock formation she could find.

Earlier that day Ipa had seen two sets of horse hoofprints in a dry arroyo and followed them to a crossing on the Lesser River. Now she lifted her eyes to Sacred Panther Mountain looming above the desert, so close she thought she could touch it, yet she knew she still had the rest of the day to travel.

Her stomach growled and twisted in pain, reminding her once again of her foolishness the second night of her journey. Exhausted and saddle sore, she had decided to sleep. But a coyote sneaked into her camp and stole away the deerskin bag with the dried beef. His curious nose knocked over her drinking water gourd, leaving it only half full. From then on she slept in the day, while Brother Coyote slept, and rode at night while it was cool. She ate ripe, red prickly cactus pears and *cholla* berries and lizards. Fearing that the Spanish soldiers might be following her down the Lesser River, she kept half a league from it and did not light a campfire. She sneaked close enough to refill her gourd and to allow the donkey to drink only under the cover of darkness.

The burro sighed as Ipa clicked her heels against its sides. Though she had found scrub grass for the sturdy beast, it was always thirsty. Ipa vowed that the first thing she would do at the sacred mountain was lead her faithful companion to the basin and let it plunge its soft gray nose into the cool water and let it feast on the green grass.

The sun was setting when Ipa kept her promise to the burro. It squealed with delight at the smell of water and almost jerked the lead rope from Ipa's hand in its eagerness to climb the mountain path to the source.

The horse hoofprints had ended in the rocky soil near the base of the mountain. If Xucate or Kadoh had come to the top, they must have ascended the mountain trail on foot.

When she reached the top, Ipa cupped her hands over her mouth and shouted. "Little Beetle! Cousin!"

Only a crow screamed its reply.

"Little Beetle! Do not be afraid. It is I, your sister!" she called out again. No one replied.

The donkey filled its stomach with water until its sides bulged. Then it began cropping the tender green grass that grew between boulders along the banks of the pond. Ipa knew the animal would be content for a long time, so she did not bother to tether its rope.

Ipa stepped into the cool water and washed the layer of dust and sweat from her body. The last time she had bathed in the sacred pool had been on her wedding day. The sweet fragrance of damp earth and junipers and wild grasses made her head reel with memories of that wonderful and horrible day. She closed her eyes and conjured up the image of Coyomo, his bright blue macaw feathers haughtily bobbing on his handsome head. If he had arrived but a short time earlier, or later, he would be alive today and Ipa would be his bride. She might have children by now and be leading a life of honor and respect.

It seemed like but a moment ago that she had

stood in the waters, her aunt gently washing her shoulders while she whispered secret advice for Ipa's wedding night. Ipa glanced down at her naked body. The pale light of the waning crescent moon streamed over her, glinting off the tiny silver crucifix resting in the crook of her neck. She thought of Rodrigo, his love and kindness and promise to come after her. In many ways her life at the mission had been full of satisfaction and peace, and she had learned many things from the friars.

A tiny whimper drew Ipa from her daydream. She paused, letting the water trickle down her arms. She could see the donkey's big ears twitching as it hungrily devoured the grass between two large boulders. If there was a coyote or panther nearby, surely the little animal would be on guard.

Ipa strained her ears. The sound came again, this time longer and stronger.

Ipa splashed out of the pool and slipped her cotton chemise over her head. The donkey lifted its head, twitched its ears, then buried its nose into the green grass again.

Ipa crept up the boulders that surrounded the tank of water, trying not to snap willow twigs under her bare feet. When the sound came again, she knew from which direction it came.

Stooping low, Ipa entered the sacred cave. She smelled burning cedar and human excrement and vomit. For a moment anger flashed through her heart that someone had violated the sacred panther cave. She crept along, one hand on the rock wall, the other in front of her, as she followed a distant golden light. As the passageway widened, she saw the source of the light—a small campfire. On one wall she saw the red painting of the panther that she had prayed to for a long life and happy marriage.

The sound came again, unmistakably a human in pain.

At the point where the passage widened into a cavern, damp with dripping water and eerie formations, she saw a shadowy human figure lying on the ground beside the dying fire. The person looked up, the half smile, half grimace of pain on its face looking more animal than human.

"Cousin!" Ipa shouted, then scrambled down the narrow path toward Xucate.

"It is coming." Xucate hissed the words as she pressed her hands onto her stomach. A swath of damp tangled hair fell across her face, but she did not make a motion to move it. Ipa smoothed the hair away.

"How long have you been laboring?"

"Two days. The filthy beast refuses to come out. It must know that death is waiting for it."

"Where is my brother?"

"The fool took the horses and rode away. He claimed to see Ximi and a band of Apaches in the desert."

Ipa sighed. If Kadoh went in the wrong direction, he would surely wander in the desert for days and die of thirst. She pushed the thought out of her mind and concentrated on her cousin. Ipa touched the large belly covered with sweat in spite of the coolness of the cavern. A wave of repulsion swept over her, as if the tiny soul inside were indeed a beast. She imagined the small red face of Juan Diestro.

"I see you haven't loosened all the knots in your clothing," Ipa said as her nimble fingers jerked at the lacing on Xucate's tunic. "The old ones say that a mother-to-be must not wear any knots, or the baby will not come out easily."

"They also say that the father must never kill or harm anything. The father of this child was a murderer. That is why it is torturing me."

Ipa did not know what to say, since her cousin's words were true. In her village, when the midwives could not deliver the baby, the shaman was brought in to sing his prayers. But there was no time to ride to the village and fetch the old white-haired man.

"I will help you take the birthing position," Ipa said and lifted her cousin into a squatting stance. Xucate had already pounded a wooden pole into the ground, and now she held on to it as the next wave of pain swept over her. Xucate's nails bit into the pole until her knuckles turned pale. She threw her head back and howled. Never had Ipa seen a human look so much like an animal, not even when the hunters wore antlers on their heads and pranced like deer or snorted like bears.

The pain passed but soon another took its place, until Xucate fell in exhaustion and could no longer stay on her heels. Ipa gave Xucate some of the pounded root powder. The bitterness made her grimace, but the pain lessened. Ipa held her cousin's hand and wiped her brow as time dragged on. The room smelled of sweat and blood, which made Ipa nauseated.

At last Ipa saw the tiny head, and with Xucate's last scream of pain and anguish, the baby passed into Ipa's hands. Ipa rapped the infant's back until it drew breath and wailed. She could not help but laugh.

"It is a man-child. A handsome son," Ipa whispered. She cut the cord with a serrated agave leaf, then held the baby close to Xucate's face.

"Take it away," Xucate said in a hoarse voice, refusing to open her eyes.

"He looks exactly like you. I see no Spanish blood in his face. Look at your son, Xucate."

But Xucate turned her head away and squeezed her eyes shut.

"Take it to the pool and drown it," she said in a raspy voice.

"No, I cannot do that."

"Then leave it for the wolves. Let them do the deed, so there will be one less Spaniard in this land."

Xucate turned her head back around, and Ipa saw that her cousin's face was the color of ashes and that blood continued to flow from her body. Ipa swallowed hard. The long trip on horseback must have torn something inside her. There was nothing Ipa could do. No medicine plant could save her cousin now.

"Promise me you will destroy it. Promise me!" Xucate's hands fumbled for Ipa's neck but found only the silver cross. Her fingers entwined around it. "Do not let the Spaniard's blood spoil our blood. If you love our people, you must destroy it. Kill it now. It is my death wish." Her breath came in short gasps.

Xucate's eyes dilated, the pupils black as the mouth of the cave. Ipa felt the fingers on her neck slowly slipping away and saw the eyelids starting to close.

"Quickly, Little Cousin. Do it before I die."

Ipa removed the wool *serape* from her shoulder and wrapped the baby in it, then staggered through the passage. The weak light of the rising sun struck her eyes as she stepped out of the cave.

She looked at the desert, the distant mesas, and the sierras even farther away, purple and blue in the shade of morning. The village always celebrated the birth of a child by dipping it into the Great River and holding it to the rising sun for the blessing of the Great Spirit. Ipa quickly washed the child in the sacred pool. The baby cried in a tiny, weak voice. He was a beautiful child, perfect in every way.

"I cannot destroy God's creation," she whispered. She lifted the small, naked body to the rising sun.

"Thank you for this child, Great Spirit. Give him wisdom and a long life." Almost as an afterthought, she made the sign of the cross over the baby.

Ipa trotted down the path, clutching the infant to her chest. Her eyes darted from side to side until she saw a crevice between two boulders in the side of the mountain just wide and deep enough to hide the bundle. She pushed it inside, then returned to the cavern.

Xucate opened her eyes to mere slits as Ipa knelt by her side, out of breath.

"It is done," Ipa said, taking Xucate's hand into her own. She hoped that her cousin would accept her word without question.

"Good," Xucate said, then sighed. Ipa felt the weak squeeze of her cousin's hand before she closed her eyes and breathed no more.

"May your journey be sweet," Ipa whispered. "May the corn rustle in your fields." She made the sign of the cross and whispered the Lord's Prayer, then sang the sister death song. She told Xucate's spirit which direction to go, which trail to take, and which door to enter to find the rope that led to the sky. She pushed aside Xucate's damp hair and adjusted Coyomo's necklace of blue stone.

"Join the spirit of the one you desired," she whispered.

Ipa buried Xucate in the desert and piled rocks over the grave. She started to made a crude cross of sticks as she had often seen the *barrio* people do for those lost in the mine. But a sudden whirlwind rushed across the desert, stirring the cross in her hands. She tossed the sticks away.

"Of course," Ipa said to the wind. "Forgive me, Dear Cousin. You would never want the sign of the Spanish god on your grave." Ipa stood and looked across the desert that Xucate had loved so dearly.

"You were a thorn in my foot, Cousin. But your heart was strong and courageous. I know you did not truly want your child put to death. I will raise him as you would have wanted a son to be raised— proud and brave and free. I will name him Panther Boy, for he was born in the sacred panther cave. Surely it is a sign of good fortune and he will be a great leader. Now, go on your journey in peace. No one will know your secret, I promise. Only Kadoh and I are left alive to tell your story, and Kadoh is gone forever."

Ipa sprinkled the baby with ashes to protect him from evil spirits. There was no time to gather willow branches and reeds to weave a cradleboard, so Ipa tied a knot in her striped *serape,* slipped the baby inside, and slung it over her shoulder so that the child lay against her stomach.

She steered the donkey down the mountain trail. If she didn't stop to rest, she could be at her village by sunset. Ipa's mouth began to crave the taste of the river water of her village. Her legs ached to stand on the roof of her uncle's house. Never in her life had the thought of the little adobe mud houses and the fields of starving corn been so precious. Suddenly the years at the mission seemed far away and no more than a dream. All that mattered now was going home.

# Chapter Eighteen

THE BABY was sleeping soundly when Ipa saw the curve in the canyon and the thin lines of smoke curling from the adobe houses. The cottonwood and willows greeted her like old friends.

"My village!" she said out loud, then smacked her heels against the sides of the weary little burro. It twitched its ears but did not hasten its step. Ipa's heart raced and she could hardly bear to stay in the saddle as they grew closer and the aroma of smoke, roasting corn, and boiling agaves filled the air.

At the top of the canyon Ipa paused and looked down. She woke the baby and took him into her arms.

"We are home at last, Little Panther," she said, rocking him softly. "There is the village of your mother's birth. But look at the cornfields. They are so small, not even one-third the size of Fray Bernardo's fields. How can such a small crop support my village?" She dismounted the donkey and climbed down the canyon trail, the baby held securely in her arms. The stubborn donkey did not want to make the steep descent but had no choice once it had started down.

Ipa grew impatient as she wended her way down the jagged trail. She wanted to leave the donkey behind, to run and shout at the top of her lungs. Her heart danced as she kept one eye on the path and another on the pueblo. She could not understand why only a few of the adobe houses had smoke streaming from the holes in their roofs. The others looked deserted.

At last she reached the bottom of the trail. She expected to see children and women run to greet her, but no one was outside save for the Old One gnawing on a corncob. When Ipa walked past her, the hag cackled in glee and pointed a twisted finger as if she knew some dark secret.

The eerie stillness made Ipa shiver as she continued to her uncle's house. As she tethered the donkey, Ipa thought about what she would say to her aunt about the baby. Surely her aunt would be pleased to see her first grandchild, yet how would she take the news of the death of Xucate, her beautiful daughter? And then there was the baby himself. His skin was still red, but what would it look like as he grew older? Would the skin turn pale like that of his Spanish father? What would Ipa say if the village women questioned her? The child was innocent, and would not telling the truth only insure him a life of misery? Yet Fray Bernardo and Fray Ignatio had told her lying was a sin.

Ipa stood on the rooftop of the *cacique*'s house and looked down through the hatch into the firelit room. Smoke streamed out the opening, warming her trembling legs. Whether they were shaking from fear or from weakness or from joy, she could not say.

"I request to come into your house," Ipa called down in the traditional greeting of visitors. Having been gone so long, she no longer felt the freedom to go inside unannounced.

"We are pleased to have a visitor," came the expected reply from a woman's voice. Ipa twisted her brow. The voice was familiar, yet it sounded strained and much too old to belong to her aunt. Cautiously, Ipa climbed down the ladder into the lodge. She breathed in the familiar smell of burning firewood and earth and corn. A million memories of her childhood rushed over her, making her feel giddy.

"I have returned," Ipa said softly as she crept into the room that seemed too small to hold her body now. Her head almost scraped the *tornillo* wood rafters and she felt as if she could stand in the middle of the room and touch all four walls at once. Her aunt was squatting on her heels next to someone lying on a woven mat. Ipa was amazed how small and stooped the woman seemed now.

"Who is it?" the man on the cot asked, and Ipa recognized her uncle's voice. He looked so very small and weak. How could she have remembered him as tall and strong like her father and like Xucate?

Ipa's aunt stared at her with frightened eyes.

"It is your niece," Ipa said. Surely she had not been gone so long as to be forgotten. Perhaps they thought she had been killed and that she was a ghost. It was only natural.

"I have escaped from the Spaniards. I am still alive."

Her aunt's face flushed with relief and she smiled.

"It is your brother's daughter, She-Who-Lived," the woman said to the man on the mat. "She has escaped from the Spaniards."

"Then our prayers have been answered. Ipa-tah-chi knows the secrets of the medicine plants. She will save us." The man made a motion as if he wanted to rise on his elbows, but he could not. The firelight streaked across his face, and it was then that Ipa saw the red spots on his body. She quickly stepped back, then pulled the cloth over the baby's head and held him close to her chest.

"You have a child?" her aunt asked, her eyes eagerly staring at the bundle.

Ipa nodded. "It is your grandson. Your daughter's child."

The woman's hands flew to her mouth to stifle a small cry, then she swooped forward.

"The spotted sickness is in this house. Quickly take the child away from here. Go see the Old One's granddaughter. She lost her baby only two days ago and will still have milk." Ipa nodded and reclimbed the ladder, her aunt close behind her.

The Old One's granddaughter was in the granary. Ipa sadly noted how low the supply of corn had grown. There was not enough to feed half a small village. The young woman took the baby gladly. Ipa's aunt drooled about the baby's handsomeness.

"At last there is a male child in our family. Someday he shall be *cacique*," she boasted. Ipa decided at that moment she would tell no one about Juan Diestro. Panther Boy would grow up tall and strong and beautiful like Xucate and be the finest leader they had ever known.

"Auntie, I am sorry to tell you that the mother of this child died giving birth." Ipa carefully avoided saying Xucate's name, for that would summon her spirit from its journey to the afterworld. And if the spirit got lost because of the distraction, it would become angry and bring bad luck to the village. "And the father of this child is dead, too."

The older woman's eyes moistened and she nodded. "I thought it was so. And your little brother? Where is he?"

Disappointment crept over Ipa. "Then he is not here in the village with you?"

Ipa's aunt slowly shook her head. "We have not seen him since the day of your wedding."

Ipa bowed her head and swallowed hard. Surely this was proof that Kadoh had gotten lost in the desert. Ipa wanted to mourn her brother properly, but there was no time. She stayed awake all day and night, gathering medicine roots and leaves and berries, pounding them into powder and making teas for the fevers. The sickness filled every house, feeding on the weakest ones—the children and the old.

The next day her uncle died. They buried him in the desert beside the corpses of many others. There should have been a grand funeral ceremony, with drums beating and men dancing and women wailing. But the sick ones could not make the journey, and those who were still healthy could not leave the sick unattended. Ipa, her aunt, and the Old One buried him alone with his bonnet of macaw feathers and his medicine pouch.

The village's sacred cane passed on to one of Ipa's distant cousins, one of the few healthy males remaining in the village. Now there were not enough men to form deer-hunting parties. The men searched daily for rabbits and small game, leaving the women to tend the sick and work in the pitiful cornfields. But they dared not leave for a long hunting trip.

For many days Ipa worked herself into exhaustion, administering medicine to the sick. But her powders and tonics did not work. By the time the spotted sickness had run its course, over half the village had died.

On the day of Panther Boy's arrival the shaman had placed a perfect ear of corn next to the sleeping baby and tied a bundle of sacred prayer feathers to his cradleboard. A month later, Ipa stood beside the river for Panther Boy's naming ceremony.

"It is a good sign that my grandson was spared," Ipa's aunt said. "It means he will be a great leader who cannot be touched by evil spirits."

Ipa was not sure she believed in evil spirits anymore, but she helped her aunt and the old shaman dip Panther Boy in the Great River and hold him to the rising sun. In secret, Ipa named the child Juan Bernardo, in honor of the kindhearted old padre, and made the sign of the cross over his tiny head.

Ipa's aunt did not question about the baby's father, for to talk about the dead would only bring bad luck. Everyone commented on the child's handsomeness, his bright eyes, and charming smile. He had superior strength, just as Xucate had had, and his tiny fists had a fierce grip. Ipa took care of the baby, only giving him to the Old One's grand-daughter when it was feeding time.

Ipa's days were filled with work, for everyone had to take on the duties of many. Ipa found a choice spot of earth and planted the five grains of blue corn that had belonged to Coyomo. She carried water to the corn every day in a gourd. As summer moved on, the corn grew and produced several fine ears, which she saved.

Although Ipa was busy, not a day passed that she did not stand on the canyon rim gazing south, the direction from which Rodrigo would come.

"Who do you watch and wait for?" her aunt asked her one day as they pounded deerskin pelts on the rocks beside the river.

Ipa felt her cheeks turn hot. How could she tell anyone that she loved a Spaniard and waited to be taken from her peaceful village to a bustling city surrounded by water, where people lived like ants in a mound?

"I am watching for Spaniards, for I fear that they may pass this way again."

"Spaniards! Ha!" The woman slapped a deerskin cloak against a rock. "All the people living on the Great River would be better off if not a single Spaniard had ever crossed our lands. They bring sickness and death. They capture our young men and carry them off to be slaves. They convince our best men to lead them to faraway lands in search of foolish metals. No, I will be happy indeed if I never see another Spaniard as long as I live."

Ipa swallowed hard as she looked into the face of Panther Boy cooing in his cradleboard hanging from a tree limb. His face had turned lighter than other children his age, and his black hair had a tiny curl on the ends. What would her aunt do if she found out he was half Spanish? It was a thought that plagued Ipa every day while she worked in the corn-fields, just as the ache in her heart for Rodrigo plagued her every night before she fell asleep.

Three months after Ipa's arrival, the little burro that she had stolen from the Spaniards gave birth to a spirited, long-legged baby. Ipa wondered if Rodrigo had known that the donkey was with foal when he chose it. The village celebrated the foal's arrival as if it were a human child, with dancing and drum-beating and singing, for they had found the burro to be of great value. She pulled heavily loaded travois and baskets of water from the river to the cornfields without complaint, climbing and descending the steep canyon walls with sturdy legs and sure feet.

The shaman, who had contracted the spotted sickness but had stubbornly refused to die, built the donkey a little manger of *tornillo* wood and decor-ated her head with macaw feathers. When her foal came, he blessed it and made it a smaller bonnet of turkey feathers, which the mother promptly pulled off. Ipa gave the mother donkey to the new *cacique* and showed him how to guide it with the lead rope. She also gave him Rodrigo's Spanish hat. On ceremony days, he rode about the village on the donkey, the black hat on his head, as haughtily as any Spaniard.

Not long after the birth of the donkey, a band of peaceful *indios* came from the south to trade. Following them was a small, scraggly herd of sheep. Their woolly coats had not been shorn for the year and hung in matted clumps. The villagers stared at the strange animals; children tried to pet them or poked them with sticks.

"What kind of strange animal is this?" asked the new *cacique*.

"They are merino sheep," Ipa explained. "They are of great value to the Spaniards. It would be very wise to trade for a male and female."

The *cacique* doubted Ipa at first, but at last consented to trade some buffalo hides and blue stones for them.

The traders did not speak the language of Ipa's village, and no one knew sign language very well, but one of the traders spoke Spanish, so Ipa was able to interpret.

Ipa and the women cut the sheep's wool as best as possible without the proper shears. She showed the women how to comb the wool and twist it into thread and weave it on a rude loom. The wool cloth was not nearly as fine as that made by the *indios* at the mission, but the villagers were pleased with the results. They died it with purple berry juice, and from that day forth cared for the sheep as carefully as they did the donkeys.

Every day during the summer, while the women ground corn and agave bulbs, or tended the squash and bean plants, Ipa repeated Bible stories about Jesucristo and taught her people words of Spanish. She taught them some prayers and how to make the sign of the cross. She showed them everything she had learned about weaving and pottery and sewing.

She tried to tell the *cacique* about the oxcarts she had seen at the mission, with wheels taller than two men, but there was not enough wood in her village to make lumber for the wheels. The villagers, even the men, listened to every word she told them about the Spaniards' way of tilling the soil and growing vegetables. When they sang the songs for the budding corn ears and later for the corn tassels, they added the sacred words of the friars and made the sign of the cross over the silky tassels. That summer, the corn did not die.

The ripe cactus fruit were harvested, but the annual games were not held for lack of young men to run the footraces. Ipa thought of Xucate laughing as she raced the wind. Her son looked more like her every day. He kicked inside his cradleboard like a captured rabbit and learned to crawl early.

"He is so much like his mother," Ipa's aunt said one cool autumn day as she chased the little crawling boy over a flat rock near the river. "He will be the best runner the village has ever seen, and he will win every race and bring our village much honor."

Ipa smiled as she tickled the child's ribs. She was grateful to Panther Boy for keeping her days busy. Yet every time she looked into his lightly tanned face, she thought about Rodrigo. He had promised to come for her as soon as he could. Many moons had come and gone. Surely the incident of Juan Diestro's death had been forgotten by now.

A thousand excuses for Rodrigo's absence crossed her mind each day. Perhaps Rodrigo had been discovered helping her to escape and had been executed. Perhaps on his way across the desert toward her village the *chichimeca* had murdered him. Perhaps his horse had been bitten by a rattlesnake or scorpion. Perhaps he lost his way, or starved or died of thirst. Or maybe he had met a beautiful Spanish lady and married her.

While Ipa's heart ached every day with her secret, her position of respect among the villagers grew. Not only did she tend the sick of her village, but she often made journeys to villages at the junction. And any time traders passed through who spoke Spanish, Ipa became the translator.

The moons slipped by, and when the hoary frost

of winter had given way to spring rains and fields of blooming cactus and green grasses, the ewe gave birth to a bouncy lamb.

No one had died of the spotted sickness all winter long. A woman gave birth to a baby girl, the first child to be born in the village since Ipa's arrival almost a year ago. The Old One said it was a good omen, and true to her prediction, one day Ipa's aunt found a secret stash of seed corn that had been wrapped and buried in a cave for hard times by someone. The raggedy village, what was left of it, danced and performed the planting season ceremony. The shaman sang to the corn seeds until his voice was hoarse and dry.

Ipa planted the seeds harvested from Coyomo's blue corn in a patch in the desert. The small stalks of corn grew straight and strong and green. The donkey carried water on her back every day for the thirsty plants, and the baby donkey was now big enough to carry small loads, too. Ipa sheared the winter coats of the sheep again and the women made more yarn. She showed them how to make pottery the way the Spaniards had taught her and her aunt was the best potter of all.

When the summer yucca flowers bloomed, Ipa grew more restless. It had been one year since she had seen Rodrigo. One day Ipa's aunt approached her as she gathered the creamy, sweet flowers. A foolish grin spread on the woman's lips.

"Ipa-tah-chi, my niece. I have good news for you. A man is here to see you. Come quickly. He is in the plaza."

Ipa's heart thundered with joy. She shoved Panther Boy into her aunt's arms and raced to the village. Her eyes searched the crowd that had gathered in the plaza, hoping to see the familiar bearded face and twinkling eyes of Rodrigo.

"Where? Where is he?" Ipa demanded from her aunt, who had caught up with her.

"Why, there. The *cacique* of the third village at the junction. His wife died of the spotted sickness and he is in need of a new one. See how grand he looks?"

Ipa stared at a middle-aged man of sturdy stature, with heavy muscles on his legs and arms. Tattoos rose across his cheeks and chest and red macaw feathers decorated the crown of his closely cropped head. He was a fine-looking man, but he was not Rodrigo.

Ipa expelled air in a long gush.

"I do not want a husband," she said, and turned away.

Ipa's aunt frowned and grabbed her niece's arm. "You are deep into your eighteenth summer and almost beyond marrying age. Of course you want a husband. What kind of life would you have without a family to care for?"

"I have my medicine plants. And I have Panther

Boy. He is all I need." Ipa pulled Panther Boy from her aunt's arms and ran up the canyon trail. At the top she stood and looked at the village below. The visiting *cacique* argued angrily with her aunt, then stomped off toward the east.

"Rodrigo, Rodrigo, when are you coming? When?" She pressed her face against Panther Boy's head. His tiny fingers reached up and grabbed her hair. He shrieked in glee and rocked up and down in her arms, oblivious to the tears sliding down her cheeks.

When the peaceful *indio* traders came again, Ipa traded them her *rosario* beads for two more sheep, though one had a blind eye.

One summer day black clouds rolled over the distant mountains and a few days later the river overflowed its banks. A band of tattered-looking people of the Caguate tribe came from the North-west. The river had been unkind, overflowing its banks and destroying many of their houses. Apaches had raided their village so often that they had very little seed corn to plant in the ground. They had lived on grass seeds and bark and dirt all winter and spring.

The *cacique* allowed the Caguates to move into the abandoned adobe houses. The newcomers planted what few corn seeds they had brought and worked in the fields alongside the men of Ipa's village. Their language was not exactly the same as

Ipa's, but they knew some Spanish, so often they communicated in Spanish.

One cool night, when the Moon-of-Falling-Leaves was high in the night sky, Ipa heard a familiar sound. She opened her eyes and let them adjust to the darkness of the house. The pale moonlight streamed through the opening in the flat roof and cold air drifted down, making her shiver. She glanced at Panther Boy sleeping between her and her aunt. The child's hair hung in long, dark curls about his smooth cheeks. Ipa pulled the wool blanket over the small arms that hugged a cornstalk doll shaped like a deer with sticks for its antlers. She had no regrets for saving the child and knew that if Xucate had lived she would have loved her son, too, in spite of his Spanish blood.

Ipa rose quietly and climbed up the ladder to the roof. The sound was echoing down the canyon, from the direction where the river curved. It seemed like a lifetime, not a mere year and a half since Ipa had heard the sound of horse hooves crunching on gravel. Many times Ipa had prayed that she would never see another band of mounted Spaniards in her life, but she could not deny that it was horsemen riding toward her village.

## Chapter Nineteen

IPA SHOUTED a warning alarm across the village, awakening all the families. She shook her aunt and scooped Panther Boy into her arms. Soon the entire village had crawled out onto the roofs to see what was happening.

As the band came closer, Ipa saw that they were not wearing the leather-padded breastplates of the Spaniards or the curved metal helmets. The men wore deerskin moccasins and breechcloths. Headbands held back long, straight black hair.

"They dress like Apaches," the *cacique* said.

"But they ride horses like the Spaniards," the shaman added.

"Perhaps they stole the horses," another man said.

"Perhaps they are traders," the *cacique* replied.

"Perhaps they have come to kill all of us," the *cacique*'s wife hissed. "What are you men going to do?"

Ipa waited for the men of her village to gather their bows and arrows or to clutch their wooden clubs and shake their spears. But the men sat motionless on the rooftops like old women, quivering and hiding their faces.

Ipa put Panther Boy in his cradleboard, though he could walk very well, and tied him to her back so her arms would be free. She decided that she would not hide inside the houses as the other women were doing, weeping and wailing. She would take the sheep and donkeys and go down by the river and hide in the cane. Let the people press their faces against the wall and give away their pots and baskets. The only future that the village had was with the livestock. The Apaches would not know about the animals and would not be looking for them.

But the donkey was stubborn and opened her mouth and brayed loudly when Ipa tried to lead her and the young donkey away. And the sheep would not cooperate and ran along the riverbanks bleating.

One of the Apaches saw Ipa and turned his horse, a fine white stallion with silky mane and tail, in her direction, while the others rode into the village plaza. Ipa grabbed a broken piece of cottonwood limb. When the horseman was close, she swung with all her might, striking his leg. He cursed in her own language.

"How do you know my language, filthy Apache?" she demanded.

"Be quiet, woman. Why do you have Spanish livestock? Where are the men of the pueblo?"

Ipa stared into the shadowy face.

"There are no men left. They have all died of the spotted sickness. Others are old and toothless. We found these Spanish sheep wandering in the desert, left behind by the slavers. They are old and sickly and of little value. The donkey is blind. You would be doing us a favor to take them off our hands. But how do you know my language?" she asked again.

A slight chuckle rose from the young man's lips.

"Have you forgotten me so soon, my sister?"

Ipa stepped closer to look up into the face, but she did not drop her club. The young man turned into the moonlight.

"Ximi!" Ipa put her hand over her mouth to stifle the cry. "You are alive! So my little brother was right to never give up on you. If only he could have seen you once again before he died."

"Died?" Ximi said in an amused voice. "Kadoh is not dead. He joined our people two summers ago.

He is with the other men now. He is the one who led us here to the village."

"Both my brothers live. The good news makes my heart sing. If our father were alive, he would be happy at last."

On seeing the smile leave Ximi's face, she added, "The spotted sickness took him many summers ago while he guided the Spaniards to the land of the Corn People."

"Yes, the sickness has taken the lives of many Ugly Arrows people, too. We have come for corn and food."

Ipa swallowed hard. "There is little corn. Hardly enough to last the winter. If we give half to you, we will have nothing to plant in the ground next spring."

"Then give us those sickly animals. We will slaughter the sheep and eat well for a few days at least. And that donkey walks well enough, considering that she is blind," he said with a chuckle.

Ipa felt her heart pound harder in her chest. She clenched the wooden club tighter and raised it in front of her.

"You saw through my lie, Brother. These animals are the only future of the village. You will have to kill me before I will let you take them."

Ximi clucked to the horse and urged it closer, but as he reached for the donkey's rope, Ipa slammed the club against his knuckles.

He swung the horse around and raised a lance tipped with sharpened bone. For a moment he poised it in the air, then slowly he lowered it.

"I will spare your life because you are my sister and we were children together once. But the captain of the raiding party will not be so full of mercy."

"How can you obey the words of an Apache, our sworn enemy? Apaches killed our grandmother and many brave men from our village. Like coyotes sneaking in the night, they steal food from others and do not work themselves. They are lazy and dirty and have no god. They are arrogant and haughty and cruel."

Ximi tilted his head back and laughed the familiar laugh Ipa remembered, only deeper, like that of a man.

"You are still a foolish child. The Apaches are brave men. They do not hide in their tipis when the Spaniards come. They stand up and fight. They take what they need to survive. I am no longer called Ximi. I am called Brave Hawk, killer of Spaniards. And Kadoh is called Horse Stealer." He patted the neck of the white stallion. The animal blew air through its nostrils, and Ipa suddenly realized that it was the horse of Juan Diestro.

"Go your way, Sister," Ximi said. "Take your sheep and donkeys to the river canes and hide them. I will tell no one this day. Today I will be your brother, but tomorrow I will be another man." He swung the horse around and joined the rest of the men, who were raiding the granaries and taking food and hides and anything they could find of value.

The village women stayed inside the houses, weeping, and the men sat on the roofs with heads hung low. Ximi called out in their own language for them to join the Apaches and become men once again. Seeing that they had no food for the coming winter, a few of the men followed on foot, but the very old and very young ones remained.

After the Apaches left, the *cacique* pulled at his hair and wailed in shame. For days the villagers wept until Ipa grew sick of hearing their moaning.

Without dried corn and beans or other foods, the villagers had to live on grass seeds and berries and agave bulbs. They sweetened bitter acorn flour with dirt, though some grew sick because of it. Against Ipa's advice, they slew the old blind sheep. On the coldest day of winter, when icicles hung from the rocks and cottonwood tree, five of the youngest families deserted the village to join relatives living at the wealthier pueblos at the junction of the rivers.

It was a winter of bitterness, but Ipa and Panther Boy stayed in her uncle's house and they survived.

When the Moon-of-the-Rushing-Waters hung low in the sky and the desert reeled with the fragrance of spring flowers and wild grasses, a small, dirty band of Spaniards rode into the village. So sudden was their arrival that the women did not have time to run to the hills nor did the men have time to pile their possessions in the plaza as gifts or prepare their bows and arrows.

But the Spaniards were not slavers. Their eyes looked weary and their faces were browned by many seasons of desert sun. On seeing that the Spaniards were not hostile, the *cacique* called the villagers into the middle of the plaza.

A Jumano guide stood beside the captain, translating his words. Ipa's heartbeat quickened as she recognized the familiar black hat, the tattooed face, and stern black eyes of Pedro, the Jumano guide who once rode with the slavers. If Pedro saw her, surely he would tell the Spaniards that she was the escaped girl who had helped murder Juan Diestro. She slipped behind her aunt and listened to the guide's words.

"Your enemy, the Apaches, are getting closer," he said. "Their attacks will come more often now. A tribe even more fierce than they pushes them southward."

A murmur rose among the villagers as they cast anxious glances among themselves. Ipa saw terror sweep over the faces of her people and felt the voice of doom creeping into their whispers.

"Do not worry." The guide's voice spoke evenly, calmly. "The Spanish soldiers will protect you from the Apaches. They will build a great white house near *La Junta,* which is their name for the junction of the two rivers. You must let their padres sprinkle water on your head and repeat their magic words every day. The brown-robed men will give you food and clothing. They will give you work animals and strong farm tools. You must work and give part of your corn crops to the good padres. In return their soldiers will keep the fierce Apaches away."

The village men nodded in agreement, astonished at the Spaniards' generosity.

"But there is one more thing. You must agree to move to *La Junta* to live with the other *indios* there. The Spaniards cannot protect you if you live so far away."

When Pedro's words had died down, the men of Ipa's village held council all night. Their whispers and the aroma of *tobago* floated on the night air until at last Grandfather Sun peeked over the eastern sierras.

"We have decided," the *cacique* said to the villagers gathered around him. "We will abandon our village and go to live at *La Junta*."

"*Aayy!* We are doomed!" the Old One wailed. She shrieked as she spun in circles, pulling her hair out and chanting her death song. That night, while the *kiva* fires burned and the men painted their bodies for the ceremonial dance, the Old One collapsed. Ipa scooped the woman into her arms and carried her to the base of the Old One's adobe house and propped her against the wall. She felt no heavier

*285*

than the ragged deerskin clothes she wore. Ipa leaned over the tiny body and held the frail, dry hand in her own.

"It is the end of our people," the white-haired woman whispered with her last breath.

"May your journey be filled with fields of sweet corn," Ipa said as she closed the wrinkled eyelids, then made the sign of the cross. When she looked up she saw the Jumano guide, Pedro, standing above her. Her eyes wildly searched for a weapon, but all she saw was a *mano* resting on a grinding stone. She picked it up and faced Pedro.

"*Shh.*" He placed his long, narrow finger over his lips as he glanced over his shoulder. "I mean you no harm." The hiss in his voice made chill bumps rise on Ipa's arms.

"What do you want?" Ipa felt her body tremble. The guide's liquid brown eyes observed her terror a moment, then a thin smile curled his lips.

"Why are you afraid of me, Angelita? Do you think I will tell everyone your secret?"

"I have no secret."

He nodded toward Panther Boy, who had curled up on a buffalo skin near the plaza fire and was sleeping soundly.

"There is a secret in the blood of the child over there."

Ipa glared back. Though her heart thundered in her ears, she pretended his words meant nothing. "My son? There is no secret in the blood of my son."

The Jumano's black eyes ignited. "He is not your son! He is the son of your cousin and Juan Diestro."

Ipa swallowed hard and her heart felt weak.

"The child is innocent," she said at last. "Please do not tell the Spaniards. If you must betray someone, let it be me. Turn me over to the Spanish captain, but please do not destroy this innocent child. It was his mother who murdered Juan Diestro, not he." Ipa thought she saw something flicker across the stern face above her. Quickly she closed her fingers around his tattooed arm.

"My cousin was beautiful, wasn't she? Diestro violated her and beat her. He deserved to die. You know he did," she whispered close to his face.

The Jumano's eyes softened for a moment and shimmered like moonlight on river water and Ipa saw his throat move as he swallowed. For a moment she thought his tears would fall.

"Yes, she was a beautiful woman, and full of courage. I wanted to take her as my wife. But Juan Diestro destroyed her." Suddenly his face clouded over and his eyes turned black again as he hissed through clenched teeth. "And that is why I killed Juan Diestro!" His fist hit the adobe wall, breaking off a flake of plaster.

Ipa threw her hands over her lips and stepped back.

"You! You were the one! Then why did you let the Spaniards think my cousin murdered him?"

"Fool, it was I who helped her escape. It was I who got the horses ready. I who told Kadoh to go with her. I who showed your cousin the escape route and gave her many hours head start before I plunged the knife into Diestro's black heart." Pedro glanced toward the Spanish leader who was getting drunk on a gourd of sotol. "Someday I will plunge knives into all their hearts."

Ipa fought the tremble in her body to no avail. She wanted to fall to the ground, to take Panther Boy in her arms and hold him tight.

"Why did you come here?" she whispered.

"I hoped to find your cousin still alive. When I saw the boy, I knew it was her son. The resemblance is unmistakable. But when I saw you tending him, carrying him and behaving as a mother would, I knew she was dead."

"It was a difficult childbirth."

The face softened for only an instant before turning cold again.

"I came for another reason, too. I have something for you."

Ipa's eyes widened as she watched the guide glance around, then reach around his neck and remove something shiny. He took her hand and quickly placed a small cold object in it.

"He waits for you. Go to him," the man whispered.

Ipa opened her fist and saw the familiar little carved turtle. She drew in her breath and let it out slowly. "Rodrigo," she said, and closed her eyes. When she opened them the guide was walking away.

"Pedro!" she called to his back. *"Muchas gracias!"*

The Jumano paused and turned. "My name is not Pedro. I am Pachoa, son of Tomanco, *cacique* of my people. I will lead the Spaniards no more." He removed the black hat and dropped it to the ground.

The next morning, while the villagers gathered all their belongings, Ipa packed food, water, her medicine plants, and the blue corn seeds she had harvested into a burden-basket. She picked up Panther Boy. Though he was not yet two summers old, he was taller than older children in the village and had long ago outgrown his cradleboard.

Ipa did not say good-bye to her aunt or anyone else. She climbed up the canyon trail for the last time and stood on the rim, looking down at the river twisting through the canyon. In the distance an eagle screamed its piercing cry, and below an owl hooted as it dived at a mouse.

Ipa remembered the night nine years ago when she stood on the canyon rim and looked for the Panther Spirit to bring rain. She was a simple child with simple dreams then. Her world was filled with long, happy days grinding corn beside the river and gathering yucca roots and cactus pears. Her grandmother sang her to sleep with songs of lost maidens and brave warriors, of magical birds and clever coyotes. And in the warmth of the old woman's love, Ipa-tah-chi never wanted her life to change.

But into every life a changing wind must come. Ipa did not mind the changes brought by small winds—once the rains fell too hard and the river gushed into the adobe pit houses; once the rains did not come for two seasons and the corn turned to yellow skeletons rattled by a dry, hot wind. And so it was. Small winds came and went, but the village continued. It had been that way as long as any man could remember, and Ipa's innocent heart was confident it would remain so forever. She would marry, bear children, grow old, and die beside the peaceful river. It was all she wanted.

Then on an autumn day, when the sun was warm and the air was cool, strangers who wore shells like turtles rode into the village on the backs of great antlerless deer. This time it was a whirling, raging wind that knew no bounds.

The village was dead now, and no smoke rose from the lodges. Ipa wondered if her brothers Ximi and Kadoh would come to raid the village again. Perhaps next time they would try to raid *La Junta* and be killed by Spanish soldiers.

With tears in her eyes, Ipa said good-bye to the

river and started her long journey. She would follow the Lesser River to its source, then turn south. She knew she would need patience to reach the road that led to Mexico City. It would take her many weeks. She knew Rodrigo would not mind her bringing Panther Boy along with her; after all the child was half Spanish. And she knew Rodrigo would be a good and kind husband.

As Ipa walked across the desert at a steady pace, she spoke to the boy riding on her back, his arms wrapped around her neck, his legs wrapped around her waist.

"In Mexico City they will call you Juan Bernardo," she said. "You will be baptized and brought up properly in the church. Rodrigo will send you to school so you can learn to read and write Spanish. Rodrigo will teach you all the ways of the Spaniards. Someday you will be an honorable *Don* with land and riches."

Ipa smiled at Panther Boy. The child would have a life of plenty and grow tall and strong and beautiful like his mother. Clearly Ipa could see Xucate's smile and eyes in the little boy's face.

As she walked across the desert and saw Sacred Panther Mountain looming nearby, Ipa paused. In the dimness she thought she could see the stones on top of Xucate's grave and farther away still, the grave of Coyomo, the Brave One. A wind gusted and rattled her necklace of copper bells. For a moment she thought she heard Xucate's laughter rising up from the sacred cave.

"But I will also teach you the ways of your mother's village," Ipa whispered to the boy, who had fallen asleep. "I will sing to you the songs of the canyon and tell you the stories of Panther Spirit and Turtle-Girl. We will plant Coyomo's blue corn and I will tell you of your mother's people. And you will never forget."

*Have you read these*
*Great Episodes paperbacks?*

KRISTIANA GREGORY
*Earthquake at Dawn*
*Jenny of the Tetons*
*The Legend of Jimmy Spoon*

LEN HILTS
*Quanah Parker: Warrior for Freedom,*
*Ambassador for Peace*

DOROTHEA JENSEN
*The Riddle of Penncroft Farm*

JACKIE FRENCH KOLLER
*The Primrose Way*

CAROLYN MEYER
*Where the Broken Heart Still Beats:*
*The Story of Cynthia Ann Parker*

SEYMOUR REIT
*Behind Rebel Lines: The Incredible*
*Story of Emma Edmonds, Civil War Spy*
*Guns for General Washington: A Story*
*of the American Revolution*

ANN RINALDI

*An Acquaintance with Darkness*

*A Break with Charity:*
*A Story about the Salem Witch Trials*

*Cast Two Shadows: The American*
*Revolution in the South*

*The Coffin Quilt: The Feud between*
*the Hatfields and the McCoys*

*The Fifth of March:*
*A Story of the Boston Massacre*

*Finishing Becca: A Story about*
*Peggy Shippen and Benedict Arnold*

*Hang a Thousand Trees with Ribbons:*
*The Story of Phillis Wheatley*

*A Ride into Morning:*
*The Story of Tempe Wick*

*The Secret of Sarah Revere*

*The Staircase*


ROLAND SMITH

*The Captain's Dog: My Journey*
*with the Lewis and Clark Tribe*


THEODORE TAYLOR

*Air Raid—Pearl Harbor!:*
*The Story of December 7, 1941*